FEB 2 2

D0331523

Lulu and Milagro's Search for Clarity

Lulu and Milagro's Search for Clarity

ANGELA VELEZ

BALZER + BRAY
An Imprint of HarperCollinsPublishers

Balzer + Bray is an imprint of HarperCollins Publishers.
Lulu and Milagro's Search for Clarity
Copyright © 2022 by Angela Velez
All rights reserved. Printed in the United States of America.
No part of this book may be used or reproduced in any manner whatsoever
without written permission except in the case of brief quotations embodied
in critical articles and reviews. For information address HarperCollins
Children's Books, a division of HarperCollins Publishers, 195 Broadway,
New York, NY 10007.
www.epicreads.com

Library of Congress Control Number: 2021944125
ISBN 978-0-06-307178-0

Typography by Corina Lupp
21 22 23 24 25   PC/LSCH   10 9 8 7 6 5 4 3 2 1
❖
First Edition

For Oscar and Norma

BALTIMORE

1

Milagro

ACCORDING TO THE St. Agnes Student Handbook, there are one hundred different ways to earn detention. I should know. In the last five weeks, here are the reasons Sister May sent me to detention hell:

Uniform violation: red lipstick. (Fine, I deserved this one. But I looked *good*.)

Uniform violation: pink lip gloss. (Unfair, because the lip gloss was the same color as my lips, only glittery. "Why bother wearing it, then?" my sister Lulu asked when I ranted about nun oppression. I don't know how we're related sometimes.)

Uniform violation: hair accessories. (My best friend

Carmen's genius idea. It turns out hair crystals are against the rules and are also the devil. It took two hours to get them out of my curls. I told Carmen if I ended up with bald spots, she had to buy me a wig.)

Improper conduct: whispering in church. (Also Carmen's fault. And Becca White's, for going up to communion with her skirt tucked into her polka-dotted granny panties.)

But today is going to be a life-changing day in the glamorous life of Milagro Zavala, for two very important reasons. The first is that if I survive today, I will have made it one whole week without getting detention. I'd like to thank Sister May and her overactive pad of orange detention slips, my brand-new collection of nude lipsticks (generously "donated" by the CVS on St. Paul's Avenue), and the St. Agnes Student Handbook, which says if you have more than twelve detentions, they will schedule a parent-teacher conference. This is why I have exactly eleven detentions to show for myself.

Mami and Sister May can't meet. They share a singular goal of wanting to ruin my life. With their powers combined, they're the sun and a magnifying glass, and I'm the withering ant, slowly dying from their depraved experiment, called "How to Turn Milagro into a Proper Young Lady." Keeping them away from each other is the only reason I'm awake and dressed on time today.

Making it to spring break without detention is also the only reason I'm sporting an unrolled kilt that almost reaches the lace on my over-the-knee knee-highs. (Sister May says she's going to rewrite the St. Agnes Student Handbook to make my knee-highs a detention offense next year. It's truly an honor to be an influencer.) Even though it kills me to dress like I've given up on living, it's a sacrifice I'm willing to make—if only because it is step one in my big plan for spring break: Operation Don't Die a Virgin.

"Mami! MAMI! Wake-up time!"

I wait two minutes before I barge into Mami's room, flinging open the door dramatically and hitting play on my phone, so the trills of Mami's favorite crooner (Gloria Estefan, always) radiate from the embroidered pocket of my St. Agnes button-down.

"What a beautiful day to go on retreat!" I sing out, determined to get this show—that is, get Mami—on the road.

It's 7:00 a.m., so of course, Mami's body is a series of lumps under a deep red comforter and a mountain of brightly colored pillows. The scent of hairspray lingers in the room, soaked into the faded floral wallpaper after years of exposure. I move around the room, checking Mami's outlets for any outstanding beauty appliances. When my older sister, Clara, was here, she was always trailing Mami around the house, unplugging the blow-dryer, turning the oven off, capping her lipsticks, and airing out aerosol-filled rooms. Now that Clara is away at college, I have taken her place as the de facto fire chief of the Zavala house. Much to everyone's surprise, including my own, I have done a fantastic job.

"Hellooo! Time to wake up!"

I walk over to the window and yank the blinds open. The lumps stir. Mami lifts her head out from under her blanket. Her hair is falling out of the silk wrap on her head, and she's squinting at me. The tendrils of her hair are criss-crossed on her face. She looks like Cousin Itt, if Cousin Itt invested in satin nighties.

"Ay, Milagro, por Dios," she whines.

"Tía Lochita is gonna be here in . . ." I check my phone. "Two hours. Let's get you packed."

I duck my head into Mami's closet and feel around for anything that resembles a bag.

I look back at Mami and she's no longer squinting at me. She's sitting up, her arms crossed over her chest. Her cleavage is impressive, even when she's not trying to show it off. I can't help but glance down at my chest and curse my pathetic A-cup boobs.

"Since when do you want to help me?"

I dive back into the closet and make an "umph" sound, tossing Mami's favorite black stilettos over my shoulders behind me for packing. "I'm being a good daughter. Don't make me change my mind."

The second reason today is going to be life-changing is because today is officially my last day as a virgin. As soon as Mami takes off for a weeklong church retreat with Tía Lochita's "Single and Single Again" ladies' prayer group and Lulu leaves on her nerd field trip, Pablo and I are going to do it, in this house. It will be me, him, and my soul slowly departing to hell—that is, if Tía Lochita and Mami (and the nuns at school) are right. I can't wait.

My plan has been ten months in the making, ever since the morning Tía Lochita called me with a huge favor to ask: One of her girls had bailed at the last minute, and would I want to make extra cash by tagging along to a cleaning gig? Technically I was her third choice (rude), since Clara was volunteering and Lulu was out collecting signatures for some random clean water proposal. I said yes immediately. I had visions of a sequined blazer, specifically the silver one that had been on the headless mannequin at Time Again, my favorite thrift store. I didn't mind cleaning a stranger's empty house, even if it meant suffering through Tía Lochita's constant reminders to dust under the plates in the cabinets. ("La Señora Gutierrez always checks. They all do. Never forget under the plates!")

That morning, when Pablo Gutierrez stumbled into his kitchen and looked at me—really, really looked at me—I felt my stomach do somersaults and I got goose bumps down my arm. I knew I was going to lose my virginity to him. It was a feeling I had, like when I knew Clara's plants were going to die, despite all of our promises to water them when she went to college. Or how eight years ago, when Papi got a new family, hundreds of miles away, I knew we would never hear from him again, not even on our birthdays.

Anyway, when Pablo smiled at me, it was a sign, better than anything written in ink. I would have bet on it, if I had any money. By the time his dimple appeared, I was a goner, ready to sink a quarter in it and collect my reward. No, what I really wanted to do was throw my hands in the air and yell: "Thank God I'm not going to die a virgin!" But I held on to my secret and kept on dusting.

I didn't tell him later that night when he asked me out, his voice soft on the phone, almost a whisper. He was so quiet I made him ask again, even though I heard him the first time. He only ever texted me after that, but I liked that better, because then Lulu and Mami couldn't creep on our conversations. I didn't tell Pablo four weeks later when he said, "Milagro Zavala, will you be my girlfriend?" I said,

"Hell yeah." We made out in the front seat of his new black Jeep, my lipstick leaving a cherry-red trail that started at his perfect lips and wandered down his jaw until it reached the monogrammed collar of his St. Anthony's uniform.

Even when he started to get braver, his fingers wandering into the uncharted territory that began above my knee-highs, I still didn't tell him. Two weeks ago, we were in his bedroom and his hands tugged at the top button of my kilt and I said no, but his hands kept on pulling, like he could feel it was inevitable too. Then the button popped off and I really had to say no. He said, "Why not?" I didn't know how to say that I wanted to keep my secret a little longer, so I told him, "Please take me home." That night, when I walked into my house, I had to hold my kilt together, lacing my pinky through the buttonhole. I pretended my hand was on my hip because I had an attitude, and not cold feet.

Last week he texted me, **Don't you ever think about it?**

That question makes me so mad. I hate that just because I'm a girl, Mami, Sister May, and the rest of the world has decided I'm not supposed to think about sex stuff. Every day at lunch, Carmen and I go over all the reasons Pablo and I should do it already. We lay our French fries out on my blue lunch tray, one for each reason.

One long, greasy French fry for reason #1: Pablo is hot. Maybe more beautiful than me. That's what Tía Lochita

7

said when Pablo first started hanging around, along with a litany of things that were suddenly wrong with my out-fits: too short, too revealing, too much of everything. Tía Lochita says she tells me these things out of love; she doesn't want me to derail my life for the first boy who comes along. I get why she's worried: Pablo is stare-at-the-sun-and-forget-what-you-were-saying hot. It's his really long and dark eyelashes and his swooping hair that he gels and parts to the right, which only draws more attention to the deep dimple in his cheek, my favorite place to kiss him. On anyone else, his look would be pocket protector mate-rial, but on him, it's like looking at the photos of old movie stars that Tía Lochita keeps framed in her living room, as if they were her friends. Even after eleven months, looking at him hasn't really worn off, except for maybe when I have to listen to him talk. And nowadays, that's really all he wants to do, except for the sex stuff.

Reason #2 is worth two French fries: I don't know any other boys who I'd want to do it with, because I hardly know any boys at all. This is one hundred percent Mami's fault, for enrolling us in an all-girls high school. Most of the girls at St. Agnes rely on their brothers' friends for boy-friend sourcing, or they somehow manage to live next door to cute boys, or in Carmen's case, work the same shift at Regal Cinemas with a cute boy. But I do not have a job, and all my neighbors wear dentures. Finding Pablo was truly a miracle, and the fact that he is Argentinian is the cherry on top. When I told him I was Peruvian, he didn't ask me about llamas or make a joke about eating guinea pigs. (Why are those the only facts people know about Peru?!)

Reason #3 gets ten French fries, because it's the most important: as previously mentioned, dying a sad virgin is my worst nightmare. Every time we see her, Tía Lochita reminds us that we could die at any minute, so we better pray every day. Truck runs you over, poof, you're gone. Bad sushi today, flesh-eating virus tomorrow. Being rich doesn't save you either, she likes to tell us. Money won't stop a bear from breaking into your fancy cabin and mauling your face off—it happened to her coworker's neighbor's sister, she swears. Every time she tells these stories, I think, *Please, God, if you exist, don't let me croak before I figure out what sex is. Also can you please give Tía Lochita new things to talk about?*

At this point, Carmen always interjects with her #1 reason: it's not a big deal. She says she didn't "lose her virginity" because it's a made-up story that aunties and abuelitas tell to make you behave, like Santa Claus or La Llorona. Carmen is adamant that when she and Levi had sex for the first time, she didn't lose anything.

The last reason (reason #5, and worth five French fries, except we've always eaten them all by this point) is that I like Pablo, like *like* him. I like that he always buys me ice cream from the Mister Softee ice cream truck that does laps around St. Agnes and terrorizes last-period classes with its obnoxious jingle. It doesn't even bother me that he tells the same jokes over and over again, or that he can talk for hours without asking me a single question. He likes to share his interests. Last week, Lulu asked me if I loved Pablo and I told her she was too young to know how any of this stuff works, which is the worst thing to say to a big nerd like her. But I didn't know what to say. All I know is that Pablo whispered "You're mine" in my ear while we were slow dancing at the St. Anthony athletics formal, and it felt nice to belong to someone. I've decided that's enough for me.

"Oye. Milagro Isabela Zavala. I'm talking to you." Mami raises her voice from the bed, where she's scrolling through her phone, probably triple-checking that the other Indigo Hotel managers haven't mysteriously forgotten about her vacation, even after she asked for time off a whole month ago.

I'm trying to figure out what I can possibly say to Mami that won't make her suspicious, or lead to an hour-long discussion about how she "trusts me" to stay out of trouble on spring break, because even if she isn't, "God is always watching." Either conversation will make me miss the bus and land me in detention (Improper conduct: tardiness). When in doubt, blame Tía Lochita.

"Tía Lochita bet me that you'd be late. She said the last time you were on time, you didn't need hair dye to cover up your roots."

"She said what?" Mami snaps.

I step back out of the closet and look at her bed, which is now empty. Mami is on the move. She makes her way to her vanity and starts jabbing various wrinkle creams on her forehead and cheeks with alarming force. It'll be a miracle if the lotions can permeate the deep scowl on her face.

"Maybe Tía Lochita can go on the trip by herself, if she's so worried about being late. She doesn't need to wait for me. I don't wait for anyone."

Crap. As usual, I've overdone it.

Way to go, Milagro.

My palms are instantly sweaty and I rub the corner of my uniform kilt back and forth between my two fingers, frantically thinking of a way to backpedal. "Oh, you know, maybe she didn't mean it. She was probably grumpy because her Tuesday house 'forgot' to get cash for her tip."

"I keep telling her big homes are too much work for her. Those CEOs are always tacaños. The richer they are, the cheaper they get. She never listens to me," Mami says, her voice growing louder as she moves toward me. Her shoulders are relaxed again, and she's not mad at her big sister anymore. Fights in our family are always like this: hot flames that go out just as quickly as they pop up. I don't think Tía Lochita and Mami have ever gone longer than twenty-four hours without talking, even at their maddest. She kisses me on the forehead, then gently pushes me out of the way with her hip, so she can change out of her pajamas. We trade spots, and I sit at her vanity now, tucking her lotions, lipsticks, and brushes into a mini bag for her.

"Yeah, I think she probably wanted to vent. She's not as mature as you." As soon as the line flies out of my mouth, I know I've laid it on too thick. Ugh. I'm never this nice to Mami. I watch Mami's back stiffen in the mirror, and I prepare for her to whip around and say she's onto my master plan and she's not leaving. But instead, she turns around and holds something up to me.

It's a lone white Converse sneaker, or at least it was white at one point. It's the one Clara lost over winter break, the night before she was due back at the University of Iowa. All of us searched up and down the house, but we couldn't find it, even though our house is so small, it's practically bursting at the seams. On the car ride to the airport, Mami said the snowy Iowa winters would be good for Clara, since she wouldn't need her sneakers for a long time. She tried to make a joke out of it, calling Clara "Cenicienta" and "Cinderella," but no matter how hard Mami tried, she couldn't make Clara crack a smile. Then Clara told her that maybe Mami didn't know her any better than the guests at her hotel, and Mami was too stunned to respond. It was hurtful and didn't even make any sense. Mami's fancy boutique hotel serves way too many guests for Mami to ever get to know, even if it *was* her job. (Which it's not—Mami's job involves payroll, marketing, and occasionally stopping the lobby piano man from guzzling too many martinis.) After that, we rode to the airport in silence.

Tía Lochita says that families are like a rubber band: tension only brings us closer together. In our house, the tension stems from Clara, specifically the fact that she's no longer here.

Clara is currently at the University of Iowa, fulfilling her destiny of becoming a doctor. Even though she's been gone since September, it's still all Lulu and my St. Agnes teachers ever want to talk about, how the brilliant and selfless Clara will one day invent a new surgical technique, revolutionize cancer treatments, or cure an obscure disease. It took a lot of convincing for Mami to let Clara go to Iowa, even with Clara earning a full scholarship (of course).

Mami's suspicions about faraway colleges were confirmed when Clara came home for winter break as a completely different person. College Clara never wanted to talk to us about her classes, her roommate, or college life—maybe she didn't think we would understand. The only thing we could get out of her was that college was much harder than St. Agnes, and she was too exhausted to do anything but sleep most of the time she was home. After months of missing Clara, it was like having a stranger with us. Clara sucked the energy out of our shared room. Even Lulu, who had signed up for a community college course over winter break, started doing her homework in the kitchen.

Mami reacted the only way she knew how: by going on a cooking spree, furiously working her way through her *Mi Lindo Peru* cookbook. All winter break, we woke up to Mami tucking tamales away into banana leaves, pounding spices in the molcajete that she'd found at a yard sale, or stirring cow intestines over the stove. She was sure the bubbling green liquid would make Clara feel like herself again. She shoved plates of crispy chicharrones in front of Clara's face. Mami said she wasn't going to let "Iowee-nies," as she started calling them, let Clara forget that she was Peruvian. Clara had ancestral Incan blood, and it was Mami's job to remind her that she was just as worthy as the Sallys and Plain Joes on campus.

After their fight in the car, I figured Clara would

make up with Mami over the phone, but if her apology call came, we never heard about it. Whenever I ask Clara about it during our rare video chats, she always looks away and mumbles that she can tell me after Mami gets over "it." And Mami is even more vague, saying that Clara "knows what she did" and she's still waiting for an apology. Even though College Clara is back at school, the damage is done. Mami has turned her scrutiny to me, and now every time I want to hang out with Carmen or Pablo, I have to sit through an avalanche of questions, or worse, Mami has invented a pile of chores I have to do. I'm not perfect like Clara, and I'm bending under the weight of Mami's expectations. Maybe all along, Clara was too, and that's why she picked a college so far away from us.

Clara's stupid shoe is enough to make Mami's lip tremble, and full waterworks are on the way. It's just like Clara to find new and inventive ways to ruin my plans, even when she's hundreds of miles away.

"Go get your sister," Mami says quietly. "You don't want to be late for school. I can pack on my own."

In this moment, I'm not thinking about Pablo, or detention, or my spring break plans. I take a step toward her, but Mami shoos me away.

"Go, Milagro."

I zip her bag closed and turn on my heel, out the door

and down the hallway. I did the best I could. Now all that's left is making the bus. According to my phone, Lulu and I have ten minutes to make it to the corner.

But when I walk into the kitchen, my stomach drops.

Lulu is sitting at the breakfast table, dressed in her favorite World Wildlife Fund shirt and a pair of paisley boxers. Her hair is erupting from the messy bun perched on her head, which is hovering over a textbook that's big enough to contain all the secrets of the universe and then some. Her homework is sprawled over the kitchen table, a jumble of charts and graph paper, blue and red pens, and a dingy gray eraser the size of her fist.

She's got her brows furrowed and she's staring at her book like it might contain the solution to frizzy hair. I've seen this look before. It's the look that moves librarians to keep the library open an extra hour later, just for her. (Meanwhile I can't get them to forgive a fifty-cent fine.) It's the kind of concentration that causes Lulu to miss her bus stop because she's too engrossed in her book, forcing Mami to drive five neighborhoods away to pick her up.

It's an intensity that can only mean one thing: there's no way we're making it to school on time.

2
Lulu

ACCORDING TO THE World Wildlife Fund, the vaquita is the rarest mammal of the ocean. They are the color of a stormy sky and they are shaped like a dolphin that ate one too many tamales. Vaquitas are stubborn and stocky. They spend their entire lives in a tiny bay, flitting between Mexico and California, and their refusal to leave the familiar warm waters of home means that one day, there will be no more vaquitas left. Only ten exist in the entire world, not that anybody cares. How could they, with such a rude name? Who could possibly want to save the "little cow" of the ocean when you could devote your life to some sleek and shiny dolphins instead? Life is not fair to the vaquitas of the world.

"Lulu! What are you doing?"

My head snaps up from my endangered species book. It takes a second to realize that Milagro is yelling at me.

"I'm reading," I say, gesturing to the book in front of me. "You should try it sometime. You might actually like it."

Milagro scowls. "We have ten minutes to make our bus. We gotta get moving. Chop chop!" She claps her hands at me for extra emphasis, but I refuse to rush.

"School?"

"Yes, your favorite place in the world. We have to go! Let's go!"

"Okay," I say, gathering my books and pencils slowly. I move like my limbs are stuck in molasses, knowing the slower I go, the more annoyed Milagro will get. It's payback for locking me out of our room last night so she could try on every article of clothing that she owns. I know she did this because she left all her clothes on the floor.

"Lulu! Ten minutes!"

I roll my eyes at her and move a tiny bit faster. Technically Milagro is right that St. Agnes—specifically the fifth-floor science lab—is my favorite place in the world. On a normal day, it's me who's shaking her awake and dragging her away from the mirror so we won't be late. I'm not rushing because, unlike Milagro, I pay attention to these things. I actually know when the bus will get here. There's no way I'm going to be late today.

In twenty minutes, I'm supposed to be rehearsing

interview questions with Mrs. Johnson, bringing me one step closer to becoming a Stanford University High School Summer Scholar. Not only is Stanford the leading school in conservation biology, it's also where my favorite biologist in the whole world, Dr. Sophia Yu, serves as the director of Stanford University's Ocean Institute. And they have a twelve-week summer program that is 2,847 miles away from my house. It was Mrs. Johnson's idea to apply. She helped me fill out the application and write the essays back in September, even though I didn't think anyone would care about my research, or as Milagro likes to call it, "stomping around in puddles and smelling like a wet dog." (Milagro does not care about Baltimore's vital role in the ecological health of the Chesapeake Bay.)

I've spent the last six months scrolling through Stanford's website, clicking on bio after bio of all the professors and researchers who work there, but I've been dreading the interview, which is officially four days away. One wrong answer could derail my dreams of becoming one of the high school students on the wrinkled pamphlet that lives under my pillow. They all beam with ear-to-ear smiles as they peer into microscopes, toss Frisbees across an impossibly green lawn, and clink milkshakes in front of Stanford's iconic Hoover Tower. The program promises research that will change the world and friends who will last a lifetime, two things I would like very much.

Last year, my closest friends were the seniors in the Sierra Club. Even though I was a lowly freshman, they still invited me to every signature drive, local protest, and playground cleanup. When they graduated with Clara, the club fell apart—a mix of lack of interest and limited club funding. I'm on the leadership committee with a few other freshmen, and we're trying to get more people involved, but it hasn't happened yet. I know I have to be patient, but it's hard not to be tempted by a summer of instant lifelong friends who have the same goals as me.

"Lulu, you're going slow on purpose! Hurry up!" Milagro whines. She's standing in front of the kitchen sink and inspecting her chin for pimples in the reflection of the window.

"Milagro. Why are you making so much noise in the morning?"

Milagro and I both turn to look at Mami, who enters the kitchen. She's dressed in an impossibly tight pair of jeans. The kind that say, "Hello! I have curves and I'm not going to apologize for it." Mami yawns and walks over to me to give me a kiss on my head. Her gold Virgen de Guadalupe necklace gently bumps against my neck. She slides one hand over my shoulder and with the other hand, she traces the bright red cherries on the oilskin tablecloth.

"I was thinking, maybe I shouldn't go on this trip."

Both Milagro and I look at each other, but neither of us says anything. Me, because I don't want to encourage Mami to bail on Tía Lochita's trip. Milagro, because her mouth is fish gaping, opening and closing as she tries to figure out exactly what to say.

Mami continues, "It's going to be a bunch of old ladies. Wouldn't it be better to stay home with my girls? We could have so much fun."

Mami's hand on my shoulder doesn't feel like love anymore. It feels like an anchor, tying me to this kitchen seat, to our little house, to Baltimore, the only city I've ever known. Mami looks down at me with a smile so wide, I can see the silver fillings in the back of her mouth.

Tick. Tick. Tick.

The old cat clock ticks loudly, his eyes shifting left to right as he surveys the room. The clock hasn't told time correctly since Mami hung it up, but it used to hang in *her* mami's kitchen back in Peru, so she refuses to get rid of it.

Mami seems unconcerned by our lack of response. "Don't you think? It could be fun. Like the old days."

My stomach clenches. I have to say something.

"Mami, I'm not going to be here, remember?" I take a deep breath and continue, "I'm going on the St. Agnes field trip. I have my interview with Stanford at the end of the week?" My stomach churns even saying this out loud.

"Oh, right," Mami says, all casual. But her hand is tightening on my shoulder, so I know she hasn't forgotten.

Six months ago, when Mrs. Johnson nominated me for the program, it was the best day of my whole life. I burst into the kitchen to deliver my news.

"It sounds boring." Milagro was blowing her nails dry. "Do you really want to spend your summer inside, leaning over a cold lab table?"

I threw my hands in the air. "I would spend my whole life in the lab if I could."

Mami frowned. "Milagro. You need to take your studies seriously, like your sisters. Pablo can't be your only hobby."

Milagro glared at both of us before stomping out of the room, but Mami didn't care. She told me, "I'm so proud of you. And I bet Clara will be too. We'll have to get you an interview outfit." She pulled out a giant stack of coupons from inside our junk drawer and started to riffle through them.

I never got my outfit. Instead, Clara came home for winter break a totally different person, and Mami began having serious second thoughts about college. She started frowning whenever she saw me in my Stanford sweatshirt, or when I showed her all the research options I could choose from. By the time Clara went back to Iowa, Mami went from bragging about her oldest daughter's full ride to college to telling us at least once a week that Iowa was nothing special, and there were just as many great colleges in Baltimore.

As usual, Milagro interrupts my thoughts. "Mami, you have to go on this trip. Tía Lochita will be so disappointed if you don't. And you know how much better you feel after you pray. And Lulu will be safe because the trip has two whole chaperones. A teacher and a priest."

Detention and hell. What else could make us behave? Milagro is trying hard to sound normal, but she's talking way too fast, her words spilling over each other. I stare at her, trying to understand why she suddenly cares about Mami's spiritual life.

Mami's eyes are shiny, and she blinks really fast before sighing. "Fine. I'll go with Tía Lochita and her prayer group. But if I come back looking like an old lady, years closer to death, it will be all your fault."

"With that outfit? You could never look like an old lady. Speaking of, Lulu! You need to put your uniform on. Chop chop!" Milagro says again. It's even more annoying the second time. Mami moves away to the sink, giving Milagro the perfect opportunity to slap her noodle arms on my chair and drag me out from under the table.

I stomp off, moving quickly to get away from Mami and Milagro. Milagro trails me down the hallway.

"Um, can I get a little privacy?" I say, turning to her before I open the door to our room.

"Psh, for what? We share everything." She reaches over me and opens the door for both of us. Milagro is right: we've always shared a room. Clara and me in bunk beds—Milagro says Clara lords over us from the top bunk—and Milagro on her own twin bed. Even now, months after Clara left, I keep expecting to see her perched up on the top bunk, twirling her hair as she reads through her AP Bio textbook.

I take a few exaggerated steps over the clothes and bras and lacy underwear that Milagro has strewn across our floor and grab my uniform, changing in the corner, where I can avoid Milagro's judging eyes. She is always quick to catch my imperfections, of which there are many, starting with the heavy-duty sports bras that I like to wear ("But Lulu, why wouldn't you show off your rack? They're HUGE!") and ending with my faded undies and black bike shorts that I wear under my kilt. I've told her a million times that I don't care that they're ugly, because they're comfortable. And since when does underwear have to be anything more than functional?

"Okay, perfect, let's go!" Milagro says the second I slip my feet into my ugly uniform black-and-white oxford shoes. I grit my teeth and try to keep from pointing out that I am not a small child or rambunctious golden retriever. I'm a high school sophomore who wants nothing more than to be left alone with a pile of books, a bag of Cheetos, and an endangered species documentary.

Things didn't used to be this way. Until I started high school, Clara, Milagro, and I were inseparable. We'd do our homework tucked away in a corner of the lobby of Mami's hotel, then race each other in the giant swimming pool during the hotel's happy hour. We started to drift apart when Clara signed up for nightly SAT classes that kept her late at St. Agnes, followed by weekends volunteering at church. Milagro was the next to drift off, thanks to Pablo. But even as we got busier and busier, we were still a bonded atom: the Zavala Sisters. In quantum theory, chemical bonds keep atoms in line, keeping them from turning into bombs or floating away. If Clara was here, she'd tell Milagro to leave me alone, and then we'd work together to figure out whatever Milagro has up her sleeve. But Clara is at college in Iowa, leaving Milagro and me unstable. We are electrons buzzing around, full of reckless energy that can't be contained. Occasionally we collide and sometimes I even think we're finally bonding, until Milagro says, "Can you please stop talking about nuclear fission. It's very boring."

I throw a few books in my bag, and then Mami walks us to the door and hugs us both goodbye. She squeezes us tight, like she's not going to see us for years, instead of a measly six days. Mami's coconut shampoo mingles with Milagro's favorite Victoria's Secret perfume. It's like I'm at the mall and not in the middle of a sweaty family huddle.

"Be good, okay?" Mami says to the top of both of our heads.

Milagro breaks free first. She tells Mami, "We always are." Her hand finds mine and she drags me away, out the door and down the street. We've moved a total of three feet when I hear Mami call me back. "Luz."

"What?" I glance back at her. Mami hardly ever uses my full name.

"Promise me that you'll stay here this summer," Mami says. Her eyes are wide open and extra exaggerated by the fake lashes that she and Milagro are obsessed with. "Not like Clara. There are so many programs you can do here, Luz."

There it is again.

"You don't need to go far away. Not yet," Mami says, her hands shoved deep in her jean pockets. *Not ever* is what she really means.

All the street noise fades away. My heart is racing, and I can't stop staring at the wrinkle down the middle of Mami's forehead, the one that appears every time Clara calls and doesn't want to talk to Mami on the phone. Sometimes I see that wrinkle on me. From her spot in the doorway, she can't see Milagro mouthing the words "Tell her what she wants" and anxiously pointing at the bus, which is two blocks away and slowly making its way toward us.

Milagro squeezes my fingers, her glitter talons digging into the top of my hand. I think of the smiling students on the Stanford brochure, who look nothing like me. I probably won't be accepted to the program. Mami's dark brown eyes are pleading with mine. Her hand grips the splintered door frame of our house, and her lip trembles. It takes a second to form the words that I know she wants to hear, the ones that make me crumble on the inside. "I promise."

My words are quiet, nothing more than a whimper, but they act like Photoshop magic. The wrinkle disappears and Mami is back to smiling. She gives us a tentative wave and closes the door.

"See, that wasn't so bad, was it?" Milagro calls over her shoulder as she drags me to the corner. She doesn't know my world is crashing around me.

"Sure," I say. Look how good staying home turned out for the vaquitas.

3
Milagro

"YOOOO-HOOO! BERTHA!" I wave my arms back and forth, doing my best to hail my least favorite bus driver, who is a block away and seems to be driving extra slowly today.

"What are you doing?" Lulu stares at me.

"What does it look like I'm doing? Come on, help me!" I grab Lulu's arm, moving her and my body through the air like we're those inflatable air dancers at a cheap car dealership.

"What! Stop!" Lulu tries to wrestle her arm away, but I lock my fingers around her wrist and jump up and down.

The bus finally screeches to a halt in front of us, drowning out Lulu's whiny protests. She yanks her arm out of my grip and shoves it deep into her kilt pocket. Bertha creaks open the doors for us, greeting us with her usual frown and mustache hairs. I swipe my card in the bus meter and move down the aisle, only to realize that Lulu isn't following me. I glance back at her. She's digging through the pocket in her kilt. She starts rummaging around in her backpack. Crumpled papers and old napkins fall out as she hunts through the debris.

I'm not taking any chances. "Wait!" I run back and dump all the change I have in the meter machine, until it makes the familiar *beep-boop* sound. "Yes!!" I pump my fist in the air and wiggle my hips in celebration. I knew skipping out on vending machine Skittles after yesterday's detention would pay off.

"MOVE ALONG!" Bertha bellows, waving us on and keeping an eye on us instead of the road. I look back at her and make a cross-eyed face before plopping into our usual seats. Lulu takes her sweet time, peering out the windows like the view is going to suddenly be different from the other thousand times we've ridden this bus.

Even though Baltimore is this giant city, our 7:02 a.m. bus is full of regulars. There's the man who never has a left shoe, who sits up front and wiggles his toes at all the oncoming passengers when we make a stop. His toenails are beyond repair. Not even Carmen's mom and her professional manicure skills could save him from the crusty yellow disaster. All the way in the back are the two oldie lovebirds, who ride the bus while sharing headphones and staring into each other's eyes. In my head, I call them Henry and Henrietta, because of their matching monochromatic clothes and shared bowl cuts. Once Carmen and I skipped school and treated ourselves to giant hoagies and monster slushies, and we ran into them at the corner store. Mami says real love doesn't exist, but she hasn't seen Henrietta surprise Henry with a Twix bar, or Henry kneel down to unroll Henrietta's accidentally cuffed jeans.

Since Lulu and I live the farthest out from St. Agnes, we're always each other's seatmates. Everyone thinks we're super close, since Mami makes us do everything together, but Lulu and I operate on two different frequencies. She's all boring talk radio, full of opinions on stuff you can't even change, while I'm the kinda music that makes you want to dance your face off and shake your head so fast, your earrings fly across the room. When Lulu finally makes it to our row, we're inches apart on the bus seat—okay, fine, we're squished because I'm spilling into her seat, leaning over into the aisle and staring at traffic through the giant bus window, willing Bertha to move faster—but we're basically entire galaxies apart.

"Nice of you to join me."

Lulu ignores my sarcasm and gently pushes me back to my seat. "Do you know why Mami and Clara are mad at each other?" she asks. She's running her hands over her kilt and smoothing out the wrinkles with her thumb.

"Huh?" I scrunch up one eye.

"I don't understand why they're not talking. She hasn't responded to any of my texts about it. What's the point of being offered an interview at Stanford if I can't actually go?" Lulu can't hide the note of pride in her voice, even as she picks at the fraying edge of her sweater, unraveling the threads.

Ugh, again with the summer program. Stanford and the college field trip are all Lulu has talked about for the last six months. She keeps telling us that we don't understand, she needs to go if she wants to get into a good college like Clara. "Clara is being dramatic. She'll come around." I'm jiggling my knee, wishing the bus could sprout wings and soar over rush-hour traffic.

"Has she said anything to you about it?" Lulu looks up at me, her brown eyes wide. Lulu never looks to me for answers. It's always the other way around, me asking Lulu how stuff works or whether she thinks something is a good idea. (The answer is always no.) I can't help her, because Clara won't tell me either. Clara has always been buttoned up, too nice to stay up late gossiping about the girls at our school, or the nuns and priests. Since she's been gone, Clara only ever asks me about Pablo. Even when I ask her about classes, her roommates, or what Iowa City is like, she always turns the conversation back to dating. My whole family is convinced my only interests are makeup and boys.

31

"I don't know, Lulu. Their fight will blow over eventually."

"You don't get it. This is really bad." Lulu slumps down in her seat and pulls her book out of her backpack, but she's not really reading it. She stays stuck on the same page for way too long.

I know Lulu misses Clara a lot, which is why I would never admit to her that a tiny part of me is relieved that Clara's gone. Lulu and I have a little more breathing room now that we're not in Clara's shadow. Tía Lochita calls Clara "una angelita" and says Clara was sent from heaven to show us all how to behave. It's hard to be annoyed with Clara about it, since all she's trying to do is make Mami happy. She's the kind of person who always bakes good-luck brownies the night before Lulu's biggest tests, or you'll-do-better-next-time cinnamon rolls for me. When I'd get annoyed at her for being so *good* all the time, Clara would be the first to apologize, even though it's my problem, not hers. She can spend hours agonizing over saying the wrong thing, long after you've forgotten about the conversation. It's very easy to imagine her as the world's nicest doctor. Clara knows how to lighten things up with a joke; meanwhile I'm always too mean. Like when we were little, I used to tell Lulu that she was adopted, or maybe even an alien, since she was so smart, nothing like me. Clara would always swoop in and say maybe Lulu was like Superman, full of secret powers that she'd uncover when she got older.

There is something uncanny about Lulu, and it's not just her big brain. It's the way she's always trying to hide from the world. Her hair is so dark, it's almost black, falling in a curtain over her face when she bends down over her reading, which is all the time. Lulu used to beg Clara to braid her hair, but Clara always refused, because Lulu would undo the braids as soon as they were in. Lulu only wanted the aftereffects: crimped waves that made her straight hair as unruly and wild as mine and Clara's. (Or at least as wild as Clara's hair was before she straightened it every morning.)

But it's not only her hair that's different. Clara and I are boring straight lines, with bodies like the frozen green beans Tía Lochita used to make us eat. No bumps, no detours. (Unless I'm wearing a push-up bra—heyyyyy.) Underneath her baggy sweatshirts and wrinkled jeans, Lulu is more like Mami: too much to handle. "Una empanada mal envuelta," Papi used to say when he visited, poking at her stomach whenever her shirt rolled up. Tía Lochita says if you speak ill of the dead, they come back to haunt you. Papi is not technically dead, but he is dead to me, so all I'll say is good riddance.

I check my phone for the millionth time. By some miracle, we might actually be early to school. I lean my head against the window and watch the buildings slowly start to change as Bertha winds her way through the city. The old redbrick row homes with chain-link fences fade away to shiny new buildings and bold and weird statues that mark the beginning of the Johns Hopkins hospital zone. This part of the bus ride is always rough, thanks to the permanent construction. Every month, it feels like there's a new research center popping up, or a fancy high-rise building. We all shift slightly to the right as Bertha maneuvers the bus around an orange crane before making her next stop. I smile at the trio of nurses who climb on. They've just wrapped up a graveyard shift at the free clinic, and each one is trying to outdo the other with their fluorescent scrubs. They take turns deciding who has to stay awake and let the others know when their stop is coming. The other two don't know that the one with purple braids always falls asleep, even when she's on duty. She sits in front of me, and whenever it's her turn to stay awake, I give her a little poke before their stop and she'll jolt herself awake and look back at me with a finger on her lips. I like it when I can pocket a secret before the day has started.

"HALLELUJAH! JESUS SAVES!"

Oh jeez. I can hear the corner preacher man even before Bertha sidles up to the sidewalk and lets him amble onto the bus. He's a walking scarecrow, skin and bones in an ill-fitting suit that's patched at the knees and fraying at the edges. He smells worse than old Crusty Toes, like preaching the Bible is so time-consuming, he can't stop to slide some deodorant on his pits. But the worst is his booming message. It's the most awful parts of St. Agnes's religion classes and Tía Lochita's dichos, full of judgment and an infuriating certainty that whatever you're thinking, it's definitely sinful.

"HALLELUJAH! TURN AWAY FROM SIN," he shouts at the nurses, startling them awake. One of them lifts her hand up to give him the middle finger before closing her eyes again. The other wipes her face. She got spit bombed. The preacher moves down to us, and he points his knobby finger at me, over Lulu's head, and screams, "FORNICATION WILL LEAD YOU TO THE DEVIL!"

My body locks tight, my elbows stiff to my sides. Goose bumps are spreading all over. My face is hot, which means it's turning red. I'm a tomato with a movie reel for a brain, running over all the X-rated images of Pablo and me that I've been dreaming about.

"FORNICATOR!" he screams again, only this time he's staring me in the eyes. His eyes are brown and unblinking.

How does he know?

All the joy from making the bus on time is gone. I want to throw my glitter backpack in his face. Tomorrow is supposed to be *my* secret, and he's taking it from me, twisting it into something I'm supposed to feel bad about.

"TURN TO JESUS! IT'S NOT TOO LATE FOR YOU!" he yells.

I clench my fists, then open them to reach down for my backpack, but Lulu is faster than me. She hands me one of her earbuds without even looking up from her book.

"Imagine being so obsessed with an essential biological function that ensures your species' survival. It's ridiculous." Lulu's cheeks redden a little, but she keeps on reading.

I pop her earbud in my ear and turn to thank her, but Lulu has already turned up the volume of her *National Geographic* podcast.

SCREEEEEEEECH.

I fly forward as the bus comes to a complete halt. My head bumps hard against the blue seat in front of me. Lulu's book slams into the seat too.

Bertha marches out of her seat and bellows, "That's ENOUGH of that."

She shoos the preacher off the bus like he's a stray cat. The preacher takes one look at Bertha's wide shoulders and flexed biceps and obliges, slipping out the back door without another word. On Bertha's walk back to her throne, the nurse on lookout duty gives her a big thumbs-up. Bertha ignores her and resumes her ride.

As we get closer to school, the homes get nicer— gleaming gold door knockers and window boxes overflowing with flowers. The tempo on the bus changes too, like

Bertha cranked up the volume and hit the disco lights: St. Agnes Power Hour. The baby freshmen pile on first, their regulation-length uniform skirts practically dragging on the ground. Even though it's April, they still haven't figured out that just because nuns run the school doesn't mean they have to dress like one. A few blocks later, the seniors show up too, huffing and puffing from running down the block to catch the bus.

Normally, this is when I do my best eavesdropping, but I can't get the preacher's words out of my brain. He took one look at me and knew. What good is a secret if it's written all over your face? He's a freak, I remind myself over and over again. He doesn't know anything. I get back to my phone vigil, anxiously watching the minutes tick by. I try to focus on Lulu's words, how sex is a "biological function" and not a Big Deal, but it *does* feel like a big deal. Pablo is my first boyfriend, and this is my first time.

When the doors finally open in front of St. Agnes's trusty steeple, I scramble off the bus like it's on fire, dropping Lulu's earbud on her lap and leaving her in my dust. She glares at me when she hops off the bus a few minutes later, but I'm too distracted by a familiar honk. Carmen's station wagon is pulling up to the curb. I've got more than a few minutes to spare, so I wait for Carmen to climb out.

Carmen is my best friend in the whole world. She likes

to say we're the baddest b*tches at St. Agnes, since we roll our skirts up the highest and we don't give a flying whatever about what Sister May says. With the exception of today, it's mostly true. I don't hide in the back of the classroom like Lulu, or bend over backward to please people like Clara.

"Hey, chica!" Carmen high-fives me.

"What's up? Hola, Abuelita!" I wave to Carmen's grandmother, who climbs out of the car and shuffles over.

"Hay, hijita, ¿por qué te pones estas cosas en la cara?" she says, her wrinkled fingers hovering over the winged black eyeliner that I finally nailed down in sixty seconds.

"Because she wants to, Abuelita," Carmen chimes in.

I stoop low, so Carmen's grandmother can run her thumb over my forehead in the sign of the cross and offer me a quick blessing. I hold my breath while she does it, hoping that she doesn't see what the preacher man saw: all my plans for tomorrow, how nervous and excited I am to finally have an excuse to wear my lacy red bra.

"¿Qué vas a hacer esta semana?"

"I'm staying here for spring break," I tell her.

"Alone," Carmen jumps in. "Because her mother trusts her."

Carmen's grandmother's eyes go wide and she shakes her head.

I'm with Carmen's grandmother. I'm still in shock that

Mami is letting me stay home alone, or that she believed me when I told her Pablo was going on a cruise with his parents. I had to agree to two FaceTimes a day, but it was worth it. I stand straight up on my tiptoes. "I can take care of myself!"

"Sí, sí, sabiduría. You know everything, just like Carmen. You need to be busier. Too much time on your hands is no good for pretty girls like you. El Diablo is always around. Ojo, pestaña, y ceja." She pries her eye open with her wrinkled fingers, so we can see the whites of her eye and the delicate red veins that lead into her sockets.

"Abuelita! Gross! That's enough. Bye!!!!" Carmen saves the two of us, bending over to give her abuelita a kiss on the cheek. She quickly shoves me toward the door and whispers, "She's getting even weirder by the second. Yesterday she tried to put avocado peels on my head!"

"No, she didn't. You're lying."

"She said it would take the frizz right out of my hair."

I grab Carmen's shoulder. "She's so wrong. Your hair is perfect."

"I know that. But tell me again in case I forget."

I slap Carmen away. We make it to homeroom on time and swing open the door. Thirty empty desks stare back at us.

Oops.

Carmen and I look at each other. I'm wincing and

39

Carmen is chewing on her thumbnail, both of us trying to think of what we missed.

The hallways were suspiciously quiet when we ran in, but I figured everyone was feeling as antsy as me about spring break. We look up at the saint calendar on the wall. Today's date is circled in red. Above the calendar, a porcelain Jesus gives us a stern look.

"Oh crap." My stomach sinks.

"Double crap," Carmen says.

"How are we supposed to remember all the mass days? It's not fair," I whine.

"What if I pretend I have cramps? Like maybe I'll hobble in and you can be helping me," Carmen says, bending over and pushing her hand on her lower belly.

"We're so screwed."

We turn around and run up the slate stairs, our feet pounding as we make our way to the auditorium.

"Let's pretend like I had a vision and you were trying to capture it on YouTube. It worked for all those saints."

"I don't think Sister May knows what YouTube is."

Carmen makes a face and tugs on my skirt. "Wait up!"

I reach the auditorium doors first. The choir is singing "Alleluia" (it still sounds terrible without Clara) and no one is looking at us. It's perfect.

I pull the door open and sneak in. I whisper to Carmen over my shoulder, "Don't let the door . . ."

CLANG!

The whole auditorium whips around to stare at us. Carmen's mouth freezes in a grimace. The choir is finished singing and the auditorium is deathly silent, except for the thundering steps of Sister May, who marches up the aisle to us.

"Young ladies!" Sister May whispers, only it's loud enough for all of St. Agnes, Lombard Street, Baltimore City, Maryland, the United States, planet Earth, and maybe even Pluto to hear.

"You should be ashamed of yourselves. And during Lent!"

Carmen goes cross-eyed behind Sister May's face. I don't want to laugh, but sometimes a giggle is like boiling hot lava and I'm erupting.

Sister May places her hands on the boxiest part of our blazers, somehow managing to dig her thumbs underneath the shoulder pads and find the muscle that makes us powerless to her. It's nun magic. She parades us down the auditorium, all the way to the front, behind the nurse's row, where all the sick kids sit. Today, Jennifer Nelfin and Dani Canner are red-eyed and sniffly. Within two minutes, they add three snotty tissues to the bulging pile threatening to spill out of their blazer pockets.

"Gross. So our punishment for coming to school late is diphtheria?" Carmen whispers to me.

"How do you even know what diphtheria is?"

"Don't you pay any attention in class? It's what we forget to celebrate at Thanksgiving." Carmen shakes her head at me. I put a finger on my lips. I'm *not* getting extra detention today.

When it's time to shake hands for the sign of peace, Jennifer looks at us and turns red, then a pale shade of green, like she might vomit all over us.

Carmen waves her off. "We don't make peace with lepers."

"Shhh!!" Sister May turns around and glares at us. "My office. Later," she mouths, pointing at the St. Agnes crest on my blazer.

Triple crap.

I want to point to Carmen and blame her, but I'm no snitch, even if it means all my carefully crafted plans have gone POOF!

One phone call between Sister May and Mami and I'm totally screwed.

Or rather, not.

4
Lulu

LACRIMATION **SOUNDS LIKE** a gross word. It's right up there with *constipation*, which, like lacrimation, is your body rebelling against you. The human body is a collection of eleven organ systems, and you are in control of exactly zero of them. Science hasn't made up its mind about why people cry, but this morning, in the sun-drenched physics classroom on the fourth floor of St. Agnes, it's Mrs. Johnson's fault. I'm doing my best to blink away the tears, but it's hard with Mrs. Johnson going on and on about Stanford.

". . . is a great opportunity! You'll spend the summer researching with the head of the marine biology department. Only one student from each state is selected to attend."

When Mrs. Johnson pulled me aside after mass, I couldn't bear to tell her what happened earlier this morning. How could I explain that Mami had forced me to give up Stanford before I could even interview for it? I'd spent all of mass wondering what Mami would ask for next. I know she can't legally keep me home forever, but I'm not brave enough to tell her that. Mrs. Johnson didn't notice my silence. She only wanted to apologize for flaking on our early morning interview practice for mysterious administrative reasons. She pulled out the itinerary for the trip, as if the schedule hasn't been engraved in my brain for the last five months:

ST. AGNES + ST. ANTHONY ANNUAL
COLLEGE FIELD TRIP

Saturday: Monongahela University
Bus departs from St. Agnes at 8:00 a.m. sharp!!!
Information session + campus tour
Dinner in the dining hall

Sunday: University of Notre Dame
Mass at the basilica
Volunteer with student organization
Attend a club meeting

Monday: University of Notre Dame
Shadow a college course

Attend a Notre Dame baseball game
Guided tour of Notre Dame's neighborhood

Tuesday: Piedmont College
Depart from Indianapolis International Airport at 9:00 a.m.
Information session + guided tour
Guided tour of San Francisco
Walk the Golden Gate Bridge

Wednesday: San Francisco
Students' choice: art, food, or history tour of San Francisco
Depart from San Francisco International Airport at 9:00 p.m.

Thursday: Baltimore
Pickup from Dulles International Airport at 7:00 a.m.

On her copy, she penciled in *Makeup interview prep: Luz Zavala. (45 min.)* in between Monongahela University and mass at the University of Notre Dame. In her wobbly handwriting, she added an additional bullet to Tuesday's list of activities: *Stanford University interview + campus tour: Luz Zavala (1 hr. 45 min.).*

"Once we get to campus, of course, we'll meet with the

financial aid office. Stanford University has great resources for their summer programs," Mrs. Johnson continues.

Mrs. Johnson hasn't caught on to the fact that I'm blinking back tears.

"I can't go," I whisper. My eyes are darting all over the classroom, looking for something, anything to stare at. I focus on the huge globe that hangs in the corner of the room. If I squint, I can still make out the Eastern Hemisphere. *Somalia. Madagascar. Yemen.* You can't cry if you're concentrating hard enough.

I take a deep breath, but my words still come out muffled. "We don't need to practice. It's pointless to even interview. I can't do the internship." I watch her smile fade and her forehead wrinkle up in confusion.

"Of course you can. It's normal to feel scared." Mrs. Johnson presses on: "That's what the practice is for. And the interview will be on campus, so you can get a feel for the school. It's all about baby steps when it comes to trying new things."

"I don't want to do it," I say, lying through my teeth, "I'm sorry. I have to go study." I'm a hazard zone for tears, and this conversation needs to wrap up ASAP.

"Luz. I understand you might feel nervous about an incredible opportunity like this. Why don't I talk to your mother about it? I'm sure she'll have some words of encouragement for you."

"No! Don't do that," I yelp. "She likes me to . . . be independent." Except that couldn't be further from the truth. If it was legal to tie teens to their mother's wrists, like those toddlers on leashes, Mami would do it.

"I still think she'd like to know what an honor it is to even be offered an interview. Earning a spot in this summer program would be a huge boost to your eventual college application."

"No. It won't be," I say, but it's Niagara Falls all over my face. I'm a blubbering mess, mad at myself for losing it, and at Mami for taking this away from me before I've even gotten it, and at Mrs. Johnson, for standing there and staring at me in horror.

Mrs. Johnson's carefully penciled eyebrows nearly reach the top of her hairline. When she picked out her sunflower-printed cardigan and matching yellow skirt this morning, she probably hadn't been planning on adding snot to her outfit. She gets up from her desk and awkwardly raises her arms toward me. I take a step back from her slow-motion pity hug. The warning bell goes off, announcing the start of the next class. It saves us both. She moves away from me, relieved.

"Why don't we talk about this later?" she says. "Take this for now." She hands me the schedule. On the back, there's a list of interview questions. My hand trembles as I take the paper from her. Unless Mrs. Johnson figures out how to reprogram Mami with "no-good American values" (this is what Mami calls the tradition of sending your kids away for sleepovers, sleepaway camp, and college), it's not going to happen. I walk out of her classroom, shove Mrs. Johnson's sheet of questions into my kilt pocket, and make a beeline to the bathroom.

The narrow hallway is full of girls rushing to class to get the day over with, so spring break can finally start. The last bits of mass have already worn off. All it takes is a few quick rolls of the skirt, some strategic unbuttoning, and a door-knocker earring or two for the pious girls of St. Agnes to return to their natural state. I didn't bother to do anything different for mass, so there's nothing for me to change.

I try my hardest to stare at the ground and not to look anyone in the eye. When I finally make it inside the bathroom, I lean over the sink and look at myself in the mirror. My eyes are red and swollen, and there are streaks of salt down my chubby cheeks. Some people look graceful when they cry, like modern-day damsels in distress. I look like Bertha backed her bus up over my face, and the rain fell, and the scavenger crows came, and what was left is what's staring at me in the mirror. Flat dark brown hair, thick eyebrows that Clara says are "expressive" and Milagro says are caterpillars. Two pimples on my chin, chapped lips, and red blotchy skin that desperately misses the summer sun.

Sure, my promise to Mami was only about the summer internship, but that was just *today's* promise. What happens tomorrow, or next week, or even next year? Every chance she gets, Mami says Clara should have picked a more sensible school, preferably in a ten-mile radius of our home. That rules out all the colleges that I'm visiting this week.

St. Agnes's annual college trip is the coolest field trip for the top-performing students at St. Agnes and St. Anthony (that's the all-boys school that's St. Agnes's "brother" school). It's a jam-packed six days spent touring campuses, sitting in on clubs and classes, and traveling the country. Most important, the trip is *always* the top ten of St. A's juniors, never sophomores like me. When I found out I'd qualified, Mrs. Johnson had been skeptical, worried I was too young to "appreciate the trip." Her eyes flitted to the hole in my sweater under the "St. A" emblem that covered my heart, to my hands, drowning in the ocean of navy-blue sleeves, no matter how often I push them up. I spent weeks convincing Mrs. Johnson that I was ready, and when she found the Stanford internship for me, it all clicked into place.

Only now, everything I've been looking forward to is a huge lie. It's getting harder and harder to pretend that one day, it'll be me clutching textbooks and rushing to a Greenpeace meeting, or trading lab notes with someone who didn't assume I'd do all the work. Could I actually leave Mami and go somewhere as far away as California, or even Iowa, like Clara did? Who would take care of her? Milagro? She'd drop Mami for a glitter taco.

I can feel the tears threatening to spill over again, and I give myself a small slap on the cheek. I've got to pull it together. Crying isn't going to fix anything. I throw some water on my face and use my sweater sleeve to dry it off. When I walk into chemistry a few minutes late and take my seat in the back of the class, Mr. Young points his piece of chalk at me, but he doesn't say anything about my face or the fact that I'm late. Being an A+ student has its perks.

He's standing in front of the classroom and lecturing from a notebook in his hand. ". . . As you can see, the vaporization . . ." In the front row, Gracelynn Hunter is texting under her desk, and next to her, Genevieve Reedy is doodling a picture of a swamp monster eating Mr. Young. The rest of the class is drifting off to sleep, powerless under the calm drone of his voice. Unlike most teachers, who put on a movie and decided spring break should start early, Mr. Young is determined to teach us the principles of thermodynamics. I want to pay attention and take notes, but my brain is racing, thinking of how to convince Mami that this summer, the next year, my whole future could happen somewhere other than our front stoop.

According to Clara, her first semester of college was unbelievable. She couldn't stop raving during our texts and calls. Everything was "so amazing" and "gosh darn incredible" and she was "loving every single part of it." Milagro thought Clara was exaggerating, or maybe even lying—"Everything can't be 'soooo amazing' all the time. And since when do you say 'gosh darn'? There must be *something* that bothers you?"—but Milagro was wrong. Every video call with Clara was confirmation that there was a whole life waiting for me, full of friends and world-changing potential. When Clara came back over winter break, I started to wonder if maybe Milagro was right. Clara didn't look like someone who was living her best life. She seemed kind of sad, and nothing could snap her out of it. I figured she missed her college friends. When winter break ended and she went back to Iowa, her texts resumed their cheerful tone, and on all of our FaceTimes, Clara *seemed* like her normal self. So it must have been Baltimore that was the problem, or maybe it was us.

"Luz? What do you think?"

I jump at the sound of my name. Around me I hear giggling. Mr. Young is staring at me. He points to the board, where he's got a chemistry problem laid out.

"Um . . ." I rack my brain for the answer.

"Solve for joules, perhaps?" Mr. Young says, throwing me a lifeline.

"Yes, definitely," I say. "Joules."

He returns to the board, but not before I catch his frown. My shoulders slump. I have been disappointing people all day.

When class ends and the lunch bell rings, I'm the first one out and making a mad dash for the emergency roll of pink Starbursts that I keep in my locker.

To get to the sophomore locker room, you have to take the back stairs, all the way down to the basement. As I walk in, I check the bulletin board, even though I know exactly what to expect. Two blank flyers, with no new volunteers signed up for next month's playground cleanup. I sigh and check my phone. I have ten missed texts from Amber Whitfield, canceling the Model UN meeting. She's going to Aruba with her family and can't stay after school. Everyone on the thread responds Jealz! and OMG no way! and Bring back a tan for me! I mute the texts and put my phone in my pocket, right next to the interview questions. This is the perfect opportunity to go home and figure things out, starting with Clara and why she and Mami aren't talking. My future is riding on it.

5
Milagro

ONCE I READ in *Cosmo* that the secret to getting people to do what you want is all in how you carry yourself. Look imposing, and people will fall to your feet. I strut my way into Sister May's office like the dingy maroon carpet is my personal runway.

Mrs. Randall, the school secretary, takes in my power pose, complete with my hands on my hips and my head cocked to the side. She is not impressed. She points me to the row of chairs outside Sister May's office. "Please wait here," she says, her voice so low, I have to lean in to hear her. The office is quiet, nothing like the giggles and screams of laughter that filled the hallways outside. Mrs. Randall is staring at me. I wish Clara was here, and I know Mrs. Randall does too. Clara has this magical way of making grown-ups listen to her. I used to call her Santa Clara, patron saint of Goody Two-shoes. If she was here—not that she would ever be called to the principal's office, unless it was to make an announcement about some food drive she was running—she'd know all the right questions to ask, like *How are your tomatoes growing?* or *Is little Emily walking?* She asks the kinds of questions that feel like a waste of time, but they make grown-ups feel safe. Except when Clara is asking them, she actually cares about the answer.

Mrs. Randall moves on to harrumphing at me. This whole time, I've been tapping my glitter nails on the armrest and apparently, it's *really* bothering her.

"Sister May will see you now," Mrs. Randall whispers to me, like this is a museum and I've been caught rubbing my fingers all over the *Mona Lisa*.

The door to Sister May's office is heavy and coffin brown, which is fitting, because I feel like I'm walking into my own funeral. When I open the door, Sister May is staring at me from behind her desk, only she's not alone. Mrs. Johnson, my biology teacher, hovers behind her.

"Let's get comfortable," says Sister May, pointing to the small love seat in the corner of her office.

Mrs. Johnson drags two chairs over and positions them in front of the couch.

I start to get goose bumps, because this feels more serious than the don't-be-late lecture I was expecting, or even,

"We called your mother and she's on her way."

"I'll cut straight to the point," Sister May says, shuffling the stack of papers in her hands.

I gulp. Whatever is coming next cannot be good. My power poses have gone out the window and I'm staring at the ground between my crisp white sneakers.

"You're doing exceptionally well in biology." Sister May lays the papers down on her desk. "And we'd like to talk to you about that."

I stare at Sister May. "I'm what?"

"Doing exceptionally well. Your grades have never been better." She smiles at me. "Mrs. Johnson was the first to alert me to the news."

I sit up a little taller. I've never been called to the principal's office for something *good* before. My eyes widen in wonder, taking in Sister May's habit and pearls. Maybe she's not so evil after all.

Sister May continues, "Believe me, I'm as shocked as you. Your grades have taken a tremendous swing since last year. To think, last summer you were in danger of academic probation, and now, with these recent developments . . ." Tiny bits of spit are flying out of Sister May's mouth as she gets more and more excited about my grades.

Huh. All those months of racing to get my homework done so I could hang out with Pablo or Carmen actually paid off? My heart rate is returning to normal, and all I can think is—*I'm saved!* Maybe even more than saved. I've seen how the honors students prance around school. At St. Agnes, having good grades is like a superpower, deflecting all suspicion and wrongdoing. I can't wait to tell Carmen that I'm never getting detention again!

"There's an opening on the annual St. Agnes spring break field trip. As you know, the spots on the trip are decided by GPA rank. Given your high GPA and the fact that several qualified honors students have prescheduled vacation plans, you're the next student on the list for the trip." Sister May smiles at me. "This is a good thing, Milagro."

Wait a second.

"Me?!" I point to myself.

"Yes. As I mentioned before, we're all as surprised as you." Sister May stares at Mrs. Johnson, who winces and hands me an itinerary of the trip with a trembling hand. The whole time, she's been eyeing my lace over-the-knee socks and big hoop earrings, like I'm a feral cat.

"You want to punish me for getting good grades?" I yelp. "But. But. But." I squeeze my eyes shut. Visions of my perfect week with Pablo are going up in flames. This can't be happening. There has to be some mistake.

"Milagro?"

Oh, right. I open my eyes again, and now Mrs. Johnson and Sister May are staring at me.

Mrs. Johnson takes over. "We think that seeing some colleges could get you even more excited about your future. And we know how successful the trip was for Clara."

I resist the urge to roll my eyes. When Sister May uses the royal "we," it makes sense, since she's BFFs with Jesus and all. But when Mrs. Johnson does it, it's extremely patronizing. I'm plenty excited about my future, particularly the next five unsupervised days of my future. I know that's not what Mrs. Johnson means, but she can't force me to care about college. It's different for Clara and Lulu. They know exactly what they want to be: Clara, a doctor. Lulu, a biologist. I watched Clara stay up late for countless nights filling out the applications and studying for the SATs, with posters of famous doctors taped above her desk. I have no idea what I want to do two weeks from now, let alone five years from now, and I don't need a big trip to rub it in my face.

"We also think you could use some time away from *distractions*," Sister May interrupts Mrs. Johnson, taking a long pause to stare at me and really linger on that word. Her gray eyes bore into my head, like she's rummaging around and finding every last thing I've been up to. This is the second time today someone has tried to read my mind.

"Maybe I like distractions!" I grit my teeth. There's no way I'm going on this trip, for a million reasons that all start with the letter *P*. I need an excuse and I need one fast, or it's RIP to Operation Don't Die a Virgin.

Think, Milagro, think.

"I . . . I don't have the money to go," I blurt out.

It's not even a lie. Mami has been working overtime ever since Clara started school. She works long hours and stumbles home, collapsing on the couch at the end of each day. I put her to bed, putting away her half-eaten bag of Doritos and dabbing her face clean with a makeup remover wipe so she doesn't wake up and look like a raccoon.

"We have some funds for students in your . . . situation," Mrs. Johnson says.

"What situation?" I ask her, my eyes narrowing. I want her to say it out loud, that I'm not like the other girls at St. Agnes.

But Sister May tut-tuts and saves Mrs. Johnson. "Jennifer Nelfin has been diagnosed with mono, so she can't go on the field trip. The trip is nonrefundable, so we need to use her spot. Plus, your mother is so relieved, now that you and your sister will be together on the trip. This is a gift. Hundreds of girls would kill to go on this trip."

Pablo's face flashes in my mind. Hundreds of girls are not dating the hottest player on St. Anthony's basketball team. Wait a second. I squint at Sister May. "How do you know my mother is relieved?"

Sister May smiles at me, the way a shark might look at an especially plump seal. Her teeth are pearly white and in full view. "We've talked to her already. It's all set up. She emailed us a permission slip. She asked for you and your sister to be partnered, so you could look out for her."

"But I told her that was impossible. The partners were chosen months ago," says Mrs. Johnson, clearly huffy that I'm wrecking her plans.

Sister May rolls right over her. "Your mother also said something about a prayer retreat and how it's already working. I told her the Lord works in mysterious ways."

Oh, I'll bet Mami's retreat is working—working to keep me a virgin forever! I'm supposed to be on a week-long vacation, uncovering the secrets of the universe, not wandering around strange cities with a bunch of nerds who think they're better than me.

"Of course. That makes sense." I smile at Sister May and pull myself out of her love seat. Mrs. Johnson's eyes are jumpy and she's tracking my every movement. "I'll talk to my mom and confirm," I say, pulling out my phone and walking backward out the door.

I walk out of Sister May's office and check the time. Lulu's Model UN club meetings always run long. Time is on my side, and I have at least three hours.

I scroll through my phone, until I find the number with a heart emoji.

SOS. You need to come get me NOW.

6
Lulu

THE LAST BACHELOR is a dating show about thirty women competing to marry a very boring man. There is nothing intellectually stimulating about the show, unless you want to ponder the odds of how they could have picked so many blonde Laurens. Technically, *The Last Bachelor* does not count as a documentary series, even if it is reality television. It has never even been nominated for an Emmy. When Clara first got into the show, I'd read my book while she watched, lifting my eyes up from the pages only to point out how cliché everyone sounded. "I like this." "I am falling for you." "My heart's journey led me to you." Give me a break.

The only interesting parts of the episodes were the dates they went on, like a hot-air balloon ride over New Mexico's reddest plateaus, a midnight bioluminescence expedition in the Florida Keys, or a test run of a NASA antigravity machine. But the contestants never asked anything interesting on these dates, like how tectonic plates might be rumbling under the San Francisco coastline or whether recent bioluminescent cancer trials held any promise. Instead, they talked about their feelings. It was all very unscientific and melodramatic. But then as the episodes went on, it grew harder and harder to return to my book. *The Last Bachelor* quantifies things that even the most thorough psychology textbooks won't touch, like how you go about getting a date or how falling in love works. Tilt your head to the left when you kiss. Don't cry until the fourth date. Never mention your past. Finally, someone was sharing the rules!

Within four weeks, I was hooked and rooting for Paulina, the Texan radiologist with an adorable tooth gap and big dreams of opening a medical clinic in the Dominican Republic. After six weeks in, I was maybe even a bigger fan than Clara. On Thursday nights, when Mami was working and Milagro was out with Pablo, we'd watch from either ends of the couch, our toes inches apart. We'd feast on huge bowls of mac 'n' cheese and down it with bottles of spicy ginger beer. We'd eat so much, our pee would turn orange, but it was always worth it.

I want to ease into my conversation with Clara before I bombard her with questions, so I text her, **Can we talk?**

I miss you! along with a photo of the cheesy pasta box, hoping it jogs some memories. While I wait for her response, I dump cheese powder over noodles, add extra butter, and go over every conversation we had over winter break. From the second Clara landed, I had so many questions for her. I wanted to know everything: about her biology labs—whether she'd actually gotten to design her own experiments, or if the professors set all the parameters. I wanted to know what it was like to roam the library whenever you wanted to—on the first day of school, Clara had texted us that the University of Iowa's library is open twenty-four hours a day. I was dying to know if she had thought more about what kind of doctor she wanted to be, or if she'd like to go into research. But Clara just kept saying everything was "fine."

At first, I chalked it up to time-zone difference, or maybe she was crashing from pulling all-nighters before her finals. Surely when Clara got one or two nights of sleep in her, she'd be back to normal—magically finding Mami's and Milagro's lipsticks under the couch cushions, or surprising me with crumbly airplane cookies, my absolute favorites. Tía Lochita tried to snap her out of it by taking her to church, so all the priests and nuns could fawn over her and tell her how much they missed having her as a volunteer. Clara turned down all of Milagro's suggestions to get out of the house, even when Milagro said Carmen could sneak us into the movies for free. After a few days, Milagro gave up and spent her winter break in the St. Anthony gym, cheering for Pablo during his basketball tournament. She invited me to come too, but I wasn't going to leave Clara alone, even if it was clearly what she wanted.

Clara spent most of winter break on our couch, buried under a pile of blankets and watching reruns until way too late. Sometimes I'd creep to the bathroom late at night and see the white glow of the screen over Clara's face, her mouth clenched closed and the frizzy hair around her temple forming a soft halo. I always went back to bed before she could hear me.

Clara finally opened up on our last night together, when we went on the hunt for gloves thick enough to protect her from Iowa's brutal midwestern winds. "It's not as easy for everyone else," Clara said, interrupting my long monologue on how unfair it was that Jenny Woolstone expected me to do all the work on our history project.

My eyebrows shot way up. "She hasn't even read the assignment! She asked me if we could write about Amelia Earhart, and our project is supposed to be on the Revolutionary War. We didn't fight the British with planes!"

"You don't know what she's going through," Clara said, ducking down to rummage through the discount bin at CVS. "She might have other stuff going on."

I crossed my arms. "Jenny said she has been too busy

learning how to play the viola upside down, and that's why she hasn't worked on our project. She wants it to be her act for the talent show. Remember, I sent you the video?"

Clara looked up at me. Her hair had fallen over one of her eyes, but the other one stared straight at me. "You never know. Things can be harder than they seem. Maybe you should try to ask her what's going on."

I sighed. "I don't want to. I just want to go to college already, so I don't have to deal with slackers anymore. You're so lucky."

Clara dug deeper into the bin. "College isn't going to fix everything for you, Lulu. Not if you don't learn how to fix things here first. People are more complex than the black-and-white pages of your biology textbook. You'd know that if you spent more time with friends instead of in the lab."

My mouth dropped open. I *did* hang out with friends— it just happened to be at club meetings. Maybe we weren't as inseparable as Carmen and Milagro, or even in the same grade as each other, but that stuff's not important. The rest of that shopping excursion was silent, with occasional small talk about the annoying holiday songs that played on the car ride home. I kept waiting for Clara to apologize, but College Clara didn't do apologies.

For years, Mami has hammered the importance of college into our brains. Life would be easier for us if we only got good grades and stayed out of trouble. We'd have so many more opportunities than than she or Tía Lochita did. Clara was supposed to be the first of three brilliant success stories, all written by Mami, but College Clara and the three weeks of winter break changed Mami's tune so fast. Overnight, Mami became an expert on local colleges, pointing out every Towson University and Goucher College bumper sticker that we came across. It was clear she had decided Iowa was way too far for Milagro and me. She'd let one daughter get away, and she wasn't making that mistake again.

Achoo!

I stop spooning the mac 'n' cheese into my bowl and cock my head. There isn't supposed to be anyone home. Milagro always goes to the movies with Pablo on Friday afternoons, and Mami is long gone on her retreat. Earlier today, she texted Milagro and me a photo from the pool. Tía Lochita is doing her usual grimace—she never smiles in photos—while Mami's eyes are hidden behind comically oversized glasses that she definitely "borrowed" from Milagro.

Achoo!

I get goose bumps down my arms. The screen door might be broken half the time, but there are four locks on our front door. More important, there is nothing in our house that is worth stealing. Last year, Mrs. Smith found a stranger asleep in her shed. He was harmless, she said, an old person who had wandered away from his senior community and didn't know how to go back. He came back twice, and each time she sent him on his way.

"Volverá, y te va a matar," Tía Lochita said, when Mami told her this story. She said it again in English to show how serious she was. The wine sloshed out of her glass as she waved her arms in the air. "He will come back to kill you. Nunca confíes en un hombre." At the time, that seemed melodramatic, but now I tiptoe back into the kitchen and grab a knife from the drawer, just in case.

You really only have a one in sixteen thousand chance of being murdered, and those numbers go down when you're in your own home. Interestingly, they go way, way up if you have a husband around, but we don't have that problem here.

I creep down the hallway, careful to avoid the planks of wood that bend and creak under my weight. I pass the smiling photos of Clara, Milagro, and me dressed in pink satin dresses and holding flowers, and the framed portrait of la Virgen de Guadalupe. The door to Mami's bedroom is wide open. There's not enough space in her little room for anyone to hide in there, unless it's under the giant mountain of dirty laundry that's piled under her vanity.

I check the bathroom next, holding my breath when I whip back the wrinkly blue shower curtain that has seen better days. But the tub is empty, and so are the linen closet and the hall closet. I'm growing more confident and moving faster, certain now that I made the noise up. I creep to the end of the hall, careful not to let the floorboards creak. When I make it to the room I share with Milagro, the door is shut and there's light peeking out from under the crack.

I pause for a second. A small shadow falls across the door crack. I'm triumphant. Ha! I'm not hearing things. Then the reality sinks in: there is someone in our room. The goose bumps are in full force now, all over my body, and my mouth is very, very dry.

I squeeze the handle of the knife in one hand and reach for the cell phone in my pocket.

He's harmless. He's confused.

I repeat this over and over again, until the phone is firmly in my palm. Then I realize I have no one to call. If I call Mami and Tía Lochita, they'll cancel their trip, and mine too. Milagro always takes hours to respond to my texts.

I pull out my phone and dial 9-1-1 on it, my finger hovering over the green call button just in case. The shadows move again, and there's a grunt this time. I can't believe this is the way I'm going to go. I don't even have a patent or an endangered species to my name. I regret the fuzzy purple socks that I wore to school today. What kind of aspiring scientist dies wearing polka-dotted socks?

He's harmless. He's confused.

The shadows move again, and this is it. Here I go. I take a deep breath. I shove the door open and scream, "GET OUT! GET OUT OF HERE!!!!"

I stand in the threshold of the door and wave the knife in the air like a musical conductor from hell.

"AHHH!!"

There is a giant lump on Milagro's bed, under her blue-and-white star-printed comforter. The puffy blanket is moving in all directions, constellations rising and collapsing with every second.

"GET OUT!!!!" I scream again.

I run to the bed and put my hand on the corner of the comforter, but then my hand touches something dry and grainy. It's a long, very hairy leg, clad in tall gym socks. The soles of the socks are so dirty, they're almost black.

"AHH!" I scream, and jump back. The room smells like Mami's flowery perfume and extra-strength cologne. I wave the air in front of me as I look around the room. There's a crumpled uniform skirt—Milagro's?—and comically large, bright white sneakers next to it. There's a lacy red bra—one I've never seen before—hanging off the bed and the goose bumps are gone, replaced with hot, hot embarrassment.

"Milagro?" I whisper, like I wasn't yelling seconds ago.

Milagro's head pops out from under the comforter. Her face takes in the knife and phone in my hand. "What the hell! Lulu! GET OUT OF HERE!" she yells. "Why aren't you at your meeting?!" She leaps up out of her bed. Only her head smashes into the shelf of porcelain angel figurines above her bed. The angels take flight, falling all over Milagro's bed and the floor. We both cover our ears and squeeze our eyes shut as the figurines crash.

Boom!

There goes Choir Angel, Mami's gift to Clara when she made the select choir ensemble at St. Agnes.

Boom! Boom!

Baby Angel and Birthday Angel are no match for gravity.

Boom! Boom! Boom!

Neither are Angel Puppy and Winter Wonderland Angels.

When I open my eyes, the room is painfully silent. Milagro is staring at the tiny pieces of porcelain and glass all over the floor. I don't know how this could be any worse.

Pablo's head pops up. His perfect hair is messed up, gelled pieces poking in different directions. Milagro's reflexes are faster than Clara's ever were. She shoves his head back under her comforter.

She turns back to me and her eyes flash. "Get out of here, Lulu!" she screams.

For the first time ever, I do exactly as she says.

I turn and run.

7
Milagro

RIP Milagro Zavala, ~~loving~~ fun sister, ~~adequate~~ academically accomplished student, and expert selfie taker. Cause of death: extreme humiliation. She leaves behind a collection of hoop earrings, a stack of unpaid lunch fines, and enough dry shampoo to survive three apocalypses. In lieu of flowers, Ghost Milagro asks that you wear an outfit that shows off your bra.

"IS SHE GONE yet?" Pablo whispers from under my comforter.

How nice of Pablo to attend my funeral.

"Milagro!" he whispers again, a little louder this time. His hand brushes my bare stomach, and my insides do flips. Not the butterfly kind. The kind when a rickety roller coaster is climbing the first hill. It's the squeeze of my stomach and half of my brain joining forces, screaming,

"Hey, get me off this thing!" while the other half of my brain refuses to do anything that embarrassing and grips the safety bars even tighter, until the two halves reach a compromise: We are not babies. We can handle this.

"She's gone. The coast is clear," I whisper back.

He pops his head out and surveys the damage, taking in the broken figurines lining the floor, the tiny porcelain shards sprinkled on the bed, the hardwood floor, the fluffy pink rug that's next to my bed. He reaches up and pulls a small piece out from my curls.

"This could cut you," he says, before tossing it in the direction of the trash can.

It lands inside, of course. Pablo pumps his fist. "Yes!"

"I know how glass works," I tell him. Pablo ignores me, like the last three minutes never even happened. He doesn't seem to feel the need to stop and wonder: What if Lulu tells Mami that Pablo was in my bed? Have I traumatized Lulu forever? And maybe most important—is this a giant sign that Operation Don't Die a Virgin is a colossal mistake?

Pablo has never had a moment of doubt in his life. He's not even looking at me, that's how focused he is on the task at hand. Instead, his eyes are staring at the lacy bits of my underwear. His hands reach out to touch the edges, where the delicate flowers meet the soft satin. Here we go again.

Pablo straightens out, fully lying over me, his legs

alternating with mine. One boy leg, one girl leg. One boy leg. One girl leg. There is no part of me that is not touching him. All my bare skin knows is the soft cotton of his summer basketball camp shirt and the slippery silver athletic shorts that spill over my thighs. I'm smothered in fabric and his heavy breathing, kissing my neck, my ear. His gelled hair is crunchy under my chin as he goes to work, making out with my neck. It's like getting slapped with noodles.

I pull myself away from Pablo and he takes it in stride, scooping me up so my legs are wrapped around his waist. "You're so beautiful," he whispers, pushing my hair off my face. This is farther than we've ever gone, the most naked we've ever been, in our eleven months of dating.

We're both breathing heavily. His thumbs knead my sides. He traces a finger down the length of my back and I shiver.

I don't like feeling out of control.

"Wait, Pablo."

He takes a second too long to respond, and when his eyes meet mine, there's no hiding the annoyance. "What? Do you want this to happen or not?"

The "or not" hangs in the air like a thunderstorm cloud. It's a threat—everything could be ruined. *We* could be ruined.

"I have to go to bathroom, I swear." I reach out and cup

his chin when I say this, so he knows I'm telling him the truth. His skin is baby soft, like he's never had a pimple in his life. Boys are so lucky.

"K. Ready when you are, babe." He shifts off me and I'm free. I hop out of bed and bend over, somehow still embarrassed that he can see me in my underwear. I slip my shorts and a tank top on and walk out of my bedroom to do a quick survey of the house. The house is deathly quiet. Knowing Lulu, she won't be back for hours, not until the librarians send her home. All I can hear is the hum of the refrigerator and muffled honks from outside.

I walk into the bathroom and stare at my reflection in the mirror, at the black curls that swarm my face and my golden-brown skin. Mami says I'm the color of sipping on the sun, my body forever storing warmth and golden rays. I wish it'd store some answers too.

I always thought I'd know what to do in this moment. It would *feel* right. But I'm as clueless as I was two hours ago, when this was a wild scheme in my head. Pablo might be my first boyfriend, but I'm not his first girlfriend. I don't want to mess this up. Why isn't there a sex-for-dummies hotline? My eyes stray to the pile of well-worn magazines next to the bathtub. The headlines scream out at me: *10 SIGNS HE LOVES YOU. IS YOUR FRIZZY HAIR HOLDING YOU BACK?! 14 JEANS THAT SHOW OFF*

YOUR CURVES. My eyes settle on the last one—*DRIVE HIM WILD IN BED!*—and my stomach unclenches a little bit.

When I walk back into my room, there's an extra pep in my step. Pablo isn't gonna know what hit him. He looks up from his phone and smiles. He pulls at my tank top, ready to get this show on the road, but I push his hand away. I muster all the courage in the world before whispering to him, "Let me tie you up." His eyes grow wide and he flings his hands back against the bed, his chin moving up and down with tremendous force. I get a shiver down my back. This power is thrilling.

In my hands, I'm holding silky scarves, the ones Mami wears when she can't be bothered to wash her hair. I kneel by the bed, clumsily tying Pablo's wrists to the iron bedposts. It's hard to tie a knot when a boy is trying to kiss you, but I am a new sex goddess, so I manage. When I stand up, Pablo is practically drooling, watching me. His eyes trace up and down my body. I wonder if this is what the polar bears at the zoo feel like, thrilled to be the center of attention, yet thousands of miles away from anything resembling normal.

If only I could get Pablo to stop looking—then I could really be in control. I make a spur-of-the-moment decision and quickly straddle Pablo. "Oof!" he says when I sit on him, but when I tie the scarf around his eyes, he's back to all smiles. I admire my handiwork. There is a very hot boy hostage in my bed. Call me Coach Milagro, because now *I'm* making all the calls. I wave my hands in the air, a private dance party to celebrate my newest accomplishment.

"Milagro?" Pablo asks.

Oh, right.

I grab the pink shimmer lotion that I keep under my bed, the one that Lulu tells me is killing the environment by leaching chemicals into the ocean. The only thing worse than a buzzkill is a glitter buzzkill.

I start in the safe zone, at Pablo's shoulders, rubbing in the glitter lotion like it's sunscreen and I'm concerned about UV rays. I don't dare look down at his shorts. We'll get there when we get there.

"Ooh, that feels good," Pablo says, sounding as surprised as me.

I glance up from his shoulders and take a long look at his beautiful face. Pablo is smiling so hard, like he won the lottery or his basketball team made it to the championships. If there wasn't a zebra-print scarf covering his eyes, I bet they'd be crinkly in the corners. That's how wide his smile is. I pump my fist in the air. I knew *Cosmo* wouldn't let me down.

Next, I tackle Pablo's super long arms. I slow down, my thumbs making small circles, growing more confident with every minute that goes by. The only thing that could make this more perfect is music. "Hang on a sec," I tell him, leaning over to kiss his shoulder. He gives a small sigh. This stuff isn't so hard after all. I reach across my bed to grab his phone. Pablo's playlists are always better than mine.

When I hit the home screen, time stops.

Maybe even my heart stops.

The only thing that keeps going is my stomach. That roller coaster I felt before? It overshot the big hill and launched directly into space.

On the phone are two perfect boobs, encased in a lacy bra that's fancier than I could ever even dream of owning. They are decidedly *not* my boobs.

I tap the photo and a message thread opens up. Tons of messages fly by as my finger frantically scrolls through the chat, until I can't bear to look anymore. A drop of water hits my finger. I'm crying.

"Uh. Milagro?" Pablo says. "Are you okay?"

I look at him, shining brilliantly in his glitter skin. He looks superhuman, which is fitting because he is stomping all over my heart. For the second time today, I'm dying. Only this version feels a million times more humiliating. This isn't nuns or fate or little sisters conspiring against me. It's someone I love taking my feelings and tossing them over a cliff.

"What is this?" I say, pulling open the photo and

zooming in. My cheeks are burning red and the fury is spreading. I rip the scarf off his face and shove the phone at him. I can't bear to look at the photo again. It wasn't meant for me.

His eyes widen, looking frantically around the room. I can practically see the wheels turning in his brain as he struggles to come up with a lie. "I can explain, I swear," he says. "Please. It's not what you think."

I spent hours thinking through every single detail about today. This was not how it was supposed to go.

"I could have anyone," I say to him, stealing a line from that show that Clara and Lulu watch together. I want to tell him I am special, or maybe I want him to say that to me, to say anything, do anything other than sit there with his head hung low.

"Get out," I say. Louder again, "Get out!"

He makes a face at me and wiggles his limbs.

Oh, right, he's tied up. Everything is wrong. I reach over and undo the knots, and he grabs his clothes and runs out the door, not bothering to pull his shirt on before slamming the door behind him. He doesn't even look back at me, to see what he's left behind.

The house is quiet.

I offered my virginity to the universe and it was soundly rejected. "No thanks. We'd like your dignity instead."

8
Lulu

I'VE WATCHED NATIONAL *Geographic*'s specials on the mating rituals of spring. I've sat through St. A's sham of a sex ed class, which involved no actual mention of the word *sex*, just diagrams of body parts and a list of STDs we could research on our own time. I even made it through "The Miracle of Life," the in-class movie about childbirth, without looking away a single time. But that doesn't mean I want front row tickets to the *Milagro and Pablo Get It On Show*! I feel embarrassment creep over me again. My skin feels hot, red, and blotchy, and I can't get this metallic taste out of my mouth. I walk faster, trying to put as much space as possible between me and whatever is happening in our house. I may never be able to look Milagro or Pablo in the face again.

I try to remind myself that one week from now, I'll

return from the field trip like the majestic phoenix, rising from the ashes of humiliation. Milagro and I can forget what happened and return to our regularly scheduled programming of carpool buddies who occasionally help each other on our homework (me) or give unsolicited fashion advice (Milagro).

In the meantime, I'm wandering on my favorite walk, past blocks of boarded-up homes. People think the homes along this walk are ugly, but they aren't looking at it the right way. Today on Hugo Avenue, someone has snuck fake daisies in the gaps between the wooden boards covering the windows, a flash of cheerful yellow. Below the daisies, six tiny plastic figurines, aka "Homies," stand on the window ledge, each one sporting perfectly slouched pants and impeccably shaved hair. I look over both of my shoulders before sneaking one of the figurines into my shirt pocket.

From old photos, I know what this neighborhood used to look like, decades ago when there were block parties, epic crab feasts, and Cadillacs lining the streets. St. Agnes's Sierra Club started off with these big ideas about saving the world from plastic consumption and overfishing tuna in Fiji, but it felt so futile. We switched gears when we learned the neighborhoods around our school were looking for extra manpower (or "young lady power," as Sister May says). Now we show up for neighborhood initiatives, which all end up benefiting the environment in the end, whether it's making the harbor cleaner or improving the air quality. Writing letters to city council about lead poisoning or delivering census forms is hardly a glamorous or immediate cure, like Clara saving someone's life (I'm too squeamish for that to even be an option), but it still feels important.

Thirty minutes later, I've made it to the only place that can make me forget Earthquake MilagroPablo. The rusted metal grate squeals as I shove it to the side and bang on the glass door. The door is frosted on purpose, so you have to go inside to see what they've got, but I squint anyway, searching for signs of life. Paddy's Pawnshop is a relic from when this neighborhood was all Irish cannery workers and giant Catholic families spilling out of their homes and into the churches that dot every corner in Baltimore. Fifty years later, the fancy deli and old saloon on either side of it have transformed into a Chinese takeout restaurant that never seems open and a Laundromat with windows so yellowed, you can barely see the washing machines. But Paddy's has stayed the same, covered in signs that scream "WE BUY SCRAP GOLD" and "WE HAVE CASH FOR YOU!!!" Whatever cheer the signs inspire is entirely undone by the metal grate that encloses the store.

Last fall at St. Agnes, I signed up for a semester of "Local Living History" for extra credit, giving up my lunch period in exchange for learning more about Baltimore.

Our big project was to interview a business that had been open for at least ten years. Most of my classmates picked cool places to hang out, like the vintage thrift stores down by the waterfront, or the North Pole, the ice cream shop where all the St. Anthony boys work. A few girls even got away with interviewing their grandparents about the law firms they'd started, or plumbing businesses they owned. I'd walked and ridden past Paddy's every day for the past year and a half, so I used the project as an excuse to find out what was inside.

The first time I walked into Paddy's, I was scared, like I might get stuck in the store, trapped in one of the glass cases and put up for sale. I'd never seen anyone walking in or out of there on my way to school. Tía Lochita told me they sold guns there, if you knew the right words to say. I went in anyway.

I discovered the original Paddy was dead, and Rick, Paddy's son, is a very bad comedian who keeps the shop open to fund his late-night improv gigs. There isn't anything seedy about him, except for his collection of ugly hats. During our first interview session, Rick told me the place functioned more like a neighborhood storage unit. People traded stuff in before payday and came right back for it once their new checks cleared. Sometimes he'd get newbies, "nosy folks like yourself," he said, gesturing to me, but he never sold them anything that the owner wasn't trying to get rid of. After the interview, he showed me all the stuff that people had left there over the years, stuff he couldn't bear to sell, like a Van Morrison signed guitar pick and a miniature bust of a former Baltimore mayor.

Paddy's has become my favorite spot to visit when I need time to think. It's where I put the finishing touches on my summer application for Stanford, where I found Milagro's birthday present (a rhinestone gecko ring that wraps around her middle finger), and now it's where I'm hoping Clara will talk to me.

Rick calls out, "Just a minute," from inside the store, and I tuck my hands into my skirt pockets. When Rick finally opens the door, he's smiling so wide, his cheeks push up against his old-timey wire glasses frames, the giant ones that I see cool kids wearing ironically.

"Hi, Luz! What a surprise to see you here," he chuckles. "Here for another interview?"

"Nope. You're off the record today. Feel free to commit as many crimes as you want."

"Crime," he muses. He laughs again. "That's a good one."

I shake my head at him. Rick is the only person who thinks I'm funny. He gestures at me to step inside. "You know the drill. You break it, you buy it." He steps behind the counter and cues up a stand-up comedy special on his ancient laptop. The audience's canned laughter erupts from the speakers, filling the shop with guffaws and hoots.

I wander away from Rick, through shelves full of weird art lamps, dusty television sets, and random musical instruments. I make my way to my favorite rocking chair, all the way in the back. It's nestled under a blinking neon sign advertising "Fresh donuts!" and there's a stack of hunting magazines from the 1950s next to it. I take a deep breath and call Clara.

The phone rings twice before she answers. "Hey, Lulu! I don't have that much time to talk. How's the pasta?"

My mind blanks and then I remember the photo I sent her. "It's good. It needed more Old Bay."

She laughs. "Of course you would say that. How's Milagro?"

"She's . . . fine." I blurt out what I just accidentally saw, making sure to include every gory detail.

By the time I'm done, Clara is laughing so hard, she swears she's crying. "I never liked those angel statues anyway. They were so creepy. Trust me, Milagro will forgive you. She's never going to live this down, though."

Her laugh fades away and then I'm quiet. "Are you going to make up with Mami? You have to," I rush out. "Just apologize or whatever. You guys can't be in a fight forever, right?"

Now it's Clara's turn to be silent. In the background, I can hear coffee shop chatter, the clinking of plates, and a coffee grinder spitting out beans.

I keep talking, hoping it'll spur some action from Clara. "It's not fair. She's mad at you and taking it out on me. I want to do things just like you. You get to live your dreams of becoming a doctor, but what about me?"

Clara's sigh comes in hot and loud over the phone. "I don't—I can't. It's hard with Mami. I just need some more time. Maybe this summer? Your trip starts tomorrow, right?"

"This summer?! That's not soon enough!" I'm glad Clara can't see me rocking furiously back and forth. "It has to be sooner. Earlier this morning, Mami made me promise—"

"Hold on. Oh, shoot."

"You wait! Are you listening to me? I need to—"

"I have to go. Robbie is calling me. Talk soon!" Clara abruptly cuts off and I'm stuck listening to the dial tone. I drop the phone in my lap, all hot and bothered again. I can't believe her. Wait until this summer? I might as well wait until I'm ninety. I don't know how to convince Clara to help me.

It's like everyone in my family is trying to sabotage me. It's hard to see any way out of this mess. I take the folded-up paper out of my pocket and stare at the list of questions that Mrs. Johnson wrote up. There's no use answering them if I can't get Mami on board, and that starts with getting through to Clara. I stand up to go, trudging down the aisle.

"I have to go," I tell Rick.

He closes his laptop solemnly. "People do things for good reasons, you know. Even if you don't understand them." He gestures to my fist, which clenches my phone.

I cringe. "You heard that?"

"I've been in this business long enough to know that everyone comes around eventually." He shrugs. "People do the right thing, even if it takes them years to figure it out."

"I don't have years!" I blurt out.

He shakes his head. "Poor wording. Sometimes it only takes days." He slaps the counters, setting off the sports bobbleheads that line the cash register. Their plastic heads jiggle up and down. "I'd say these guys agree with me."

I stare at their dusty sneers. Most of them sport Baltimore jerseys, but there are a few rival Pittsburgh team players in the mix, with mustaches scrawled on them. I reach my finger out to steady one of the bobbleheads.

Clara had to get off the phone because of Robbie, her ultra-boring long-distance boyfriend. They're long distance because Robbie is in Pittsburgh, at Monongahela University on a swimming scholarship. Monongahela University is the first stop on the trip. I perk up as the synapses in my brain start firing. If Clara won't talk to me, then maybe Robbie will. If Robbie can tell me exactly what happened between Mami and Clara, or even give me a few hints, maybe I can figure it out on my own. All I have to do is find Robbie and everything will be fixed before Mrs. Johnson even realizes I've snuck off the campus tour. Then I can go back to prepping for my Stanford interview and fly off into the sunset.

"There's that smile!" Rick shouts at me.

"I gotta go!" I wave to Rick and rush out the door. When I get home, Milagro has vacated our room and stationed herself in Mami's room. There's no sign of Pablo or the damage from the shattered statues. The only hint to her mood is the music blaring from the door. It's the sad stuff Mami listens to, but frantic beats that pulse and make simple words like *You did me wrong. I love you baby baby baby* seem epic.

Good. Not talking is fine with me. I tug the door closed and wrestle the giant duffel bag out of our closet. The sooner tomorrow comes, the closer I get to solving the mystery of Clara.

9
Milagro

BEEEEP BEEP BEEP!

TRUMPETS! TRUMPETS! GUITAR!

When I hear the alarm go off, I yell, "Lulu! It's the freaking weekend. Can I get a break here?" But the alarm goes off again, and again. I rub the sleep out of my eyes.

"AHHHH!"

I'm screaming and my eyes are on fire, like I jumped in a chlorine pool after shoving jalapeños in my eye sockets. I shoot out of bed, only it takes me a few seconds to realize it's not my bed—I'm in Mami's bed. Actually, I'm on Mami's floor, surrounded by all the rejected shoes and outfits that she didn't take on her trip. To make matters worse, it's not Lulu's alarm that's going off, but mine. As the mariachi accordions go off—chosen to annoy Lulu, and no, the irony is not lost on me—I wipe my eyes with Mami's silk robe and look down. Mami's robe and my hands are still covered in glitter. Body glitter. Last night's events come flashing back to me, like the world's most embarrassing movie: Pablo. Mystery boobs. Dying a virgin. Poor clueless Milagro. My reality is worse than every nightmare I've ever had about going to school naked.

I look at my phone again. There's no text from Pablo. No explanation, no apologies, nothing. I want to stay in Mami's room forever and wallow in self-pity. I want to burn all the candles in the house and run around shouting curses at Pablo, that hairy black spiders burrow deep in the engine of his car and crawl out of the air vents, or a nail infection takes hold of his thumb and leaves it so festered and green, he can never hold someone's hand ever again. I want to drop out of St. Agnes and start my own glitter convent in Tahiti, where we all wear matching gold bikinis and never talk to boys, even though we look so, so hot. I grit my teeth. I'm not going to cry before I've eaten breakfast.

My phone alarm goes off again. Then I remember: OH CRAP. THE TRIP!!! I silence my phone and slouch down against the bed. I've spent all night thinking about it, and there's really no getting out of it. I will be grounded forever if I miss the field trip, even if it's the last thing I want to do. I take a deep breath and run out of Mami's room and into mine. "Lulu, we have to go!" But when I throw the door open, the room is empty. Lulu's side is still a mess, of course. Her bed is a pile of sheets and a comforter, and the floor is covered in scattered sheets of notebook paper and dog-eared books. If it wasn't for the half sheet of computer paper perched on top of her mountain of pillows, I'd be worried about her. I grab it, and read:

M, see you in a week. Don't touch my stuff
or eat my Double Stuf Oreos. I mean it!!!
—Lulu

Lulu is going to be so, so pissed when I show up to the bus. There's no amount of Cheetos or cinnamon-flavored waffles that will stop her from smothering me with her crumpled lab reports after she finds out that I'm crashing her trip. And if I tell her it wasn't my idea, it'll make her even madder. She won't care that it's actually my worst nightmare (not counting, of course, whatever happened . . . or should I say *didn't* happen last night). But I can't worry about Lulu right now, because I have to focus. I need to plan a week's worth of outfits that say I Don't Care If My ~~Boyfriend~~ Ex-Boyfriend Has a Phone Full of Boobs Because I Am a Strong Independent Woman Who Could Have Anyone (Even If I Know No One). Then I have to dig up my extra-waterproof makeup to stop my stupid tears from giving everything away.

Thirty minutes later, I'm out of breath as I lug my

giant suitcase off the bus. I've never been to St. Agnes this early on a Saturday. It's every bit as terrible as I expected. There's sweat dripping down my back, and my hair is sticking to my neck. My sunglasses keep sliding down my nose and my arms are rubbed raw from where my sequin sleeves meet my skin, a million mini paper cuts all stinging at once. My armpits are basically on fire. My lime-green shorts, so carefully chosen for their delicate scalloped edges, have betrayed me. They've left me exposed, and now tiny mosquito bites dot my calves and ankles, the first sign of Baltimore spring. I wanted my look to say "casual diva on vacation," but instead, I'm a sweaty monster who fell into a vat of grease and emerged with hives. Today is officially the second worst day of my life, and judging from the scene in front of school, the next six days are not looking too promising either.

St. Agnes was built in the 1840s, back when people wore bonnets because they didn't have essential technology like curling irons. The school's architects probably traveled by water buffalo or whatever. They definitely didn't plan for the hulking coach bus that takes up the entirety of the one-way street in front of the school and blocks traffic in two different directions. The bus is gleaming silver, and one side reads, "TAKING YOU WHERE YOU NEED TO GO! FAST! ON TIME!" There's a chorus of angry honking cars that strongly disagrees. The bus is bigger than the mini yellow school bus that lugs around St. Agnes's failing sports teams, but still smaller than the double-decker bus that Tía Lochita rides every Thanksgiving to New York City so she can watch the Macy's Thanksgiving Day Parade from her best friend's fire escape while chomping on a turkey leg.

"Milagro! Over here!" I look up and spot Mrs. Johnson, waving to me frantically from the cool marble steps of St. Agnes. She's juggling four tote bags, three clipboards, and an overstuffed pillow. St. Agnes's prissiest moms surround her, each one with a perkier, blonder ponytail than the next.

I pretend I don't see her and duck behind a spindly street tree. I'm on the lookout for Lulu, hoping I can explain myself before she loses it, but it's hard to find her. It's strange; her signature messy crow's nest of a bun usually sticks out in a crowd.

"Milagro Zavala, come here!"

Busted. I lift the branch out from over my face and look up at Mrs. Johnson.

"Oh, me?" I mouth, and point to myself. Mrs. Johnson nods emphatically.

Great. As I trudge over with my suitcase, I wonder if there's a way to explain to Mrs. Johnson that I've taken a vow of silence, so I can't possibly talk to anyone on the trip, not about college or anything personal. Especially not about boys. Maybe better yet: I can tell her I took a vow of chastity. I push my sunglasses up and wipe my nose on my beautiful sequined sleeve, which is now covered in boogers. I hate today.

As I walk up, Gracelynn Hunter's mom is blathering on about Gracelynn's tree nut allergy, while Mrs. Johnson does her best to look interested. I duck under Sarah Jefferson's mom's wide arms—outstretched to demonstrate how big of a lawsuit there'll be if Sarah doesn't come home in one piece—and tap Mrs. Johnson on the shoulder. "What's up, Mrs. J?" Mrs. Johnson is so relieved to see me, she drops all four tote bags and pulls me in for a hug. I stand there stiffly, hoping no one sees what's happening right now. I do *not* do unsolicited touching, and I definitely do not do teacher hugs. When she pulls away and opens her mouth to give me instructions, Maddie Stone's mom swoops in and interrupts her.

"Theresa, can you clarify something for me? The dorms will be single sex, right? I don't want my Maddie to be exposed to anything . . ." She drops her voice and looks me up and down, her eyes taking an extra-long pause at the space between my crop top and the waistband of my electric-green shorts. ". . . anything nasty," she finishes.

Any other day, I would cross my eyes at her and stand a

little taller, making my torso as long and offensive as possible, but today, her words pile up in my waterfall of Terrible Thoughts, settling in nicely in the Things That Are Wrong with Me flood that's flashing through my brain and leaking out of my eyes. I clench my hands and wonder if there's any scenario where I can kick a mom and get away with it. Mrs. Johnson ignores Maddie Stone's mom and says, "Milagro, be a dear and please take these to the bus," pointing to the pile of bags. She smiles at me and rubs her freckled arms, still red from where the tote bags were hanging.

My mouth drops open. "ALL of these? But what did I do?!" The moms close ranks around Mrs. Johnson before she can respond to me, leaving me stuck looking at a bunch of Lululemon yoga mom butts.

I start lugging Mrs. Johnson's bags back toward the bus, two bags slung on each arm and a bunch of clipboards under my chin, all while dragging my suitcase behind me. Only when I actually make it to the bus and start loading her crap into the undercarriage, my classmates decide it's a sign that I'm a bellhop. They start tossing their overpriced, brightly colored designer suitcases at me.

"Thanks, Milagro!" they chirp. As usual, they've pronounced my name all wrong, the "lag" sounding like "hag" or "jet lag."

No way, José.

I abandon the pile and head for the only hiding place I can think of.

I rap on the bus doors and wave to the bus driver. He's moving his hands wildly, holding his phone between his shoulder and ear, but he still manages to let me on before returning to his conversation, something about tickets to a game and whether the Orioles will manage to not embarrass themselves this year. (Never.) I haul myself up the bus steps and walk past him, getting a good look at what we're working with. There are twenty rows of tall seats, all covered in what was once plush gray fabric but is now threadbare and spotted black. Yellow rope lights run down either side of the aisle, leading to a white door in the back of the bus, with "BATHE-ROOM" handwritten in permanent marker. There's also a handwritten note taped to the door: "Lock Door Behind U."

Given how much St. Agnes hypes this trip up, I thought we'd be on a tour bus, like the kind rock stars travel on. Or maybe even a cool RV, the kind you see on all the wilderness camping shows. This is the opposite of glamour. The air is full of the competing smells of deodorants, musty cologne, and—I take a big sniff—what smells like fried chicken and waffle fry remnants.

I walk down the aisle, hoping to scope out a seat as far away from everyone as possible. Two steps in, I find a dozing Lulu, her face bent over a fat book. Of course. I should have known she'd be the first one to arrive. I take a deep breath and tap her on the shoulder. "Hey!"

"Hi," Lulu says right away, rubbing her eyes and swiping some stray hairs out of her face. Then she takes in the bus and my outfit, and her eyes narrow. "Wait a second. What are you doing here? Did Mami change her mind about the trip? Did she make you come to take me home? Why wouldn't she call me first?" The questions spill out as her head darts from side to side.

"Whoa! What are you talking about?"

Lulu charges on. "Or did something bad happen with the house? Did you burn the house down?" She stares at me, her eyes widening.

She's breathing heavily now and hugs her book closer to her chest.

"What! No! Jeez—I forgot about the straightener *one* time. It wasn't that big of a deal. It has an automatic off switch! Everyone needs to calm down about it." I put my hands up and motion them downward, like I'm petting an invisible dog.

Her eyes flash and she sits up taller in her bus seat. "Don't tell me to calm down!"

Yikes. I change my tactics. "Okay, okay. Sheesh. Nothing burned down. I haven't talked to Mami."

"Oh," she says. Her shoulders slump. "Then what are you doing here?"

"Is that the kind of stuff you worry about?"

"What?"

"Buildings burning down and stuff."

"Yes, of course," Lulu says, like it's perfectly normal. "Anyway. Why are you here?"

I take a deep breath. "I'm here because I'm going on the trip. Sister May is making me come," I say. "Detention on the road. Lucky me." It's the lie I practiced the whole way to St. Agnes. I'm not sure why I'm lying to Lulu, only that it feels important to do it. I know how much this trip means to her and I don't want her to think it's less special because they let a glitter fool like me on it. And maybe a small part of me—okay, fine, a really big part of me—doesn't believe I *should* be on the trip. I'm convinced midway through the week, when we're cruising through the cornfields of Indiana, Sister May will call up Mrs. Johnson and tell her that her math was way off, that I'm as unsmart and careless about my grades as everyone thought I was. I push away those thoughts and muster up some cheeriness, sliding into the seat next to her. "Lucky you. It'll be like all our vacations to Ocean City. Only this time, maybe I'll get to make the plans. Clara was always so bossy on those trips. We always had to do what she wanted."

"There's already a set itinerary," she says impatiently. The full impact of what I said hits her. "Wait a second. What do you mean, 'you're coming'?" She puts the last part in air quotes, even though she knows I hate them. "You can't 'just come.' The trip's full, which you'd know if you were supposed to be on the trip." She crosses her arms. "Aren't you supposed to be at home? With *Paaaaaaaablo*," she says, stretching his name out.

I wince at his name. I can feel my face heating up, thinking about yesterday. Lulu's face is getting red too. I don't need ESP to know from her lack of eye contact, she's remembering it too.

"I'm . . . ," I say, trying to figure out how to deliver the news. But I'm at a loss for the words that could explain what happened last night, or what I'm going to do now that Pablo is gone and I'm a rejected virgin forever. The only thing I'm not at a loss for is tears. Big-time tears, streaming down my face. Lulu's eyes widen in horror and she scoots away from me slowly, until her back is firmly pressed against the bus windows and there's a gap between us. I can't stop running my hands through my curls, as if I could fix everything if my hair settled properly.

"Are . . . are you okay?" she says, biting her lip. She's studying me like a science experiment, her eyes roving over me. She takes in my chipped nail polish, my dripping, snotty nose, and the mascara that I can feel clumping on my lashes. "Did something happen?" All the indignation and anger are gone from her voice.

I sniffle. "It doesn't matter. I don't care about him." My

shoulders are shaking from crying. I cover my face with my hands so she can't tell that I'm lying. I'm doubled over in my seat, gasping for enough air to keep tears coming down. When Celine and Whitney and Adele sing about heartbreak, they're always lounging in bathtubs and standing around in gowns. I'm in discount clothes and stolen makeup, crumpled up on a bus seat that is at least seventy years old.

Lulu reaches over to rub my back, slowly at first. She pulls me out of my huddle and into a hug, squeezing tight. We haven't hugged like this in years, not since we were little. Usually we avoid touching, unless it's me dragging her somewhere. Lulu is careful not to get tangled in my earrings. "You don't need him. You're better without him. You're so much cooler than him," she says softly, right in my ear.

I laugh, only it comes out as a snort, since I'm still crying. Lulu doesn't know anything about being cool or dating. She doesn't know what it's like to spend the last year thinking you'd finally discover the secrets of the universe, only to fall flat on your face.

"Let's forget about boys," Lulu says. "For this trip."

I pull away from her. Now it's me who's staring at her.

"Sisters before misters," she says, louder this time. There's no smile on her face. Her pinky sticking out in front of me. "Sisters are supposed to stick together. We're all we've got if we want to get anywhere." She sounds like Mami talking about Tía Lochita. "This is *our* trip, and we're going to have so much fun without any stupid boys."

My voice is strained and I'm still hiccuping back tears as I say, "Sisters before misters. Our trip." In that moment, I really, really do mean it. *Sisters* sounds better than *nerd* or *dumpee*.

We link pinkies, kiss our thumbs, and smush them together, her thumb pressed hard against mine. We haven't done that in ages either, but I remember all the moves.

The weight of our promise is still sinking in when we hear a weird sound in the distance, like stomping and chanting. It grows louder and louder, drowning out the sounds of the St. Agnes girls' chatter. Lulu and I press our faces against the bus window.

The first thing we see are their hunter-green blazers, brighter than any color found in nature. Then we see their thick black leather shoes, stomping in unison. Then two short lines of high school boys in blazers and khaki shorts appear.

The St. Anthony boys.

They're dressed in uniform, marching and shouting as they make their way down the sidewalk. They've each got matching camouflage green bags strapped to their backs and high black socks that reach mid-calf. It takes me a few minutes to realize they aren't screaming nonsense. It's some kind of prayer, only the yelling renders the words totally bananas. It's Catholic roulette, on steroids.

O GENTLE AND LOVING
ST. ANTHONY! YEAH!!!!
WHOSE HEART WAS EVER FULL!
OF HUMAN SYMPATHY!
WHISPER MY PETITION INTO THE EARS OF THE
SWEET!
INFANT!
JESUS!
WHO LOVED TO BE FOLDED IN YOUR ARMS.
THE GRATITUDE OF MY HEART WILL EVER BE
YOURS.
AMEN!!!

As if being stuck on a bus with St. Agnes nerds wasn't bad enough, I'm now going to be held hostage by ten of Pablo's classmates.

As the boys get closer and closer, there's a new, urgent hum in the air. A high-pitched giggle spreads across the parking lot. All the St. Agnes girls are standing up taller, pulling their shirts down a little lower, and grabbing on to their friends, pointing at the boys.

The chanting and marching ends when the boys line up against the bus, their backs as straight as rulers. There's a silence on the street. Even the moms have gone quiet. From behind the line emerges a stout, beefy man with salt-and-pepper hair. His black button-down shirt is impeccably pressed. He's got a small white band tucked under his collar: classic priest uniform. I send a silent prayer of gratitude that Sister May isn't our chaperone leader.

"That's enough, gentlemen," he says.

Mrs. Johnson strides down from the entrance stairs and sticks her hand out. "Hello, Father Coleman. I see the boys are ready."

Father Coleman sizes up Mrs. Johnson. He shoves his hand at her and shakes her hand vigorously, squeezing it like he's juicing it. "Theresa, let's get this show on the road. My men are ready!"

Mrs. Johnson pulls her hand away from him and winces as she flexes her fingers and shakes out her wrist. She takes a deep breath and turns to the girls on the sidewalk. "Ladies. Please line up."

Lulu and I scamper off our seats and out the door, quickly joining the St. Agnes line. I slide my giant sunglasses on, hiding my runny makeup and red-rimmed eyes. There's a lot of whispering and shoving around us as the boys are gawked at and earmarked for crushes.

Frown lines appear on Father Coleman's face and he glares at the boys, daring them to be as disorganized and giggly as we are. Mrs. Johnson ignores him. "Ladies, for this trip, you'll each have a St. Anthony partner. You'll sit together, attend all the events together, and be responsible for each other. If your partner gets in trouble, that means you'll get in trouble."

"Harrumph!! That won't happen with my men!" Father Coleman says, glowering at them.

His men? I roll my eyes.

"St. Agnes girls know how to behave themselves too, don't we, ladies?"

We all stare back at Mrs. Johnson, unsure of what the right response is. An amen in unison? An aggressive nod? A curtsy?

"Right, then!" After an awkward silence, Mrs. Johnson quickly flips through the clipboard in her hand and begins reading names off the list. Lulu clutches my hand and I look at her. "Promise?" she says, mouthing the word.

"Promise," I whisper back.

"Lucas Teller and Milagro Zavala." Mrs. Johnson looks up from her clipboard and points to me.

A gangly boy with curly blond hair approaches me.

"Shall we?" he asks. I take two steps away from him and wait for him to climb on the bus first. The engine is grumbling and the AC is fully kicking in. I'm kicking myself for wearing a crop top and not packing a sweatshirt for the ride. I shiver and pull my arms close to me, rubbing my hands up and down.

"Here, take this," Lucas says, pulling his St. Anthony blazer off. I stare at him. "Trust me, you're doing me a favor. I can't stand wearing these hideous jackets. We look like dorky trees."

"What?" I say.

"Brown on the bottom," he says, pointing to his khaki shorts, "and green on top. Dorky trees."

I take the blazer from him. It's softer than Pablo's letterman jacket, not that he ever let me wear it. He said the team was superstitious about stuff like that. I wonder if he let Mystery Boobs wear his letterman jacket. I bet she wore it with nothing on underneath, not even a bra. And Pablo probably loved it. Before I know it, tears are creeping back out of my eyes.

"Do you ever take those things off or what?" asks Lucas, pointing at my shades.

"These old things?" I say, pulling them off and trying a smile at him. It comes out as more of a grimace.

He doesn't ask any questions about my blotchy face or messed-up makeup, not even when I wipe my eyes with my thumbs, which are now stained black from all the eyeliner and mascara. I want to break the silence, but I'm afraid it'll make me cry more. I don't want to add a St. Anthony bozo to my People Who Feel Sorry for Milagro list.

Zzzzttt!

There's a buzz in the pocket of Lucas's blazer. I reach

my hand in, grateful for the distraction. I pull out a flip phone and turn it over and over again in the palm of my hand. "Wow. I haven't seen one of these in a long time."

"What can I say, I'm a sucker for retro technology," says Lucas, grabbing the phone.

"Seriously?"

"No. My parents confiscated my smartphone when I got caught with my headphones on during class. It was the tenth time that did it." Lucas shakes his head. "You'd think being a virtuoso on the piano would give you a free pass out of Calc 2, but apparently not."

The phone buzzes again, and again. Then two more times again.

"All right, all right, already!" Lucas says, flipping the phone open. His fingers fly across the number pad, putting even the fastest texter at St. Agnes to shame. It must be the piano playing.

"My boyfriend, Jared, is obsessed with me," Lucas says casually. "I'm pumped to see him at our first stop. He's a freshman at MonU."

My eyes grow wide as I think about how Pablo would text me every day **See u after school?** even though he knew Mami said we were only allowed to hang out on the weekends, and only in public places. I guess it left a lot of room for him to hang out with other people. Other girls.

"What, does that bother you or something?" Lucas

sits up, his back against the window and his blond curls plastered against the glass. "You're not one of those super conservative people, are you?"

I shake my head vigorously. "No! Not at all! I don't care who you date! Do whatever. Or whoever. I'm just trying to mind my own business." I stare at the ground in front of me and hope that Lucas will get the hint. The last thing I want to do is talk about boyfriends.

He sighs with relief. "Most of the people at St. Anthony are cool about it. There's a few parents who are shitheads, but it could be worse." He shrugs. "Jared is the best, so that's all that matters."

My tears are back at it, even as the rest of the St. A students shuffle onto the bus and Maddie demands that her partner give up his aisle seat so she can sit next to Gracelynn.

Lucas is gawking at me with a horrified look on his face.

I sob, my shoulders heaving until I can mumble out, "My boyfriend cheated on me. I'm ready to join a nunnery."

I'm expecting some sympathy here. Maybe Lucas will offer me his pack of snacks or a soft handkerchief that I can lay over my face. Instead, he scrunches up his nose and points his finger at my chest. "You'd let some stupid boy lock you up in a convent? So he gets to have all the fun?" His brows are furrowed as he says, "Not to mention, running to a convent is very seventeenth century of you."

"What?" In between a sniffle, a laugh sneaks out of me, even though it sounds more like a dolphin noise. "Why do you even know that?"

Lucas hikes his feet up on the seat and hugs his knees. "I'm convinced you can play music better if you know where the composer's writing from. Sixteenth- and seventeenth-century composer bios have become my thing. I just started reading this book about Vivaldi last night that I have to talk about, or I'll explode."

I give him a small smile, grateful for the distraction. He sounds like Lulu. "Okay. I'll bite. What's his deal?"

"Vivaldi signed up to be a priest at sixteen because it was the only way he could pursue music without having to worry about a job. Then one year into priesthood, he's like"—Lucas fake coughs—"'Oh no. I shan't be a priest. I have asthma.'"

"He sounds like a bigger drama queen than me."

Lucas laughs. "He was still technically a priest, but he didn't have to do any of the work. He just got to compose all day. What a dream."

Two hours later, Lucas has me googling Ethel Smyth and George Bridgetower, and he's made me look up his best piano pop covers. In return, I've told him the tragic story of Jenni Rivera, and I've forced him to watch her live performance of "Resulta," pointing out her perfect glittery tears and enviable face-framing curls.

When Lucas returns to his book, my pity party starts again. I text Carmen, but she doesn't respond. She's probably already sipping smoothies on the beach. I'm so desperate for commiseration, I even text Clara. It takes her ages to respond, and all she says is an infuriating Maybe the silver lining is that you'll have more time for school. She's useless. In front of me, Amelia Brown is watching a lacrosse game intently on her phone. Behind me, I can hear Genevieve humming *Mamma Mia!* songs, which I bet is playing on the iPad resting on her knees.

I stopped by Lulu's seat on the bus and she shoved whatever she was working on deep in her bag, like I was going to copy her homework or something. Lulu told me we could talk later, since it was against the rules for me to be in the aisle and she needed to prep for her Stanford interview. Mrs. Johnson confirmed both of these facts as she shoved past me on her run down the aisle to the bathroom in an attempt to calm her motion sickness. I stayed in my seat after that, giving Mrs. Johnson all the space she needs.

Lucas's earlier words sink in: *He gets to have all the fun?*

I know I promised Lulu "sisters before misters" and all, but she's already distracted by the trip. Maybe Operation Don't Die a Virgin doesn't have to end with Pablo.

"Hey, Lucas?" I tap him on the shoulder. "Tell me about the boys on this trip."

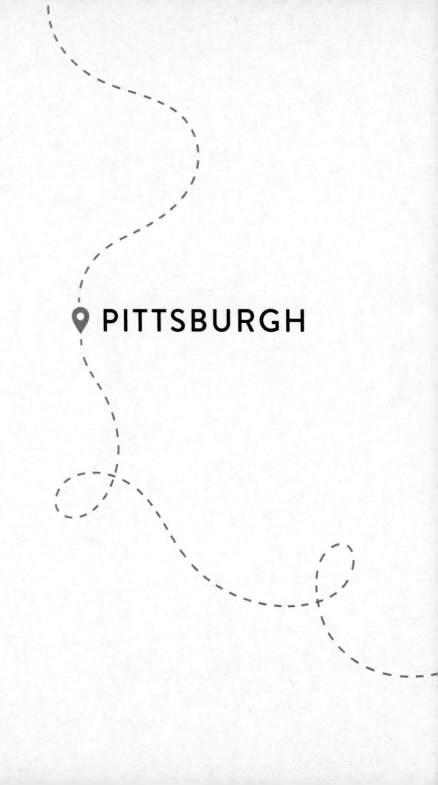

PITTSBURGH

10
Lulu

"**WITH OVER FIVE** hundred clubs and organizations and sixty majors for students to choose from, Monongahela University is a world-class leading university. You can be anything and everything you want here. From an accountant to a zoologist!"

At *zoologist*, my ears perk up. Then again, my ears are about the only body part left with any feeling, after surviving the four-hour bus ride from Baltimore to Pittsburgh, only to be stuck in this never-ending information session. For the past forty minutes, a middle-aged lady in a pink fuzzy sweater has talked at us about the wonders of MonU. These wonders include a spa on campus, dorms with new elevators, and a homecoming tradition of slamming pies in each other's faces.

She drones on, "Monongahela University's computer

science department boasts fifteen labs and two Nobel Prize–winning professors, each of whom mentor students through research opportunities."

I resist the urge to raise my hand and tell her she's wrong. In the inches of space between the seat in front of me and my lap, I've got a stack of brochures that say MonU's CS department, in fact, has seventeen labs. But maybe she's not counting the—I flip through the gleaming brochure with a giant squid on it again—"NEW! Robotics Labs!" I sigh. This whole presentation is a huge waste of time. Everyone knows that MonU is a powerhouse athletics school with a serious party reputation. (According to Maddie Stone, who blathered on about it for at least thirty minutes, the most popular majors are keg stands and toga styling. Maddie says she's definitely going here.)

There's no way Mami is going to let me go to college out of state, much less to a college that regularly makes *U.S. News & World Report*'s "Top 10 Party Schools." Mami doesn't read *U.S. News & World Report*, but she has a sixth sense for bad behavior. Which reminds me: I take a glance down both sides of my row, but I don't see Milagro. I scoot forward a little in my seat and poke my head between two sleeping parents, taking a peek on down either side of their row too, but I can't find my sister's neon-green shorts anywhere. I lean back and chew on my fingernail. If Milagro is sitting alone, crying over Pablo, it's probably all my fault.

What do I know about boys? If Gloria Estefan didn't sing about it, or *The Last Bachelor* didn't cry about it, then I'm totally stumped. What would a normal human do in this scenario?

I shoot Milagro a quick text. **Hi! Are you here?** but there's no response.

It's really boring! I text again.

I follow up with **Boys suck! :)** and **Oops! I mean :(**

I'm cringing. I hate emojis and I hate emoticons even more. Words were invented for a reason. Even if I can't figure out the right ones to make Milagro feel better.

I was in shock on the bus this morning when Milagro sat next to me and sobbed about her life being over. Watching my strong, beautiful sister fall apart is only further proof that boys are bad news. I know humanity needs them to survive, but I like to think of dudes as an invasive species. Whatever happened in our bedroom between Pablo and Milagro is not something that I plan to do for a long, long time. At least until I get my PhD. On the bus, I patted her on the back like she was a dog. I promised to look out for her, even though I'm the little sister and she's the big sister, and now I'm already failing. Without even trying. Clara could fix this, if she wasn't a million miles away.

Think, Lulu, think!

I shove all the brochures back in my tote and pull out a stack of papers instead. On the bus, before she got carsick and spewed her guts in the bus bathroom, Mrs. Johnson told us to come to each college information session with ten questions prepared. Mine are technically for Robbie, even though I still don't have a plan for finding him yet, aside from staking out the athletic facility and hoping to bump into someone who knows him.

QUESTIONS FOR MONONGAHELA UNIVERSITY

Why doesn't Clara talk to Mami anymore?
Do you know what their big fight was about?
How can I fix it?
Why won't Clara tell me?

My pencil hovers over the last one. Should I cross it off? I don't want to come across as too babyish.

"Um. Aren't the questions supposed to be about college?" someone whispers.

I jump back in surprise, knocking down my MonU-branded mini-golf pencil to the ground.

Crap.

"I think our questions are supposed to be about academics and stuff," the whispery voice continues over my head while I scramble to find my pencil. When I sit up, my St. Anthony buddy is leaning over my shoulder and

114

studying my questions. He casts a shadow over my paper, thanks to the six extra inches of height that he's got on me. He reaches deep into his khaki uniform pants and says, "Don't worry, I came up with some too."

"What?"

"Some questions," my buddy says slowly. "I. Also. Came. Up. With. Questions."

I don't like his attitude one bit. "For your information, I have college questions too. They're . . . a work in progress," I whisper, trying to stuff my Robbie questions back into my tote, only the paper frills from where I ripped the sheet keep getting tangled in the wire spirals of my notebooks. "And why are you creeping over my shoulder anyway? Haven't you ever heard of privacy?"

"Soooooorry. I thought we were supposed to be partners," he says, before turning away and raising his hand. He gestures to Mrs. Johnson.

What the crap! This is the first conversation that I've had with my "buddy," aka Leo Joseph, since we first walked onto the bus, and now he's trying to get rid of me.

"Wait! Wait! I swear I have questions!" I whisper. "You don't have to tell on me or anything, I can show you them!" I tug on his sleeve. "Leo! Don't do this!" I plead, in my friendliest voice ever. I spot Caroline Jansen and Amelia Brown giving Leo a once-over before they lean into each other and giggle, but not in the I'm-making-fun-of-you kind of way. I heard Amelia create a ranking of all the St. Anthony boys on the bus, and according to her, Leo is at least a nine. It's more than anyone would rank me. If Leo refuses to be my partner, one of the St. Agnes girls will snap him up and I'll be stuck with Mrs. Johnson. Then I'll never be able to sneak away. Or worse, I'll be a permanent fifth wheel to a St. Anthony and St. Agnes duo. "Please!" I say, one last time.

Pink sweater lady spots Leo's raised hand and stops mid-lecture. She points at him. "Yes, young man? Do you have a question?"

I'm done for.

Leo clears his throat. "I heard you say that MonU has fifteen labs, but according to the brochures, there are seventeen?"

The woman brightens and stands up straighter. "That's right! Last year, the university president . . ."

Wait a second—I thought only I noticed that. I watch Leo reach into his pants pockets again and pull out a piece of paper that's folded impeccably. As he unfolds the piece of paper, it opens up into a beautifully organized fact sheet about Monongahela University. In one corner, he's got the school's vital statistics: number of students on campus, the acceptance rates, the deadlines for each application (early, regular, financial aid), and a bulleted list of scholarships that the school offers. Underneath the stats, he's got five questions about MonU's chemistry and computer science departments. After the lady stops talking, Leo thanks her and takes out a small red pen to correct the number of labs.

Leo's fact sheet is like if my chemistry lab report had a baby with my AP History cheat sheet. I can't help it—I snatch it out of his hand and flip it over. On the back, Leo has done the same for the University of Notre Dame, the next college we'll be visiting. I'm willing to bet that he's got another folded up in his pocket for the final school we're visiting. I don't know whether to be mad that someone has out-nerded me or to report him to *U.S. News & World Report* for plagiarism.

Leo takes the piece of paper back from me and shrugs. "I like to be prepared," he says. "Facts are important. Once you give up on facts, then—"

My phone buzzes and I tune out Leo. When I check the screen, my only new message is from Tía Lochita, who has sent a photo of her and Mami giggling in front of a statue of Mary.

I text them back that we made it to Pittsburgh and Tía Lochita responds with a prayer hand emoji. Still no word from Milagro.

As the admissions lady finally wraps up her lecture, the auditorium comes alive again. A fleet of student tour guides appears, each dressed in matching school sweat-shirts and sporting giant "ASK ME ABOUT MON U" pins.

They're like *Captain Planet* characters, or stock images if you were searching for "college students." There's a girl with dramatic eyeliner and a funky beret standing next to a short guy with thick glasses and—I squint—the differential equation for Newton's law of motion tattooed on his biceps. Next to him is a girl taller than anyone I've met before. She's got a soft smile on her face, but her hands on her hips mean business. I bet she was always the first one picked in gym class.

The admissions officer points to the tall girl and says, "Who would like a tour of the athletic facilities with Anika?"

"Me!" I shout, thrusting my hand in the air.

Beside me, Leo frowns. "You're an athlete?"

I hadn't planned on explaining myself to anyone, much less my buddy. Aren't all St. Anthony boys supposed to be jocks? He should *want* to go on this tour. "Yes," I say. "It's a very obscure sport. Not a lot of people know about it."

He stares at me.

"It's . . . Ping-Pong."

"Is Ping-Pong an obscure sport? I thought people called it table tennis?"

"Not when they give scholarships for it. Then they call it Ping-Pong," I continue stubbornly.

Before he can respond, the admissions lady shouts: "Enjoy yourselves! And remember: GOOOOO MON U!"

She throws her fist in the air and does a little hop, tucking her legs under like a cheerleader.

The auditorium erupts into giggles and chatter. Mrs. Johnson yells over the hubbub, "St. Anthony and St. Agnes students! Remember, we are operating on the buddy system. Where you go, your buddy goes too. Do NOT lose your buddy."

Leo turns to me. "Sorry, but I don't want to see the gym. Seen one gym, you've seen them all." He stands up and stretches his arms over his head. His blazer and button-down ride up to show a sliver of brown skin, and his dark green boxers.

"But. But. But . . . ," I sputter. "Gyms are great! You can work out in them!" I stand up and try to come up with another reason, but I don't know what would possess someone to sweat in front of strangers when you could be home on the couch watching *The Last Bachelor,* or doing something sensible, like reading a good book.

Leo wrinkles his nose, so I pull my arms up and flex my biceps like I'm in a bodybuilder competition. "Eh? Who doesn't like giant muscles? Amirite?" I nudge him on the shoulder with my fist.

"Don't take this the wrong way, but who goes to college to work out?" Leo says, walking down the aisle to follow a tour group.

I tag after him, calling over his shoulder, "But there's a

pool. And did you hear the spa? We could go to the spa!" I can hardly believe the words coming out of my mouth. But if I want to figure out what the hell is up with Clara, I *need* to be on that athletics tour.

Leo stops suddenly and turns around. "First of all, I hate pools." He puts a finger up, cutting me off. "Bad summer at space camp. Second of all, who advertises a spa at a college session? Tell you what. You can choose the next college tour. I want to get a good look at that new chemistry lab. It's important," he says.

I blink at Leo. There is so much I want to ask him, but all I can focus on is Anika's tour group disappearing with Amelia at her side, rapid-firing questions, surely about MonU's lacrosse program. It's unfair in every single way. I've waited so long for this trip. But the trip is worthless if I can't get to Robbie. I think about the Stanford brochure of smiling students—there will be future friends and time for geeking out *after* I figure everything out. Right now, Leo is a major impediment to my mission.

Leo gets tired of waiting for my response and sticks his thumb in my face. I stare at it, unsure if this is some weird version of flipping me off.

"Shake it," he says.

"Excuse me?"

"It's a pinky swear, but better. Because thumbs are a sign of human evolution."

"What?"

"What could be more evolved than a thumb? A promise!" he says triumphantly.

Against my better judgment, I smile. I can't help it. It's the kind of line that I would use to convince Clara or Milagro to do something I wanted. (Not that I've ever been successful.)

I wrap my fingers around his thumb and shake.

"Great. Let's go!"

"And this is the classroom decorated in the style of a traditional Ukrainian schoolroom. The crystal chandelier includes seven hundred pieces of imported glass."

While the rest of our tour group oohs and aahs under the chandelier, I whisper a quick apology to whoever has to clean up this room. My beat-up Converse were not meant to tread on this plush red carpet.

At this point on the academic tour, I've looked at fifteen internationally themed classrooms, each one reflecting a different architectural style. We've sat in a mock pagoda, squatted over gleaming desks low to the ground, and pressed our backs against rigid Turkish wooden desks. It's like Disney's Epcot decided to host an SAT test. Everything about this building is over the top, from the name—the "Cathedral of Learning"—to the eye-popping lobby design. I'm talking creepy Gothic French architecture, complete with huge stone awnings, a marble fireplace, and two massive wooden thrones. Our tour took a ten-minute detour so everyone could snap a photo sitting on them. I'm half waiting for a gargoyle to come to life and offer me a study guide.

Our tour guide's mini history lesson for each classroom has consisted of memorized facts about each country. Every follow-up question has been deferred to a "later time," as if in an hour, he will magically turn into an encyclopedia with all the answers. Leo is enthralled, leaning over the desks to get a look at the chair construction and lingering by the classroom cabinets to check out the art inside. He's got his socks slouched down to his ankles and his uniform button-down untucked, with his blazer hidden away in his backpack. Like a chameleon, he's somehow shifted from a prep school student to an underdressed high school boy. It's astonishing. Wherever I go, I'm always the same. Even when I don't want to be.

I pull up the campus map on my phone and plot the distance between the Cathedral of Learning and MonU's athletics complex, so I can find Robbie. They started dating a few weeks before Clara left for college, after spending the summer lifeguarding together at our neighborhood's public pool. They made sense together: if Clara was a star at St. Agnes, then Robbie was her equivalent at St. Anthony. There was no swimming record that he couldn't break, and no diving board that was too high for him to master. Robbie also had very pretty blond hair and abs that would make any *The Last Bachelor* contestant green with envy.

The only big difference between them was that Robbie didn't have much to say. At least not when we were around. Milagro used to say that Robbie communicated in grunts, and the only words he knew were pizza toppings. But if Clara found him interesting, then he must have some redeemable qualities . . . somewhere. Especially since they kept dating, even after heading off to colleges in opposite directions. Finding Robbie shouldn't be hard—aside from Clara, he's got one main interest in life, and that's the swimming pool.

I have to find the gym, or wherever athletes work out. A weight center? Nordic sweat lodge? I start inching my way toward the door. If I can peel off from the group without anyone noticing, I'll be free!

"Come on, buddy, you don't want to get lost!" Leo pulls away from the glass cabinets and nods to our tour guide, who is collecting everyone and leading us to what will probably be yet another classroom. It's almost as if he can read my mind.

I shake my fist feebly. "Wahoo. I can't wait."

Our tour guide, aka the short guy with tattoos, leads us back through the lobby and out of the enormously tall building. He tells us the next stop is the artificial intelligence lab, where MonU students have been training robots to harvest lettuce. I'm torn. This is something I might actually enjoy! But I need to find Robbie more than I want to investigate. I hope Clara appreciates the sacrifices I'm making for her.

Before our tour guide can take off, a stream of college students pours out from the double doors of the building next door. Within seconds, our motley tour group is jostled by students carrying overstuffed gym bags, an errant lacrosse stick, and what looks like a mascot head. It's my perfect getaway.

I duck out from our group and dart into the building emptying of students.

The door slams behind me and I'm left squinting at blinding white fluorescent lighting. The bulbs are working overtime, but not even they can hide the gray and drab walls of this lobby. The only hint of color is a faded red sign that announces this building as "POSVAR RESIDENCE HALL." A girl to my right, dressed in plaid pajama pants and a MonU sweatshirt, punches the vending machine, trying to get a Twix bar out. Next to her is a printer, along with a long line of students who are distracted, tapping their feet impatiently or scrolling on their phones. No one has noticed that I don't belong in this building, much less on a college campus. There's only one person left to fool:

the security guard sitting behind a giant wooden desk. Her back is to me, and she's focused on the singing competition that she's watching on her tablet. From my position by the door, I can see the small screen. Tiny judges cheer enthusiastically for one of the contestants, but I pretend their claps are for me.

Another stream of students goes by—more gym bags and awkwardly shaped sporting equipment and what looks like a giant hamster cage. It's quiet again. The printer line never seems to end, but at least the vending machine girl gets her candy bar. I peer out the window and wait for Leo and our tour group to move on without me, so I can make a clean getaway. All I need is a few minutes. A hundred and twenty seconds tops.

"Student ID?"

Outside, our tour guide stops to tie his shoe. Leo is looking over his shoulder. He frowns and crosses his arms before walking up to the tour guide and tapping him on the shoulder. When our tour guide looks up at him, Leo puts his hands up in a shrug and begins talking animatedly. I squeeze my hands into fists. Leo has blown my cover before I've even managed to get any dirt.

"S'cuse me. Do you have a student ID?"

My phone buzzes. I'm done for. The text is almost certainly from Mrs. Johnson, who has already been informed about my missing-student status.

"Hey, you! With the bag and black hair. I said ID!"

I pull away from the window and turn around. The security guard is glaring at me. She's put her phone away and she's pointing to the sign in front of the desk. She taps the sign with her finger: "ONLY STUDENTS WITH IDS WILL BE PERMITTED IN THE BUILDING."

"No student ID, no entry. The rules are simple."

I walk toward the desk, ready to spill my guts. If I tell the security guard that I'm lost from a tour group—the *athletic* tour group—maybe she can get me into the gym.

"Excuse me, but I don't . . . ," I begin.

"If you need a new ID, you can go to Panther Central. If you're a visitor, you can call your friend down to let you in."

"Okay, but I'm not . . . I don't . . ."

"And if you're locked out of your room, you gotta talk to your resident advisor," she says, pointing to the wall behind her, "but you can't loiter without an ID." Then she turns back to her tablet, already bored with this conversation.

I think about lying about my identity being stolen or meeting an old friend, but I'm no Milagro. My emotions are scrawled on my face and it's always obvious when I'm lying. Plus, I can tell from the security guard's total disinterest in me that she's heard it all. I walk away, but not before taking one last glance back at my new mortal enemy.

I stop in my tracks.

I rub my eyes and break out into a megawatt smile. I

would recognize that white-blond hair flip anywhere.

On the bulletin board behind her is Robbie's floating head. His hair is blinding, and he's so tan, he's practically orange. Next to his face, someone has cut out a speech bubble and typed "Hey, Floor Five! Got a problem? Call me! 555-229-3838!" There's other floating heads and friendly messages, but Robbie's is the only one that matters.

I'm so thrilled, I could kiss the security guard. I scribble down Robbie's number and race out of the building, scrambling to catch up with my tour group, which has only moved about thirty feet from the residence hall.

Leo breathes a huge sigh of relief when he sees me. He waves at me, and his head juts toward the tour guide. We drop to the back of the group.

"Did you find what you were looking for?" Leo asks, taking big strides. He cranes his head to keep track of our tour guide before taking a peek at me. I can see why Amelia and Caroline were ogling him. He's objectively handsome—with a perfectly symmetrical face and warm brown skin that practically glows in the sun. There's a playfulness in his smile that's disarming, like we're in on a joke together, even though we're total strangers and I've been trying to ditch him at every opportunity.

"Huh?"

"I tried to stall our tour guide," Leo explains. "I asked him a bunch of questions. You seemed like you were on a mission when you zoomed off. I thought I'd help out with whatever you're trying to do." He tucks his hands into his pockets, but his arms are so long that his elbows stick out, even as he tries to look casual.

"Thanks?" I say hesitantly. "You don't have to do that."

He shrugs. "I know. So are you gonna tell me what your mystery mission is? Or are you going to make me guess?"

I shake my head.

"Hula-hooping competition?"

"Nope."

"Gold medalist sighting? I heard MonU is highly ranked in table tennis—excuse me, 'Ping-Pong.'" Leo hops around me, batting imaginary Ping-Pong balls my way with an invisible racket.

I whirl around, keeping my eye on him. "Not a chance."

"Tracking down the world's best fried chicken recipe?"

"Nope. I already know where that is. It's—"

"Frank's Chicken Shop Stop on the corner of Lombard Street and Greenmount Ave?"

My mouth drops open. "How did you know that?"

"C'mon, everyone knows about Frank's. I just moved to Baltimore and even I know about it. It should be a freaking national landmark. And the fries . . ." Leo's voice trails off.

"Okay, but do you know about his feud?"

"And with a little Old Bay on them? The stuff dreams

are made of." Leo gives a fake chef's kiss to the air. "Wait, his what?"

Leo and I spend the rest of the tour talking about the greatest chicken rivalry in Baltimore City, aka the one between Mr. Frank and his across-the-street neighbor, Mr. Freddy. Their fight started years before I was born, when Freddy quit Mr. Frank's shop and opened his own, right across the street. "Frank told our Sierra Club chapter the whole saga while we worked a school supply drive last year. He sponsored the event, with giant trays of slaw and drumsticks." Leo practically turns green with envy when he hears that. "He said Freddy's recipe stealing was the greatest betrayal in culinary history."

Leo solemnly says, "I believe it."

"Their chicken ranks up there on my list of favorite foods, right next to the tamales that my aunt buys in her church parking lot."

"Swap tamales with my grandmother's samosas, and I fully agree."

Our tour guide delivers us to Market Place Fresh, MonU's dining hall. Leo swings the door open and says, "After you, heir to the fried chicken secrets."

When we see they're serving fried chicken in the dining hall, Leo and I laugh and skip straight to pizza. There's no point in comparing. Our trays are heaped over with pepperoni slices, chips, a small bowl of marshmallows for Leo, and a handful of chocolate-covered raisins for me. I have a moment of panic when I wonder if Leo will sit with the St. Anthony boys and I'll be stuck alone, but Leo leads the way to a table and gestures across from him. I take a look around for Milagro, but she's nowhere in sight.

I plunk my tray down. "So, will you tell me what happened at space camp?"

"That depends." Leo takes a big hulking bite of his pizza. The cheese dangles all the way down to his tray, and I laugh at his attempts to snap it all up. "Will you ever tell me what made you disappear?"

I put my hand in my pocket, where I've tucked the scrap of paper with Robbie's number on it. "Nope. But I found exactly what I was looking for."

11
Milagro

"I'M DEAD. I'VE died and gone to heaven."

I load my fork up and take another heaving bite and sigh.

"Call me Saint Milagro, patron saint of hotcakes, because there's no way I'm ever eating another thing in my life."

I lean back in the spindly metal chair and collapse dramatically while Lucas and his boyfriend, Jared, laugh.

"Who knew that ditching the information session and tour would be the best decision of my life?!" Butter and flour might not solve any of the world's problems, but they sure can provide a temporary distraction from them. There is nowhere in the world that I love more than this diner, with its tiny Formica tables and cheery murals of smiling children. I take another bite of pancake and decide to pledge my life to butter.

"You haven't even tried the potatoes yet," Jared says, pushing a heaping pile on an orange plastic plate toward me. Jared is so freaking tall, he barely fits at our table. There's a two-inch gap between the ends of his neon-blue MonU sweatshirt sleeves and his wrists. His pants are short too, but he makes up for it with trendy black-and-white-striped socks. Lucas and I are two stubby crayons, whereas Jared is a remarkably lean and long paintbrush.

"Trust me, no one leaves Pamela's without pledging their life to the potatoes," says Lucas. He takes another bite of his strawberry and whipped cream pancakes. He smiles so wide, you can see the strawberry smears all over his perfectly white teeth. "Now tell Jared your plan."

"I'm trying to meet a college boy," I say. Whatever bit of cool confidence I can manage to dredge up is immediately erased by the pancake bits crammed in my mouth.

"We were hoping you could help in that department," Lucas says, wriggling his eyebrows.

"Oh yeah?"

"Yeah," Lucas says, before leaning over to plant a kiss on his boyfriend. Lucas and Jared are so stinking cute, they only make me feel a little sad for myself, instead of my usual pity party.

"The drama club is having a get-together tonight," Jared says. "Nothing big, but there will be tons of people there. You might find a few of them interesting."

I gulp. I thought Pablo was interesting. Look what good that did me.

"Jared is an electrical engineering whiz. He's already done the lighting for two theater productions on campus," Lucas says. He's smiling at Jared like he invented the light bulb.

Jared shrugs off Lucas's praise. "It was no big deal."

But Lucas will not be deterred from his hype-man duties. "You should see his dorm room! He's got these tricked-out light bulbs that change colors based on his mood and strobe light according to the beat of whatever music he's got playing."

"It's a stupid app."

"Yeah, that you built!"

"The drama kids think it's trash. They want me to stick to traditional lighting cues."

"Creative genius is never supported by the system. What do they know about innovation?" Lucas waves his fist in the air.

"Tell me about it. I have the biggest grudge with St. Agnes's musical theater department." I glance at Lucas. "I know musical theater isn't as impressive as classical music, but—"

He frowns. "Whoa. Hold on. All music is art. I don't judge the container, just the contents."

I sigh. "I wish you were our theater director. She's

about as small-minded as the theater kids you're talking about," I tell them. "I'm still mad that she vetoed my costume designs, even though the whole class voted for me."

"What designs?" Lucas asks.

"It's this stupid costume design project." But even as I say this out loud, it's still not true. The project was the coolest school assignment I'd ever been given. "You're supposed to design and sew the costumes for the musical of your choice. The winning costumes get displayed at the St. Agnes talent show. I picked *A Funny Thing Happened on the Way to the Forum*."

Jared laughs. "I already know where this is going."

"It was so beautiful. Flowy Roman togas, beaded bikinis, intricate body jewelry, and the most elaborate headpieces with giant feathers. I spent weeks buried under sequins and Swarovski crystals recycled from thrifted prom dresses, only for Mrs. Boller to say the costumes were 'sexually inappropriate.' What does that even mean? It's just clothes!"

"Seriously? That is so messed up." Lucas frowns at me.

I look at Lucas. "Big surprise, she picked Mina Spott's designs instead, even though *Cats* is so overdone. And how hard is it to sew a tail? Anyway, she gave me a big fat zero for the project. That's when I decided school was not worth my time."

I shove more food in my mouth, but thinking about

Mrs. Boller has turned my pancakes to flavorless mush. Mami was so mad when she saw my report card, and it didn't help that Clara egged her on: "How do you get a D in a sewing class? It's supposed to be an easy A." I push those thoughts aside and choose to focus instead on meeting a college boy who is way cuter and more mature than Pablo.

Lucas and Jared have moved on to talking about Calc 2 and how it's so much harder than Calc 1. I check my phone and my heart stops for a second when I see I've got three messages. Then I see the texts are all from my family.

The first text is a photo message from Tía Lochita. Tía Lochita and Mami are standing outside some church, looking solemn. **Milagro and Lulu. We're praying for you to make good choices.** The next photo is them clinking wineglasses by the pool. **Leave the bad decisions to las viejas.** I snort, but not before noting that Mami "borrowed" (is it borrowing if you don't ask?) my third-favorite pair of sunglasses.

The next text is from Lulu, wondering where I am again. **Come find me after the tour. I have an idea for later! :)** I think about the pledge we made on the bus, and how we linked pinkies and promised we'd stick together on the trip. "We're all we have left, now that Clara is gone," she told me. "Let's not waste time with boys anymore. We don't need them anyway." In the moment, I was riding a girl power wave, ready to run away to a nunnery. But the more I thought about it, the more annoyed I got that Lulu was so sure I was "wasting time" with Pablo. It's not like her preferred activities (watching documentaries, researching obscure animals, refusing to brush her hair) are so much better than mine. This party invitation practically fell in my lap, and, well, pancakes and cute boys can't be wrong, right?

I don't want Lulu to know that I'm already breaking my promise, so I text her back: **Was feeling sad, so I decided to take a break. See you back at the dorm!** Then I close my phone and get back to plotting.

By the time Lucas, Jared, and I finish our brunch, the waitstaff at Pamela's practically has to roll us out of the restaurant because our bellies are so stuffed with food. Lucas and Jared split off, so Jared can show off MonU's music practice rooms to Lucas, while I go investigate our sleeping arrangements. I dig up the neon-yellow lanyard that Mrs. Johnson passed out before the information session and flash it at the security guard. He points his thumbs toward the elevators. According to my tag, I'm staying on the eleventh floor of "the Towers." The building is tall, gray, and sterile. The lobby is littered with motivational posters, like what I might expect a boring office to look like. None of my classmates are in sight, and I want to keep it that way. I slam my thumb over the door-close button and the doors oblige me. Midway through a sigh of relief, a scuffed-up sneaker appears between the crack in the elevator doors. The doors spring open and a lanky blond boy tumbles in. He hits his head on the wooden paneling of the elevator. His legs collide with my bag before he springs back up. It's like watching a pinball machine come to life.

"Hey, you're Milagro, right?" he says, sweeping large clumps of dust off his sweatshirt.

"Huh?" I look at him. He points to my chest, a little too close to my boobs. Oh, right, my stupid lanyard. It might as well be a billboard for all my personal information.

"I'm Hector," he says, shoving his lanyard up toward me. "I'm on the school trip. So you ditched the big tour too?"

"Um, well . . . ," I start.

"Yeah, I didn't want to do it either. I've already visited this school like a thousand times. I've probably been to like a hundred football games in my life. My whole family has gone here. My dad even has a MonU tattoo. My mom would kill me if I got a tattoo, though. You date Pablo, right?"

I snap my head up from the floor. "Yes. No. Not anymore."

Hector raises his eyebrows. "Interesting."

I scowl. "It's not." The numbers are taking forever to creep up on the elevator screen. It feels like we're hardly moving at all.

Hector leans over me and hits the tenth-floor button. "All the boys are on the tenth floor. Don't want cross-contamination or any 'funny business' with the ladies on floor eleven," he says, mimicking Father Coleman's gruff voice. "But maybe we could make some arrangements. You know, in case you wanted to stop by." His eyebrows are raised suggestively. I don't like how close Hector is standing next to me. I take a big step back. Between Lucas's rundown of the boys on the trip and Pablo's betrayal, I'm ready to swear off high school boys forever.

"I would rather shove this lanyard into my eyeballs."

Hector goes silent. When the doors open for the tenth floor, he bounds off without a word.

The elevator finally makes it to my floor. I take a step out and do a double take. I've fallen into an old episode of *The Twilight Zone*—the black-and-white ones that Tía Lochita always falls asleep to. Everything in the hallway is shades of black and white, from the steel-gray carpet that's thicker than a Brillo pad to the black steel doors that mark each of the rooms in the hallway. Even the exit sign by the stairs is painted black and white, instead of the normal cheerful neon. At the end of the hall is some kind of lounge room with a small television and an even smaller couch. (Black, of course.) I walk toward it. There's a flimsy card table that looks like it could collapse at any second. Someone has left an empty coffee cup and the wrapper of a blueberry muffin behind. I shudder, wondering if I should be worried about roaches or mice. Mami is always telling us horror stories about hotels in the city.

When I finally make it to my room, it's not much better than the shabby lounge. The room is tiny—big enough to fit a small metal bed, a desk, and a small sink. The smell of bleach lingers in the air. In fact, the whole room is so sterile, it could double as an operating room. I look at the suspicious brown stain under the bed and shudder. On the bus, Mrs. Johnson told us that having a "single" instead of sharing a room with a random roommate is a luxury for a college student. I take this as yet another sign that college is overrated. When I think about the future, I always imagine running a business, like Carmen's mom does, or owning some kind of store. You don't need college for that.

I have a few hours to kill before I'm supposed to meet Lucas and Jared. I should spend it exploring the campus, or even checking in with Lulu. Instead, I pull out my phone and settle onto the crinkly blue mattress. I lean against the wall and open Instagram. I scroll past photos of Maddie and Gracelynn posing with the MonU mascot, and a video Caroline posted of Genevieve beaming as she meets her idol, some anthropology professor. I click on Pablo's account and scroll through his photos, looking for clues. I tap his followers and spend what feels like hours meticulously going through the list, scrutinizing selfies and bikini shots, all in the hope of identifying the mystery girl on his phone. By the time I'm done, I've learned nothing new about Pablo. But I have learned a lot about myself. Enough to know I hate this feeling.

The sun has long set outside and my stomach is rumbling. My hotcakes are a faint memory. Pablo is winning, while I'm sitting in total darkness. Murmurs and giggles from the St. Agnes girls trickle through the door, but I can't bring myself to join them.

RAP RAP RAP!

I jump up, my hand flying to my chest.

Lulu pokes her head around the door and grins.

"Jeez, Lulu! Don't you know how to knock?"

"I did? I thought I did? Is there a normal way to knock?" Lulu stands in the doorway, nervously pulling at her fleece hoodie.

I shake my head. "You scared me, that's all."

"You didn't come to the tour today. And you're sitting in the dark all alone." Lulu flicks the light switch on, flooding the room with a buzzing yellow glow. She sits next to me on the bed. "Do you want to talk about it?" Her words are sweet, but they don't match her face, which is a grimace. It's been a long time since we talked about our feelings to each other.

"I'm okay." I shrug.

"You're not crying anymore. That's good." She peers at

the corners of my eyes, checking just to be sure. I wonder if this is what lab animals feel like.

"I guess you can run out of tears."

"Want to watch a movie in my room later? I'll even let you pick." Lulu clasps her hands on her lap and jiggles her knees.

I sigh. That *does* sound like fun. "I kind of made plans to hang out with my St. Anthony buddy."

"Oh. Cool," she says, her voice going extra high on the second "oh" syllable, in a way that indicates this is not cool at all. Lulu stares at the white space in front of her. "Technically we have a curfew. I don't think we're allowed out of the dorm. But okay, have fun!"

I can hear the giggles and the trickling sound of pop music from down the hallway. There's a better chance of Pablo materializing in my room with an apology bouquet of flowers than Lulu joining the St. Agnes girls to hang out. If I take off without her, Lulu is going to sit in her sterile room like the world's nerdiest plant, soaking up the fluorescent lighting until the morning.

I run my hands through my hair. Jared hadn't said anything about not inviting St. Agnes girls. Lulu and I have never hung out before, but maybe out of Mami's eye, Lulu could loosen up. She can be kind of funny sometimes . . . on purpose . . . I think. Before I can change my mind, I blurt out, "Do you want to meet us later? We're going to a par—" I cut myself off. Lulu would never come to a party. "Uhh. To a club meeting. For theater kids. It could be fun."

"Me?" Lulu says, turning to look at me. Her eyebrows are raised. "You want me to come?" she says, her hand on her chest. And everyone says I'm the drama queen.

"Well, yeah!" I say, a little too loud for the small room. "Who else? We made a pact and everything, right?"

"We have to stick together," she says quietly, mulling over my invitation. "And it's a club meeting. That's school related."

I cross my fingers behind my back and jump up off my bed. "Yes! And we have to get ready." I turn to my suitcase, digging through the clothes for anything that will make me feel like my usual sparkly self. I call out over my shoulder, "Want to borrow something?"

"What's wrong with my outfit?"

I look back at Lulu. She follows my gaze down to frayed denim pants with a rip in the pocket. Not a stylish on-purpose rip, but the kind that comes from shoving too many things into your pockets. Then I look at her scuffed-up Converse, which have the beginnings of a hole where Lulu's pinky toes should be. It's not party attire—unless your party is in a swamp. It's definitely not drama kids party attire.

"Um . . . nothing," I say nervously. "But if you wanted to be more . . . comfortable, you could wear something else?" I reach all the way to the bottom of my suitcase and toss my electric-pink sweatshirt at her. It's the most casual thing I own, but it's better than the shirt she's wearing now. I can count two holes in her World Wildlife Fund shirt, including one in her armpit.

Lulu fingers the sweatshirt. It's got soft black fuzz on the inside, and it pokes out at the sleeves. The inside matches the black zippers on the shoulders. Carmen and I found the sweatshirt, along with a rainbow-colored beret and gold leggings, at the thrift store next to her mom's nail salon. Whenever we visit Carmen's mom, she makes us do a fashion show down the aisle of nail booths. It's the reason I've gotten so good at shimmying my hips. Sometimes Carmen's mom even buys the clothes from me, paying me extra for a finder's fee. She likes to introduce me to her clients as her "personal stylist."

I quickly slide my pants off and slip on my tightest black skirt, throwing an oversized T-shirt and neon statement necklace on top before getting to work on my eyeliner. The cracked and blurry mirror isn't much to work with.

"Voilà!" I twirl around and blow Lulu a kiss. "What do you think?"

Lulu looks me up and down. She doesn't say anything, just continues studying my newly reapplied makeup and necklace.

I tug my skirt, wishing it could magically grow a few

more inches for this conversation. This is not what getting ready with Carmen is like. I miss her over-the-top compliments and booty-shaking playlist, but she's off the grid in Puerto Rico. Carmen says her aunts in Puerto Rico pretend to be too cheap to pay for Wi-Fi, when they really just want an excuse to invite themselves over to their kids' houses.

Lulu bites her lip. "I think I'm going to need this sweatshirt." She tosses it over her head, where it proceeds to get tangled in her glasses. I lean forward and free her—and her messy bun.

"But!" Lulu sputters.

I put my finger up. "Trust me. This hair deserves some breathing room." I run my fingers through Lulu's hair, catching all the tangles and tucking her strands behind her ears. Lulu sighs dramatically, like Mami does when she thinks I've forgotten to take out the trash.

I text Lucas that we're on our way, and when I look back at Lulu, she's peeking at herself in the mirror and smiling. A wave of relief washes over me. Maybe this sisters pact thing isn't so bad. I slip my arm around the crook of her elbow and pull her up off the bed. "Let's go!" I lead her to the service elevator on our floor, which Lucas swore would bypass the security guards.

When the elevator door opens into a dark alley full of cardboard boxes and a few smelly dumpsters, Lucas is tapping his foot at us. He's wearing his St. Anthony button-down, with a neon-pink pocket square hanging over the embroidered school crest. "Finally. She emerges. And with a friend."

"Technically I'm her sister. Not her friend!" Lulu whispers so loudly, it barely qualifies as a whisper.

Lucas looks at me and Lulu, studying our faces. "I can see the resemblance. And similar aesthetic."

"These are *not* my clothes," Lulu clarifies.

"Hey! Where are you going?" a deep voice booms out from the shadows of the dumpsters.

Oh crap. I reach for Lulu's hand, but she shakes it off. Lulu's St. Anthony partner emerges, clad in gym shorts and a flaming-orange shirt with a smiling oriole on it, aka Baltimore's baseball mascot. "Are you sneaking out?" he asks her. His eyebrows are raised high, nearly reaching the tops of his black hair.

"What! No! Yes? What are you doing here? Are you stalking me?" Lulu says, flustered. "It's not breaking the rules if it's for a school project."

Lucas snorts, and I jab him in the side. "Hey, Leo. They're with me," Lucas tells him. "We're going to a . . ."

"Drama club meeting," I rush out.

"Drama club?" Lulu's partner smiles. "I guess I'm in."

"It'll be way less intense than the quiz bowl crew you hang out with," Lucas warns him.

Leo puts his hand on his forehead. "Oh man. I keep trying to get those guys to cool it, but shouting random facts is their thing." He shakes his head wistfully. "I can't take them anywhere."

"Excuse me." I've got my hands on my hips now. "I think it's better if you stayed. One less person to get caught."

"Fewer," Lulu whispers loudly. "One person fewer. Not less."

I roll my eyes. Between Lulu and her partner, it's a toss-up who will be more of a party pooper.

"He's cool," Lucas says. "C'mon." He takes off speed walking.

"You heard the guy." I scramble after him.

"How come he gets to wear that?" Lulu pouts, pointing at her partner's gym shorts. "And I had to change out of my favorite shirt."

He grins. "Are you mad?"

"Yes. And you should be too. The patriarchy hurts everyone, not just me."

"I'll wear my pink sweatshirt tomorrow, then," he says back to her.

I want to roll my eyes again, but I'm actually grateful the four of us are together. Take away the sunshine, and MonU's campus goes from springtime splendor to horror-movie setting. I'm used to blinking signs, car headlights, and streetlights on every corner. Here, we're lucky to find one lonely streetlight illuminating our walk every few blocks. Our choices in scenery are creepy shadows of the ancient trees that line the sidewalks, or worse: mind-boggling darkness. There are no city sounds. No neighbors grumbling about football. No cars honking at the kids who leap across the street to meet their friends, instead of waiting for a crosswalk. It's so quiet, I might as well be at church, or maybe a funeral.

Yeah, maybe my funeral.

Yikes. I push the thought out of my mind. I need to stop letting Carmen talk me into watching horror movies.

Lucas veers off the sidewalk. "There's a shortcut this way, c'mon."

Lulu and I glance at each other. I nod. She gives me a small smile. We're in this together.

With just a few steps, we've swapped light posts papered with sagging flyers for wet trees and no-trespassing signs.

"Are you sure it's this way?" My voice is warbly. I don't sound like myself. I sound like Lulu.

Lucas leaps over a puddle. His gleaming white sneakers expertly avoid black muck and slippery leaves.

"Lucas?"

He turns back and wriggles his eyebrows at me. "Just trust me."

I look down at my sneakers, now splattered and

dripping from rain puddles. I have two options. I can continue to mope over Pablo, who isn't texting or thinking about me, or I can go back to being myself—someone who likes adventure and partying with strangers and is so completely, totally over her loser scumbag ex-boyfriend.

In this moment, I choose to be the fun girl. And if I happen to be photographed while I'm doing it . . . well then, everyone (okay, maybe Pablo) will think I'm having the time of my life without him.

12
Lulu

THERE ARE MANY things I am morally certain about: Global warming is definitely happening. The laws of physics cannot be disputed. Peanut butter and mayo should never be mixed. And when Milagro invited me out tonight, she said it was a "drama club meeting." She definitely didn't mention that there would be plastic red cups overflowing with beer, or that there'd be so many people, I'd have to elbow my way to find her in the corner. She also didn't mention that she'd ditch me as soon as she got to the party, or that twenty minutes later, there'd be a boy wrapped around her body, his hand snaking onto her right butt cheek. She definitely didn't mention that the music would be so loud, we'd have to scream at each other to say hi. So much for our pact.

"Lulu!" Milagro yells, untangling herself from the

comically tall cologne-wearing parasite that seems to have taken a special interest in her. "You've got to try some of the punch," she says, shoving her cup in my face. The liquid inside is the color of window cleaner. "It tastes like cotton candy."

"Ugh. For the last time, I don't . . . ," I begin, but Milagro isn't looking at me anymore. She's staring at the boys in the corner, who are using their lacrosse sticks to toss beer cans in the air. "You know what, it doesn't matter. I'll pass."

Milagro doesn't respond, so I wave my hand in front of her face. "Hello?"

Milagro is startled. "What? You want to go to class? But it's nighttime!" She erupts into giggles and leans back to laugh more, pushing her head into the beer gut of the burly boy standing behind her. She's laughing so hard, I can see a tiny smear of purple lipstick on her back tooth. "My sister is so funny," she screams up into the left pec that's hovering several inches above her head. He nods at her, or maybe he's nodding to the music, or maybe to nothing at all. He's built solid, the kind of dude who eats bacon every day and always orders an extra egg on the side. If he was part of the plant kingdom, he'd be an oak tree, or maybe a maple. He looks like he has sap for brains. His once-blue eyes are glazed over, the same shade as Milagro's favorite pink lipstick. I want to offer him some Visine, but

I can't decide if it's rude to suggest. This is why I *don't* do parties. I hate social norms, small talk, and most of all, I hate strangers. Am I supposed to just introduce myself to people, or wait in the corner next to the wilting potted plant until someone talks to me? Whatever happened to good old-fashioned fun, like reading a book in your bed?

Milagro takes a big swig of her drink. "Yum!" she says to no one.

"I don't know if she should have any more of what's in that cup," Leo yells. "I wouldn't trust the beverage makers at this party." His voice is barely loud enough to hear over the intense rap song, which has inspired Tree Boy to come to life. He shifts side to side, like an earthquake in slow motion. I wonder if I should tell Milagro about earthquake safety protocols. Whatever is inside her plastic cup is definitely at risk for spillage.

"On second thought, I'll take that," I say, reaching out to take the cup away from her. "Are you sure you . . . ," I begin, but then my pocket vibrates. I reach for my phone and Milagro slaps it out of my hand, sending it spiraling across the room. "What are you doing?!" I can feel my body getting hot.

"You don't need your calculator tonight. Live a little!" She snorts loudly. "Live, laugh, love—isn't that the stupidest thing you've ever heard?" She's not wrong, but I still want to murder her. But first, I need my phone. I dive down to the ground and instantly regret it. There's a sticky glob of an unidentified substance on my left knee and a small puddle of what I hope is water to my left. I take a sniff. Nope, it's definitely not water.

When I finally grab my phone, Robbie still hasn't responded to my invitation to this sham of a "club meeting." All I have is an email alert from Mrs. Johnson. *I thought you might want an extra copy of the interview questions, for tomorrow's practice session. See you bright and early!*

At the moment, the only thing I'm qualified to interview for is a permanent seat in detention, for breaking nearly every single rule on this field trip, all in the name of "sister bonding," which Milagro obviously never intended to do. I take a deep breath and close my eyes. It's just one night. I'll make up for it the rest of the week. Mrs. Johnson will never know.

When I open my eyes, Leo has disappeared.

Great. I push my way through the crowded house, hunting down the only other responsible person at this party. I walk past a room with a keyboard in it. Milagro's St. Anthony partner plays show tunes, leading a few of the MonU kids in song. I shudder and walk faster. In the next room, there's a huge group huddled around a TV and a sound system, with a mic plugged in.

Just as I step in, a girl screams out, "Next!" She swings the mic in the air like it's a lasso and she's a karaoke cowgirl.

Her pointer finger out, she points to me. "You, in the pink sweatshirt! You're up!"

Every molecule in my body freezes. I don't blink. I don't breathe. I guess these are my last seconds on earth before I spontaneously combust of embarrassment. I know you can't *really* dig a hole and end up in China, but I've decided now is the time to confirm it. I could use my phone as a shovel. There's no way I'm karaoke-ing, especially in front of strangers. I curse Milagro for making me wear such a distinctive outfit. No one notices me when I'm in my regular clothes.

Leo appears out of nowhere. "I'll do it for her."

The crowd boos with more energy than should be legal. I take a huge gulp. My nerves are fried and I feel every single kind of embarrassment—firsthand, secondhand, and imaginary. "No, really, I'll do it," he tells the girl, whispering his song choice into her ear.

Once I read about fremdschämen, the German word for secondhand embarrassment when someone you know commits a major social mishap. As the girl bows and surrenders the spotlight to Leo, I wonder if you can die from fremdschämen. If so, Milagro will have blood on her hands.

Leo steps toward the girl, taking the mic out her hand. He turns around to stare at us. What seemed like a sparse room—bare floors, a few folding chairs, and a dead plant in the corner—now feels hugely, enormously full. The crowd continues booing, and Leo seems to shrink in front of our staring eyes. After a few painful minutes of jeering, the girl who pulled him up crosses her arms and looks nervous. She walks up to him and whispers in his ear. I desperately want him to give up, to spare us all the embarrassment, the raucous booing, the shame of trying something and failing. Leo shakes his head and straightens his shoulders.

Leo covers the mic and makes a noise, only the sound he makes isn't intelligible, not words or a song. He's making funny noises with his mouth—beats and breaths that tumble out and fill the room. Beatboxing! It's a song I can't place, but music, nonetheless. More important, it's good. *Really good.* The boos quiet down as Leo ups the energy and volume of his beats. The louder he gets, the bigger he gets too, like he's reclaiming the room. He fake tosses the mic to the girl, and she hits a button on her phone. The music comes on, from out of the sound system, and Leo opens his mouth wide, belting out a song lyric I know better than I know the periodic table. I gasp.

It's the song that's synonymous with Mami's aguadito de pollo, because Milagro, Mami, Clara, and I would dance to it around our tiny kitchen while we waited for the rice to soften up in the stew. I could be abducted by extraterrestrial life-forms, knocked out in a coma, dead asleep, and if someone plays Gloria Estefan's "Dr. Beat," I would bolt upright and start dancing. The music works its way through me, until I've given up on the quiet toe taps to the beats and am full-on dancing from my spot in the corner.

When Leo finishes, the boos have transformed to woos and karaoke cowgirl gives him a high five before taking the mic and hunting for her next victim.

"You were amazing!" I yell. I'm waving my hands and mimicking explosions with my fingers. "Boom! Boom! Boom!" I am planet Earth and Leo is a meteorite—on fire, explosive, an out-of-this-world experience. "That was incredible. How did you learn to do that?"

Leo waves me off. "That was nothing. You should hear my old friends. We used to sneak onto cruise ship karaoke lounges and clean up." Leo makes it rain over my head, showering me with imaginary dollar bills. "My best friend Rafi could hit falsetto notes without even trying. We only got caught because we were so good."

"I can see why! They loved you!" I say, pointing to the crowd behind me. "I've never heard anything like that," I shout over the opening verses of the next karaoke singer's sappy ballad.

"Nah." He shakes his head. "I'm not a singer. I usually just stick to beatboxing in the background." He stoops down to my height, so I can hear him better. His brown eyes—almost as dark as mine—are suddenly, startlingly close to mine. "This was a one-time exception, just for you." Under the party's black lights, Leo's grin is bright and electric, bioluminescence in human form.

I start to blush and stutter, the worst possible combination. "Okay. Err. Well. How did you know that song anyway?" I finally get out. "No one listens to Gloria. It's one of the greatest injustices in the world."

Leo laughs, and two observations hit me all at once: 1) There is a freckle on his cheek that leaps toward the corner of his eye when he smiles, and 2) I have really lucked out with my St. A partner. Anyone else would have abandoned me by now, leaving me in karaoke hell. I fiddle with the lanyard in my pocket as Leo continues, "I think 'no one' is a stretch. She's one of the best-selling pop stars of all time, across the entire globe. She has her own Broadway show." He shrugs. "My family lived in Miami until last year. Gloria is practically the president of Miami, no matter who you are. Pro tip: if you want to win at karaoke, give the people what they want."

"I can't argue with that logic. Why did you move?" I ask. We both take a second to giggle at the next karaoke act, two boys singing and executing a flawless dance to a boy band song I don't recognize.

Leo puts his hands over his ears. "Not this song," he groans. "My sisters have made me listen to this so many times, it haunts me. They're going to be so smug to hear that college kids share their taste in music."

"But could you land those splits?" My jaw drops as I watch the boys in action.

"Def not. And we moved because my dad got a promotion. He's a doctor at Hopkins now, splitting time between research and—"

Then the lights go out.

"THIS IS CAMPUS SECURITY. NOBODY MOVE!"

Oh no.

My stomach feels like I chugged whatever was in Milagro's cup. The room is swirling around me. The honor code that Mrs. Johnson made us sign is all I can hear in my head, and how "I will not purchase, nor facilitate the purchase of, nor imbibe alcohol or participate in any alcohol-adjacent activities" was a HUGE part of it.

I turn to Leo. "We have to find Milagro!" I clench my fists, equal parts scared and furious at her. Goodbye, college. Goodbye, perfect record.

Shrieks and squeals of panic have replaced the dance music and low hum of the party. There's a stampede to the hallway, and a bottleneck as people shove their way through, desperately trying to find an exit that doesn't have campus security in front of it. I cover my head to avoid splashes from partygoers abandoning their drinks.

The lights come back on and the same deep voice booms out, "PLEASE STOP WHERE YOU ARE. THIS IS CAMPUS SECURITY. WE JUST WANT TO MAKE

SURE EVERYONE IS SAFE. NO PUSHING."

Leo and I run into the other room, Leo sprinting ahead of me because of his long legs. He looks back at me and motions with his hand, waiting until I've caught up to his blazing-orange T-shirt. "Lulu! Get up! We have to go!" Milagro yells, appearing behind me and tugging on the stupid sweatshirt that she made me wear.

I jump up and pull my arm away from her. "I can't believe you dragged us here. What happened to 'sisters forever'? All you wanted was an excuse to find a Pablo replacement."

A flash of hurt crosses Milagro's eyes. "Can we talk about this later?" she says. "We have to GO!"

"Uh, Lulu," Leo says. "I think she has a point." He's tapping his foot nervously, his eyes darting all over.

"When is 'later'?" I ask her, complete with finger quotes. "I'm not an accessory you can try on for the night. 'Oh, today, I guess I'll be a good sister.' UGH. Why can't you be more like Clara?" I'm getting angrier and angrier, my mood quickly rising to match the anxiety and rapid yelps of the crowd.

Milagro's eyes widen. Oak Tree Boy chooses this moment to come to life, and he slips his hand in hers and yanks on it. "Come on, babe. We gotta go."

Milagro slips out of his grasp and crosses her arms. "I'm not leaving without my sister. C'mon, Lulu!"

"Go!" I point toward the stampede of people. "I'm not going anywhere with you. What's next on your fun schedule? A lava pit? No, thank you. I'll take my chances on my—"

Oof. Someone shoves into me, and my knees buckle, nearly tipping me over. Milagro reaches around and yells to the stranger "Hey! Watch it!" but he's long gone. Leo slides his hand into mine and yanks me upright. I don't even have time to thank him before Milagro turns to me. "Lulu, I can't leave you here. Come on, before we get in trouble!"

I step backward, away from her and the giant crowd of people. "We're already IN trouble, thanks to your *brilliant* thinking," I snarl.

"I invited you because I was being nice," Milagro says, her hands now fists at her sides. "You should be thanking me!"

I wish I had a drink in my hand or giant pie, so I could smash it in Milagro's face, the way *The Last Bachelor* contestants do when they're mad. Instead, I spin around and walk toward the booming voice. I don't need Milagro to get out of this. If I explain that I didn't *mean* to be here, I'm sure they'll let me go. There's no need to drag Mrs. Johnson or anyone else into this.

The crowd splits open and it's like the great science gods heard my prayers. Robbie appears.

I practically gallop toward him. "Robbie!"

"Thanks for calling me, Lulu," Robbie says, putting his arm around my shoulder.

One of the campus security guards comes up to Robbie and shakes his hand. "We found a keg in the bathroom. Calling us was the right move. This could have gotten ugly fast."

Milagro's mouth makes a perfect O shape before her eyebrows come slamming down, forming a tight V over her eyes. "YOU called the cops on the party?!" she says, her finger jutting out in front of my face.

"No," I say slowly. "I invited Robbie. When I thought we were going to a CLUB meeting!"

"Robbie IS the police, you bozo." Milagro is exasperated. "Look at his freakin' T-shirt." She shifts her finger of judgment to Robbie, right below his chin.

RESIDENTIAL ADVISOR is stitched in tiny yellow letters under Robbie's left collar. Oops. Technically Robbie is not the police. He's with campus security. But pointing this out seems ill-advised. I glare at Milagro's gold sneakers.

"I can't believe you." She turns away in disgust and grabs Oak Tree Boy's hand. "Good to see you, Robbie. Glad you continue to disappoint on all counts. And Lulu—don't call me. You can get a ride home in his squad car." Milagro walks away.

"Wait, wait a second!" the security guard says.

Robbie shakes his head. "She's with me; let her go."

The party literally ends when Milagro leaves the room. It's the ultimate power move. In the animal kingdom, Milagros are the predators, and everything else is just lying in their wake.

Robbie, the campus security guard, Leo, and I survey the mess. There are plastic cups littered on the counter, spilling out from under the sofa, overflowing the sink, and lining the windows of the apartment. The security guard scoops up a sweater strewn over a light bulb and sighs. "You folks can go now. No need to stick around for the write-up."

I wince and put my hands on my head. I didn't want to get anyone in trouble. Especially not me.

Robbie taps my shoulder. "Let's get you out of here."

"You're not going to write us up? Send us to college jail? Tell our St. A's chaperones about the party?" I ask.

"Please don't," Leo says. He shoots me a worried glance.

"You're with me. Let's call it RA perks." Robbie shakes his head and walks me out the door. "Coach makes all the swimmers be RAs in order to keep us out of trouble. It sucks being the fun police."

I nod. I know what it's like to feel like a permanent buzzkill. The three of us walk outside and I tug at Milagro's sweatshirt sleeves until my fingers are fully wrapped in the black fuzz. I wish I'd thought to bring mittens, or maybe a scarf. I take a peek at Leo's bare legs and arms. He's shivering too.

Robbie shakes his head. "You're gonna need something to warm you up. I know just the spot." Leo looks at me, and I shrug back at him. Robbie is an RA, so I don't think we'll get in trouble for following him. The only sounds are the crunching of leaves and a car alarm in the distance. I run over my questions for Robbie in my head, so busy focusing on which one to start with that it takes me a while to notice that the streets have become way more lit up. By the time Robbie slows down, we're surrounded by really drunk people. Way worse than what was at the party. Maddie wasn't lying about MonU being a party school. The only non-bar storefronts are munchie destinations: pizza, grilled cheese, and bacon-covered hot dogs. There's an ever-present smell of fried oil and body spray that hovers over everything, along with a constant chorus of "Woooooo!" that emanates from the bars that line the block. Several groups of girls grip each other as they teeter past us in their heels. I can count at least two vomit splotches on the sidewalk. My stomach gurgles and I look away.

Robbie stops in front of a crowd and snakes his way through people, until he reaches the glass door and pushes it. "C'mon. Follow me. Grab a table and I'll order for us."

Robbie sidles up to the counter and Leo and I peel off,

plopping down into seats in the back corner. There is a new world within the cramped wood-paneled restaurant. Everyone is loopy and full of exaggerated hand waving and feet stomping. The girls in front of me laugh louder and longer than they might in the daytime. Their sandwich bites are messier, leaving them with mustard smears and lipstick stains all over their faces, but they also seem really happy to have reached French fry nirvana. There are packs of giant, cozy boys in sweatpants and matching sweatbands, lugging bags overflowing with mysterious sports objects. They look like they could bench-press me with one arm, but instead they're scoping out the girls in the sandwich shop, in between annihilating the mountains of curly fries in front of them. The smell of French fries and melted cheese is even stronger in here. I can feel it snaking around my hair and burrowing deep in the fibers of Milagro's sweatshirt. Good. I hope it's ruined.

"So who is this guy?" Leo says. "And why are we here?"

"He's my sister's boyfriend. My older sister, Clara. Not Milagro. And it's kind of a long story."

Leo nods. "Secret mission stuff. Got it." He peers around the restaurant. "I think we're the only high school kids here."

There's an awkward silence as we wait for Robbie. Finally I ask, "So . . . quiz bowl?"

Leo shrugs. "It seemed like an easy way to make friends

when I transferred to St. Anthony. It's fun, but really corny—have you ever seen the sets? They haven't been updated since the nineties. Thankfully, our matches are only broadcast on the local channels, so my old friends in Miami can't watch."

"You don't want them to see you?"

"No way. I wish there weren't any cameras at all. Somehow, my mom hasn't gotten the memo. She DVRs all of my matches and sends it to our family's never-ending WhatsApp thread. He laughs. "Then again, we get my cousin's water polo matches and flute recitals, so I guess we're even."

"But isn't the St. A's team really good?"

Leo shrugs me off. "It's just a thing I do for fun. The trophy stuff is inconsequential."

Robbie appears with two of the biggest sandwiches I've ever seen. They're towering high, almost as tall as the cans of soda next to them. He's also got curly fries, Tater Tots, and eight containers of ketchup crammed on his tray. Robbie shakes his head, flipping his beautiful blond hair out of his face. "Bon appétit." He points to one of the sandwiches, split in half. "I figured you guys could share."

Leo and I stare at the hulking mountain of carbs and meat. My eyes blink once, then two times in quick succession. I'm not sure I can fit the sandwich in my mouth. I pry the top piece of bread off and my mouth drops open.

"Is that? No." I look up at Robbie. "Wait. Is it?" I drop down, so my face is low to the table so that I can better inspect my sandwich from every angle.

"Yep." Robbie pulls his long hair to the top of his head and wraps it up in a man bun.

"Seriously?"

He nods. "It's a thing here." He takes an enormous bite and smiles, keeping his lips pursed, so none of his toppings spill out.

When I first planned my line of questioning, sandwich toppings were not high on my list. But when I see French fries lovingly placed between a heaping pile of meat, slaw, and cheese, all tied together by thick, crusty white bread, I want to know everything, starting with the invention and ending with the etymology of the sandwich's name.

I take a hulking bite, relishing every bit of fried crunch and salty, tangy crispiness before I'm overwhelmed by flashes of light.

"Oops. Sorry about that." Leo frowns at his phone. "I hate when the flash goes off." He takes another photo of his sandwich before sliding his phone back into his pocket. "My friends and I have a shared photo album of our greatest food hits. This is perfect."

"Your greatest what?"

Leo smiles. "It was a thing my friend Rafi started last summer, when I moved away."

"Karaoke king, Rafi?"

"The one and only. It's a way of keeping in touch, with no strings attached about response times, no worrying about "likes" or perfect lighting, or anything like that. You always have to eat, right?"

I nod.

"My friends and I upload pics—the more fried, the better. Here, look." Leo whips out his phone and quickly scrolls through photos of powdered sugar–covered pastries, overloaded hot dogs, and a few bubbling stews. "Ugh, my friend Dom uploaded a jibarito the other day and I—" Leo looks away wistfully. "What I wouldn't do for some fried plantains."

I study the photo, before handing the phone back to Leo. I love it and I wish I'd thought to do this with Clara.

"Did Clara send you?" Robbie asks, interrupting our sandwich shop talk.

"Huh?" I ask, my words muffled by all the sandwich bits in my mouth and my brain distracted by a sudden craving for plantains. I swallow. "I texted you on my own. It's kind of a personal quest. I wanted to know—"

"So Clara didn't ask you to meet me?" Robbie interrupts. I shake my head again.

"She's not the reason you're here?" Robbie asks again. Sheesh, he is dense. I shake my head.

"But Clara must have asked you. Why else—"

"I think we can safely say that Clara didn't ask her to come," Leo says.

I can't help but laugh. Then I feel bad when Robbie won't look either of us in the eye.

Robbie continues staring at the table. His fingers trace over the grooves in the wood. His mouth is pulled tight, and he's gritting his teeth. "Two days before my swim meet, she sent me a text that said it was over. I thought maybe she changed her mind."

I sit up straight. "Wait a second."

"She said she had some stuff to figure out. Something about school being a lot and needing to find herself. I told her that no matter what, she was still amazing. You know, so many people look up to her and stuff. But it only made things worse."

"She dumped you today?"

"No. Like months ago. Back in January. She said, 'Don't call me.'"

Leo winces.

"What? But you just called her! Yesterday?"

"No." Robbie frowns. "She told me not to call her anymore, so I listened." He perks up for a second. "Do you think she wants me to call her?"

"Definitely not," Leo jumps in. He pats Robbie on the shoulder with a napkin. "Tough break, man."

Robbie slumps in his seat, his eyes blinking fast.

"But Clara *said* you were calling her. Yesterday, when I called her."

"Then she lied." Robbie shakes his head. "We haven't talked since January."

My mind is whirling. None of this makes sense. Why would Clara lie about Robbie calling? "Did Clara break up with you before or after the fight between her and my mom?"

Robbie chooses this moment to take a big bite of his sandwich and mumbles, "Cslkdhrushoru. Laldkjsdhd and slkdsjsld." A little string of slaw falls out of his mouth.

It takes every bit of focus not to roll my eyes at him.

He takes a giant swallow and gives me a sheepish grin. "Sorry. I don't know anything about a specific fight. Once she said your mom didn't approve of the choices she was making, and it was stressing her out."

"You mean about you guys?" I mumble. My cheeks redden and I stare at the grimy floor. I've seen what happens in the Fantasy Suites of *The Last Bachelor*—and whatever I accidentally stumbled into in Milagro's room.

Robbie blushes. "Nah, nah," he stutters. "Nothing like that. She said biology was harder than she thought. She wasn't sure if she could be a doctor. I caught the tail end of a few of their fights."

A change in major? That's what made Clara and Mami so mad? It doesn't make any sense.

"Has she asked about me?" Robbie interrupts my thoughts. He's combing his fingers through his mini hair bun as he waits for my response.

I shake my head slowly.

Robbie deflates. His shoulders hang low and even his man bun seems less perky. We're both victims of Clara's newfound impulsiveness. I offer Robbie my curly fries and he takes them without comment.

When Robbie finishes eating, he hugs me goodbye. He's got his hands tucked into his jeans pockets and he's hunched over, squinting to keep the rain out of his eyes. "Don't worry about Clara," he says. "She'll make up with your mom when she's ready."

I'm not worried about Clara. The Stanford interview is in three days. I'll be back in Baltimore, with Mami, in five days. "You don't understand. I don't have that kind of time."

He shrugs. "Good luck, Lulu." He takes off jogging, and in a few seconds, he disappears, lost to the misty fog that is quickly descending over campus.

Leo and I race back to the dorms, running through sheets of rain streaming down from the sky, drops trickling their way down my back, into my socks, and even the inside of my glasses. I'm grateful for the rain, which is too loud for either of us to chat about what happened tonight.

On the elevator, I mumble, "Thanks for coming along. You didn't have to do that."

Leo somehow still has boundless energy. His voice booms off the small metal walls of the elevator. "Hey, it wasn't boring and we didn't get caught. Two markers of a good night," he says. "And I got to try a new sandwich. Don't tell Robbie, but I'm still gonna stick to French fries on the side." I shiver as the elevator's AC kicks on, and try to give Leo a half-hearted smile. At least one of us had a good time tonight.

He's quiet for a few seconds, the silence stretching as the floors whiz past us, before he says, "I'm sorry about your sister. Whatever you guys are going through sounds hard. I hope you figure it out."

I wrap my fingers around my lanyard and stare at the dusty elevator floor. "Me too," I tell him. I give Leo a limp wave goodbye when he walks off onto his floor.

When I make it off the elevator, three St. Agnes girls stare down the hallway at me from their lounge encampment.

"Where are you coming from?" Amelia calls out, fiddling with the drawstrings on her tie-dyed joggers. "Lulu! C'mere. Did you go out? Like out, *out*?" She fixes her steely blue eyes on me, daring me to walk away. Suddenly I understand why St. Agnes's lacrosse team is undefeated this season.

I walk down the hallway toward them, sliding my hands sheepishly into my pockets. "Um. Maybe? But it wasn't my idea. And it kind of sucked. Wait. You're not gonna tell—"

They all sit up straighter, and Genevieve puts down her pink Gatorade.

"Were there boys there?" "Who'd you go with?" "How'd you figure out how to sneak out?" It's hard to keep everyone's questions straight.

Caroline rubs her hand in anticipation, waiting for me to respond.

I'm too exhausted to lie. "Honestly, the party was not worth sneaking out for." An image of Milagro's bland date flashes in my mind. "I didn't have much in common with anyone there. And it was weirdly sticky."

Genevieve nods approvingly. "Frat parties are so over-rated. I'm holding out for an artsy girl at Piedmont College."

"You're holding out for anyone that wears as much black eyeliner as you." Amelia reaches over and grabs a handful of popcorn from Genevieve. Genevieve playfully swats her hand before tossing a kernel in Amelia's open mouth. They both erupt into giggles when it lands in her ear instead.

"That's why I'm the lacrosse captain and you're the debate team captain," Amelia tells her, stealing the pop-corn bowl away from her.

"Overrated or not, it sounds more fun than our night. The most exciting thing that happened was Maddie find-ing a roach in the hallway," Caroline laughs, pushing up her gold-rimmed glasses.

"She screamed so loud."

"I can't believe she said her dad would sue MonU for being uninhabitable."

"She's gonna scream even louder when she finds out *you* went to a party," Genevieve says, nodding to me. She reaches into Caroline's bookstore tote bag and pulls out another bag of popcorn.

I bite my lip as the hallway fills with laughter, until I realize they're not laughing at me for being unsocial. It's Maddie who is the butt of the joke, after she apparently called everyone a big loser, among other things, for wanting to stay in.

I'm blinking back sleep when I tell them I'm going to bed. I get a chorus of "Bye, Lulu!" in return, and they immediately start debating the best vending machine topping for the new bag of popcorn.

I smile to myself as I walk down the hallway, but the thrill of possibly making friends wears off as soon as I collapse on my bed. Every metal coil in my saggy mattress digs into my back, each one a sharp reminder that I don't belong here. Above me, the fluorescent light buzzes loudly and I can hear my heartbeat echoing in my ears. Even though it's late, I reach into my pocket and call Mami for answers, waiting patiently for each of the phone rings. But the call immediately goes to voice mail. She warned us about the terrible cell service.

I text her instead. **The trip is so fun! I miss you already. Please send besos and hugs to you and Tía Lochita.** I attach the photo Milagro and I took before we went out tonight. My hair is an enormous cloud around my head and my fingers are wrapped around the edges of Milagro's sweatshirt. Milagro is looking down at her phone, ignoring the camera. I should have known we'd never be a real team. Not like me and Clara. I close my phone. A team only works when you can count on people.

I set an alarm for 6:00 a.m. and turn the lights out.

13
Milagro

COSMOPOLITAN SAYS THAT you should consider yourself the CEO of your life. If that's the case, then I'm officially firing Craig—or is it Greg?—who is currently crouched behind me and whispering an unintelligible medley of slurred words punctuated by puffs of vodka breath. I'm getting secondhand drunk by sharing airspace with him. Given his size, it's disgusting to imagine how many tiny Jell-O shots he must have eaten to reach this level of wobbly intoxication. I'm not saying I should win an Oscar for my very convincing performance of Drunk High School Girl, but it *was* pretty darn good. (Of course, in my dream scenario where I end up winning an Oscar, Lulu would probably storm the stage and rip it out of my arms.)

At the party, Craig/Greg seemed so promising. "A bona fide hunk" is what Jared called him. Craig/Greg walked in the room, looking like he hunts his own meat and could punch through a wall. He walked up to me and said "Hola" and mispronounced my name, even after I corrected him twice. I was sure he was a jerk, but then Craig/Greg actually paid attention to me at the party. He led me to the kitchen again and again to pour me a drink or snag a few BBQ chips. I poured all of my drinks into the fake plants in the living room or swapped them with blue Gatorade when no one was looking, but it was still very considerate of him.

When Robbie showed up, everyone ran. Watching them scramble reminded me of the time Mami poured bleach on the ant colony behind our fridge, only it was fumbling bodies squeezing out of doors and windows, ducking into closets and rushing into upstairs bathrooms. When the lights flashed on, Lucas mouthed the words "call me" before he hopped out a window with Jared and took off running. I made a beeline for the door, with a lumbering Craig/Greg shouting "Hey, wait up!" behind me.

Now Craig/Greg and I are crouched outside of the house, waiting for campus police to wrap up their party citations before we make our exit. There's no point in asking Craig/Greg to tell me his name again, even if I am using him as a human chair (okay, fine, I'm sitting on his lap). It's only to keep from accidentally toppling into the dog poop littered throughout the tiny alley.

Craig/Greg nudges me, but I ignore him. I don't know why Lulu would call Robbie. I doubt they've ever had a real conversation before. Maybe Clara asked Robbie to show Lulu around MonU to get her acclimated to college life. Of course, she didn't think to include me in her plan. I guess nothing about me screams "college material." I make a mental note to text Clara, and then I remember our last conversation, and I decide to spare myself another lecture.

THUMP.

"HEY!" I yelp.

I'm flat on my butt, my legs splayed out in front of me.

"GRAMMMPPHHHHH."

Craig/Greg is out cold, leaning against the wall and ripping snores that could wake the dead. Now I'll never know his name. I put my hands down to push myself off the ground. My fingers sink into something much, much softer than cement or dirt.

Oh no.

This is not happening.

No no no no no no.

I pull my fingers up to my nose and snap my head back and gag. It smells worse than the time I stowed an egg sandwich in my purse and forgot about it for a week. It's even worse than when I'm on detention dumpster duty and have to empty the St. Agnes cafeteria trash cans. I let out a whimper and a sniffle. The neighborhood is quiet in response. There is no one who can appreciate my pain.

I smear my hands on anything I can find: the brick, Craig/Greg's salmon-colored shorts, and the grass in front of the house. But nothing rids my fingers of the smell of dog poop.

I gingerly reach into my pocket, careful not to let any of my fingers touch the fabric of my skirt. I pinch my phone and drag it out of my pocket.

Success!

I jab my pinky at the screen, but it doesn't turn on. It's as dead as my morale, and there isn't a phone charger in sight. Goose bumps run down my arm. I have no way of making it back to the dorms. Worse—if a masked murderer happens to come by, I have no way of calling someone for help. I'm a smelly, hopeless mess. I blink back tears. I need to come up with a plan.

When Mami was first dumped by Papi, she became obsessed with self-help audio books. This was before *Gloria Estefan 20th Anniversary* and after her Zumba phase. She would play them on loop, everywhere from our beat-up station wagon to her weekly bubble bath. The self-help experts had smooth-as-honey voices, the kind you'd want to hear when you're crying in front of the refrigerator, clutching a soggy pint of chocolate ice cream in one hand and a mug of lukewarm hot chocolate in the other. The problems they tackled were scandalous: husbands who gambled away homes, or marriages that collapsed after mysterious "business trips."

Mami's favorite parts were when the strangers would describe their rock bottom. It thrilled her to listen to problems worse than hers. She'd crow as a woman would sob, "And after I took him back for the sixth time, I discovered he got my cousin pregnant." Mami would shake her head and shove another spoonful of ice cream in her mouth. "These women are so foolish, Milagro." She was smug with the knowledge that while her love life might not be perfect, she hadn't messed us up or lost our house.

I may not have a lyin' cheatin' husband, but this is my rock bottom. My butt is covered in wet grass, there are poop particles under my glitter nails, and my cracked phone might as well be a doorstop for all the help it can provide me. When I wander the streets of Baltimore without a phone, I know all the bodegas and bars that will let me duck in and borrow a charge. At least once a week, I spend thirty minutes demolishing a chicken box while waiting for my phone to rise from the dead. But here in Pittsburgh, it's so freaking dark and quiet. I guess everyone collectively decided to go to bed at 9:00 p.m., including the streetlights.

I strain my ears for any kind of noise. All I can hear is the occasional splash from cars running over puddles.

But there's a vague brightness in the distance, so I decide to walk toward it. My arms are wrapped tight around my waist and my neck is swiveling from side to side, desperate to hear signs of life.

I'm almost halfway up the block when I decide I've totally lost it. The silence has driven me absolutely bonkers.

I'm gazing at large butterflies. They're radioactive orange, the color of the sun before it sets. The pink ones are electric magenta and purple. Black stripes with white splotches rise up to the sky like a midnight miracle. I trudge up the hill, squinting my eyes at them. They shimmer with every step I take, bigger than me, or a car, and maybe even an elephant.

As I crest the hill, the butterflies stop moving. Not because they're dead but because they were never alive. They're painted or something, huge on the side of a random building.

Even though I told my brain never to think about Lulu again, I can hear Lulu laughing at me, making fun of me for thinking butterflies could be that big, or survive in temperatures this cold.

My mouth drops open when I finally make it to the entrance of the building. I touch the thousands of small glass tiles that make up the enormous wings of these mosaic butterflies. It's bigger and better than anything I've ever doodled during class. Up close, the shades of orange, red, and pink glass tile lines put the St. Agnes art supply closet to shame. The tiles are crooked, wandering up and over, some rows merging together before splitting apart. Some of the tiles are covered in grout, from where the artist got too excited. There are even a few spots where the glass tiles have popped out. It's wild how things that are drop-what-you're-doing-and-stare beautiful can be so messy when you look at them up close. If my phone was working, I'd take a selfie in front of them. But I knock on the glass door instead. There's a shuffling of shadows, so I stand up a little straighter and get my sob story ready.

The door opens and I scream, "AHHHHH!!!!!"

"AHHHHHHHH!" screams the bear, leaping away from me, its shiny claws out.

CRACK!

For the second time today, I've been tricked. It's not a real bear. It's a person in a giant bear head. The sharp edge of the metal door is wedged firmly into its papier-mâché skull. The person inside is stuck, even as they try to free themselves. It's a humiliating dance of pinwheel arms and hip shaking. It does nothing to dislodge them, but it does make the pom-pom on their bear costume butt jiggle in place.

My giggles pour out of me. I'm doubled over, heaving with laughter and stumbling backward. My sneakers catch on a dip on the sidewalk and again, I'm out cold on my butt.

"Um. A little help here?" the bear calls out, waving its mitten paws in the air. Once Lulu showed me a video of a bear that thought it was human. It wobbled on two legs and walked like its big booty was wearing a heavy diaper. This monster looks like that real bear mated with the MonU's tragic teddy bear mascot, and this was their love child.

The monster's voice is high-pitched and muffled. "Can you move faster?" she sniffles.

I pick myself up off the ground. "Where should I start?"

"I *told* Martin that sewing the head to the body was a bad idea, but does anyone listen to me? Noooo." The bear has a pointer finger jabbing at the air in front of it. I don't know who Martin is, but he's in big trouble.

I grab the pointer finger. "Just tell me where to start."

The bear goes quiet.

"Are you still in there?"

"The seam starts in the tail. But my arms are too short to reach it. Which I *told* Martin would be a problem." The pointer finger is back in action.

I squat down. "Okay. Bear with me." I double over laughing again.

"Any time now," the bear says, tapping its foot impatiently.

I grab the pom-pom tail and yank. Underneath the Velcro, I find a yellow zipper pull that runs the whole length of the bear's left leg. I tug on the zipper, opening a seam big enough for the mystery person to crawl out and stumble into the open air.

A red-haired girl in leggings and a black tank top emerges.

"You're not the pizza delivery guy," she says matter-of-factly. She and Lulu came from the same school of manners. I guess I won't be getting a thank-you.

She shoves past my spot on the sidewalk and cranes her head, looking left and right. "Crap. He probably went down the wrong road. Why doesn't anyone ever listen to me?" She steps back inside and surveys the damaged bear head, still stuck on the door frame. "Martin is *not* going to be happy about this." She wrenches it off the frame and grabs the fur suit.

I scramble up off the ground to follow her.

"Hold it right there!"

"Oof!"

I bounce off the girl, or rather, her bony arm. She's sticking it out in front of me, a bouncer to whatever's inside the beautiful butterfly building.

"I need a phone charger." I hold my phone up like an offering and push the power button twice to show her how dead it is. I remember my gross hands. "And to use the bathroom. You kind of owe me."

Her red hair is sweaty and matted to the sides of her face. There's a piece of fur stuck to the tip of her nose, the same shade of brown as the freckles across her cheeks. She's cradling the bear head on her hip, like the world's ugliest baby.

"What's the last words that Macbeth says to his son?"

"Um. What?" I stare at her.

"You heard me." She taps her foot. "I don't have all day."

I didn't think tonight could get worse, but now that my survival depends on literary trivia, things have progressed from terrible to OMG horrific. I rack my brain, wishing I paid any attention to Lulu when she went through her Shakespeare phase.

"I don't . . . know?" I say. "To be, or not to be?"

"Oh man, you are so wrong."

My shoulders slump. Back to the cold and unfamiliar streets of Pittsburgh it is.

The monster girl's arm goes slack. "You can come in. Follow me!" She swivels and charges up the stairs. I scamper after her.

"What? But why?"

"I thought you might be one of those drama freaks," she said. "Wait. You're not one, right?" She stops mid-stair and sizes me up.

I shake my head. She finally swipes the fur off her nose. "I mean, we're all drama freaks, but MonU's historical 'actors' are the worst of the lot." Only she uses finger quotes when she says the word *actors*, and she pronounces the word like she's got a British accent. I laugh. She glares at me like Mami does when someone dares to correct her pronunciation. "I'm Kailee. You can follow me. But NO pictures!" She sticks her finger out at me, pointing to me and my phone. "That's the only condition."

I nod solemnly.

Kailee leads me up the stairs. "Bathroom is that way," she says. "Come find me for a charger."

In the bathroom, I scrub my fingers until they're red, raw sausages. My nail polish is missing on my pinky and there's a scrape on the palm of my hand from one of my many spills to the ground. My hands are a mess, but they pass the sniff test. I fold up pieces of paper towel and dab at my skirt until all the mud splotches are gone. I stare in the mirror. A stranger stares back, someone with smeared mascara and stray leaves in her hair. I don't know who I am outside of Baltimore, outside of the confines of my tiny house. Outside of Pablo.

Kailee is fiddling with her phone, standing in front of two giant black-painted doors. When I walk up to her, she throws open the doors and ushers me into a large, well-lit room. The first thing I notice is the bar. It's wooden, splintery, and just a tiny bit crooked, leaning too heavily to the right. The bar is covered in a glittery tablecloth and there's a mountain of red plastic cups stacked on top of it. Next to the cups are liters of Sunny Delight, Diet Coke, and lime soda. It looks like the party I was at earlier, only there's no line of sweaty people jostling for a chance at a keg.

In front of the bar is a crowd of people—well, technically woodland creatures and assorted monsters, in various forms of undress. There are five wolves with sneakers on their feet, two Draculas with a bag of (fake?) blood thrown over their shoulders, and a lone lion in a tan sweatshirt. His tufts of fur poke out from the tops of his sweatshirt and he keeps spanking people with his tail. He's got a lion head on his hip too, and I can count at least ten spots where the fur has worn off, exposing the sad gray mesh of papier-mâché below it.

"Sorry, folks, false alarm. The pizza isn't here yet. Let's get back to making magic!" Kailee claps her hands before turning back to me and nodding to a couch in the back corner. "You can plug your phone in over there," she says.

I sink into the couch, wincing as the leather creaks under my weight. I cannot believe how far south my night has gone. I was supposed to be making out with a studly college boy, not watching the dress rehearsal for a tragically low-budget production of whatever off-off-off-off-Broadway show this is. I plug my phone into one of the chargers on the wall and cross my fingers that Mrs. Johnson's anti-nausea medication keeps her conked out for the next two hours, or however long it'll take me to get back to the dorm room.

Kailee claps again. "Back to work, people!" She tucks the bear head back under her arm and takes long strides to the corner of the room. With a flick of a switch, pop music fills the space. It's almost loud enough to drown out the grumbling as the costumed "animals" lumber toward the center of the room.

A squad of people dressed in black pop out from backstage. Each of them holds a small plastic case in one hand and a folded-up director's chair in the other.

"False alarm?" one of them calls out.

"Trust me, you'll know when the pizza is here," Kailee says. She settles her broken monster head back on her head, poking her fingers at the cracks.

People in black T-shirts spring open their director's chairs and shove the actors into the seats. I hear one of my top favorite noises in the world—the snap of a plastic compact opening—and my heart starts beating faster. These are real makeup artists. They reach into a giant jar of clean sponges. Another whips out a shiny foil-covered makeup palette in disco shimmer colors. Like a moth drawn to a buzzing light bulb, I can't help myself—I stand up from the couch and wander toward them.

"Is that black snail primer?" I ask, pointing at the orange-and-black jar.

"Imported from Korea." A girl with pink hair grins. "I got it off an online beauty forum." She jiggles the jar in front of me.

"Wow!" I gasp. "It's so much thicker than I thought."

"And look how well it holds shimmer." She dabs a splotch on her arm. "But I can't figure out why it keeps pilling when I layer the cream colors over it."

"Have you tried powdered eye shadow and a wet brush as a swap for your cream pots?" I blurt out, before I can stop myself. *Ugh.* As soon as the words are out of my mouth, I want to take them all back. These are professional makeup artists. They don't need advice from a high school drug store makeup loser like me.

Pink hair stops what she's doing and looks at me. "I never thought of that. Let's try now."

"It's a stupid idea. It probably won't work," I backtrack. "But I read that creams have their own oils, and the snail mucus draws oil out of your skin. I don't know. Two kinds of oil mixing together can't be good for getting anything to stick."

"Let's find out!"

I hold my breath as she layers primer and powdered shadows. When she presses a sponge over the monster's face, nothing happens. The makeup stays put.

"Hell yes!" She high-fives me. "I'm gonna tell everyone about this."

I let out a huge sigh of relief. "What is this place, any-way?" I ask her, taking mental notes on how she's applying plum eye shadow to Dracula's eyelids.

"The Glitter Box Theater? It's a DIY performance space. You rent it out and can put on any kind of show. Martin and Kailee are the brains behind the operation; they hired me and my makeup crew for dress rehearsals and performances."

A trilling ring goes off.

Oh crap.

I glance back at the sofa, but my phone is still out. Kailee waves her phone in the air while flicking the lights on and off. She places both hands around her mouth and yells, "PIZZA'S HERE!" She runs out the door—this time without her costume head. Phew. We hear her clomp down and back up the stairs, and when she emerges, she's got a stack of pizzas piled so high, you can't even see the top of her bright red ponytail.

I rush over and grab a few boxes from her, laying them out on the bar. It's the least I can do, considering she saved me.

"Thanks," she says. She dives behind the bar and pops back out with a roll of paper towels. "Quick, grab a slice."

Everyone beelines for the bar, and Kailee and I find ourselves shoved into a corner with our slices.

"So who are you, anyway?" She's got one eyebrow

raised and a slice of mushroom pizza lifted to her mouth. Every few seconds, she surveys the room, to make sure everything is under control. She's a total boss.

"I'm Milagro. I'm visiting MonU. I'm not from here."

She nods. "That explains the clueless look. But what are you doing *here*? Most people don't even know this place exists."

"My sister called the cops on a party. And my friends ditched me. My date fell asleep. And I got lost."

"You've had a rougher night than Aaron," purple Dracula chimes in. She points to a hairy werewolf in the corner, with an ice pack wrapped around both his knees. "He bruised his knees while trying to do the worm."

I study the werewolf. "I got dumped yesterday too. So I think I win."

"Tomorrow will be better," Dracula says, nodding with confidence. "It always is."

I snort. "I doubt it. I'm stuck on this epically boring field trip and tomorrow we're headed to another college. I don't even care about college." Oh no. I'm back to blabbing my feelings to strangers. "You guys have the right idea." I wave my arms around the room. Everyone stares back at me, bemused. "This weird stuff? I thought it was tragic, but it's so cool. I want to do something like this. Something I actually care about. I'm not about taking tests and writing boring essays for another four years." Dracula is nodding along. "I don't get why everyone says you *have to* go to college," I blurt out. It's what I've wanted to say to Lulu and Clara for so long, and it feels good to finally have it off my chest.

"Wait a second," the injured werewolf says. By this point, he's hobbled over to the pizza corner. He puts up a furry palm between us. "Who do you think pays for this?"

I shrug. "Ticket sales?"

He laughs. "We wish. We'll be lucky if we can convince our friends to watch our show. Try again."

"Hey, my mom watches every livestream," Kailee says defensively.

"Bake sales? You have a patent on fur glue?"

He shakes his head. "We're just a bunch of college kids. Doing something meaningful in between all the homework and tests."

My cheeks redden. "You guys go to MonU?"

"Hell yeah! HAIL TO THE MON!" the monsters roar. They erupt into giggles. "We might not be jocks, but we've still got school spirit," one of the Draculas explains. "We get club money to put on shows like this."

"Yeah, shows that no one will see."

"That's enough. Break's over!" Kailee claps her hands. This time there's no grumbling, just a few extra bites of pizza and sips of soda before everyone goes back to their places. The monsters and animals run through their number, while the injured werewolf teaches me how to do a leap. It's crooked and I keep landing with my knees bumping into each other, but he promises that with practice, I'll move like a graceful swan. After the final run-through, I show the Draculas how primer can help their brows stay on longer and we practice lining our lips with black pencil.

The red cups from the bar—the ones that I eyed suspiciously—never get filled with alcohol. There's no dramatic reveal of Jell-O shots, table-pounding beer-chugging competitions, or sweaty bodies "accidentally" brushing my butt. Craig/Greg feels like a distant memory. Maybe he was the real monster all along—a sweaty, stumbling drunk monster.

When Kailee drops me off at the dorms, a tiny bit of the Monster Troupe magic has stayed with me. The security guard nods himself awake when I come in, but he goes right back to snoozing as soon as I swipe my lanyard. I practice my pirouettes in front of the elevator and down the hallway to my room. The gray carpet softens the sound of my jumps, so I'm free to fall as much as I'd like.

I pull my phone out so I can set an alarm, and the selfie of Craig/Greg stares back at me. He has a vacant look in his eyes, but in a model-y type of way, rather than about-to-pass-out. His chin hangs over my shoulder the way that Pablo's used to. And my lipstick looks *great*. It's the perfect photo for pretending I'm moving on, and yet I can't bring my fingers to do it. I don't want Pablo to have the last line in tonight's magic. Instead, I shove my phone aside and fall asleep instantly. I dream of dancing Draculas, a friendly werewolf rave, and owning a supermarket full of snail primer. When I wake up in the morning a few hours later, even though it's ungodly early, there's a smile on my face, like I've spent the whole night giggling.

SOUTH BEND

14
Lulu

MOTION SICKNESS IS caused by a disturbance to your body's balance. Your brain can't handle conflicting signals from your eyes (countryside rushing by the windows), your feet (planted firmly on the floor of our grungy bus), and your butt (our bus driver seems to hit every speed bump, pothole, and divot in the road). It's not just humans who are afflicted by motion sickness—dogs, cats, even horses can suffer from stomach flops, woozy bellies, and the foreboding sensation that you're going to vomit. Mrs. Johnson is exhibiting all of those symptoms when she wobbles her way to my seat.

"Luz. I know we were supposed to practice interview questions on the bus, but—" She pauses and closes her eyes.

"Mrs. Johnson?"

She turns several shades paler as she manages to eke out the words, "Perhaps you and your partner can—" and then she slaps one hand over her mouth and grabs the headrest of my seat with her other hand.

"I've got it." I wave her away, and she storms down the aisle, practically running to the bathroom in the back of the bus.

"What was that about?" Leo asks.

"Nothing." I turn the volume up louder on my *National Geographic* podcast and raise my book higher over my face. But not even graphic descriptions of lionesses tearing the slowest gazelles to shreds can distract me.

"It didn't sound like nothing. What's your interview for?" Leo scoots up in his bus seat and peers over my shoulder. "You've been reading that page for the last twenty minutes."

I slap the book shut and hug it tight across my chest. "Nothing important. It doesn't matter anyway." I shove my book into my bag, crumpling up my papers, my field trip folder, and more along the way.

"Is this about last night? Maybe we can go sandwich exploring in Indiana." Leo smiles. "Where is Clara anyway?"

"Iowa." I'm biting my lip so hard, I might just get a blister. This morning, I called Clara five times, but she didn't answer. I finally texted her that I knew about her and Robbie. I even asked her why she didn't tell us, if she was mad at us, and if she wouldn't please call Mami for me. Clara's texts came in hot, one right after the other.

I need time before I can talk to Mami.

I promise things are all right. I'll make it up to you in person. How many days until Stanford?

Please let me have some space. You'll understand when you're older.

There's nothing that makes me angrier than "when you're older," except for maybe the ambiguous and amorphous "space" that Clara needs. Isn't two thousand miles between us enough? What is "space" anyway? She has always had space. Milagro, Mami, and I are asteroids and planets orbiting around Clara the Star.

Leo wrinkles his nose. "Iowa? Why? I'd probably stop talking to my family if I went there too."

I want to glare at Leo, but it's not his fault that my sister has betrayed me. He was cool last night. Cooler than I would have been, if our roles had been reversed.

"It probably has some redeeming qualities," he says quickly. "Like corn." He gestures outside.

I hear the flush from the bathroom and Mrs. Johnson's wobbly steps making their way down the aisle. I turn to Leo. "Okay. We need to pretend like you're interviewing me. For a college thing. I don't want to talk about why. It doesn't matter. Mrs. Johnson needs to think that we're practicing. Only I really don't want to."

"Interview me instead," Leo says. "Sometimes you learn better by doing. That's what my dad always says. 'See one, do one, teach one.' It's a doctor thing."

I take a deep breath. "Fine. Why do you want to go to college?"

Leo clears his throat. "I want to go to college because there's a lot I don't know about the world and how it works." He crosses his eyes. "And no offense to Baltimore, but I would do anything to get back to warmer weather. Berkeley? UCLA? I'm all over it. Next question?"

I shake my head. He really doesn't get it. None of my classmates do, not even Milagro. College isn't a vacation for me. It's not a joke either.

"Too bad. It's my turn." He takes his phone out. "But let's make it a game. My sisters and I played this during the move, when we were stuck on long car rides between Baltimore and Miami." He shows me the screen. His map is open to a random street I've never seen before, in street view.

"Where is that? There are no mountains like that in Baltimore or Indiana."

"I have no idea. It's random." He squints. "I think it might be Juneau? In Alaska? But that's the whole point. I'll ask a question. If your answer is good, you can choose which direction we walk down the street view. If your answer is bad, I choose. Either way, we get to explore a new city."

I lean over his shoulder. "Is that a dog in a lime-green puffer coat?" I zoom in. "I think his toenails are painted."

Leo laughs. "You wouldn't believe the weird stuff that shows up in street view. One time, my sister found someone screaming at a raccoon." He wrinkles his nose. "You also see a lot more people dumping trash and peeing outside than you would expect. Anyway, I'll start. If you were a type of tree, what kind of tree would you be?"

"What!" I sputter. "That's definitely not an interview question."

"Try telling my dad that. Whenever I complain about college applications, he says it's nothing compared to cutthroat med school admissions. He likes to spring that one on his medical school residents."

"How am I supposed to just pick one tree? There are so many to choose from!"

"Obviously you should want to be a mango tree, because it's a great pollinator—so you can work well with others—and the trunk is strong enough for furniture, so you have strong values, and it's water resistant, making you cool under pressure." He pauses. "Should I keep going? I haven't even touched on the fruit-bearing properties."

My mouth gapes open.

Leo is suddenly sheepish, running his hand through his hair as he explains. "It's less pressure if you think of interviews as personal trivia rounds. You've done cool things, right?"

I give Leo the tiniest nod, though I don't know if anyone would refer to my activities as 'cool.'

"Then connect two facts—something about you and the thing you want. Unlike real trivia, there's no wrong answer, since you're the only expert on you." Leo leans back, stretching his hand under the seat and rummaging through his bag. "Want one?" He shows me two granola bars. "My parents made me pack so many snacks, as if the school wasn't going to feed us."

I nod yes and he hands one over, before tapping right on his phone, bringing us to a crosswalk in front of a small wooden post office. "Your turn. Quiz me. "

We soar past fields of corn, soybeans, and clusters of happy brown cows as Leo and I work through Mrs. Johnson's basic interview questions. At first, I clam up. I'm not used to talking about myself this much, but then I see how at ease Leo is and the way he casually brings up the travel tournaments he's attended with the St. A's quiz bowl team, or finally reveals his disastrous summer at space camp. ("They made everyone run underwater drills in a giant pool to simulate weightlessness, and the counselors made fun of you if you were slow. It was awful.") It never sounds like bragging or looking for pity, just things that happened to him. He's always looking for the silver lining too, like when he brings up moving to Baltimore for his dad's promotion, he spends more time talking about how great it is to have his grandmother move in, instead of how much it sucks to transfer high schools. When my answers are curt, Leo tilts his chin down and stares at me, refusing to hand over the phone. It's an effective strategy, because I'd rather blurt out a better answer than get stuck in a staring contest that makes my stomach flip. It helps that Leo seems genuinely interested in my lab work from last summer, or the brainstorms I've had with the Sierra Club freshmen.

"Luck shouldn't determine whether someone has safe drinking water," I tell Leo. "Last year, we were able to do so much during the local elections. I don't want the neighborhoods to think we got bored."

As Leo looks at me, the sun catches on his dark curls. I run my fingers through my hair, wondering if my hair is glowing too.

"Miami has swim advisories all the time. It's these huge companies that don't give a fu—" He stops and glances at Father Coleman, snoozing a few seats away. "A crap about the environment. Throw in an old city sewage system, and it's a health catastrophe and it feels like people have given up."

"At this rate, making things 'not terrible' would be a step up," I say quietly. "That's why college seems so cool to me—the chance to learn how to make our messed-up world a little better."

When we run out of interview questions, we move on to Leo's trivia bible, which he says his quiz bowl teammates memorized years ago. Leo smokes me on US presidents, but I get him back with world capitals. We've conquered most of the streets of Juneau by the time we switch to our likes and dislikes. I learn Leo's favorite dessert is cherry pie, he's been to three JoJo Siwa concerts ("As a chaperone for my sisters, okay?!"), and he hates any movies that feature a dance sequence (an objectively terrible opinion). By the time we finally make it to Juneau's gorgeous, marble-laden capitol building, Leo's phone battery is blinking and threatening to die. We agree to take a break for the last hour of the trip.

As Leo quickly dozes off, I move on to my next order of business: fixing whatever happened between Mami and Clara. I'm humming to myself as I save newspaper articles and op-ed pieces on the value of the humanities and why literature and philosophy and sociology are worth studying. In case those aren't enough to convince Mami that Clara doesn't need a biology degree, I've also written mini bios on six people on *Fortune*'s Top 100 Leaders of the World. Did you know Barbara Walters was an English major? Mami loves Barbara Walters. I glance out the window when my research is complete. Our windows are framed by blindingly green oceans of grass, a million shades of yellow and green and sun. The world around me is blossoming, and so are my hopes for the future.

Our weary bus finally pulls into our home for the next two days: the University of Notre Dame. As Maddie breathlessly explains to Sarah Jefferson, "Notre Dame is Harvard, but for people who like Jesus and football." There's a quiet rumbling and rummaging as everyone digs into their bags and pulls out electric-green school paraphernalia—floppy hats and long scarves, oversized sweatshirts and, in Jason McDaniel's case, a prized letterman jacket from when his dad was a football player at Notre Dame. Maddie and Gracelynn agree this is "so cool" and a few of the boys even ask if they can touch the worn leather elbow patches.

Caroline rolls her eyes and leans over the aisle to tell us, "Can you believe they actually put a statue of Jesus in the end zone of the football stadium? 'Touchdown Jesus' is made of stone and his arms are wide open for any passes."

Genevieve sighs dramatically. "How many days until Piedmont? Don't tell Amelia, but I think I'm allergic to jocks."

"I heard that!" Amelia shouts from two rows away.

The bus driver has us illegally parked in front of the University of Notre Dame's basilica, aka an over-the-top, million-dollar church. The kaleidoscope stained-glass windows and stone arches reach up so high, it almost hurts my neck to see how they brush the wispy clouds in the sky.

Mrs. Johnson hops off the bus and doubles over in the grass, before quickly making a sign of the cross. I think she's grateful to not have vomited on the ride. Father Coleman cups his hands around his mouth and bellows, "BUTTS UP AND OUT! LAST ONE OUT HAS TO SIT WITH US AT MASS." We're a blurry haze of blazers and hands in hair, desperately trying to smooth out bumps and frizz. Mrs. Johnson recovers enough to fling open the basilica doors and point us to pews in the back. She's got her finger on her lips and a withering death glare, but we don't need it. We're stunned into silence.

When I picture a perfect day, I think of the quiet hum of our little house, in the hours before anyone gets up, when the sun streams into the kitchen and I'm barefoot and eating the ripest strawberries before anyone else can get to them. I think about the ecstasy of getting a new book, the reverence I have for turning a crisp white page over for the first time ever. This is the overwhelming feeling I get, complete with shivers down my arms and a small smile on my face, when I walk into the basilica. The ceilings are as bold and blue as the sky on a perfect spring day. The beams are so far above us, I want to marvel at their architectural feat, but there's so much more I can look at. The priest up on the altar is small potatoes compared to the white arches that rise up from the church's sides and crisscross at the top. He can't possibly compete with the painted glittering wings of the angels or the gold molding that wraps around the ornate columns. Pink and blue and gold shadows fall over the pews, from the stained-glass windows. Even I can't help but put my hands out to watch the moody light dance across my arms. Leo does the same, his arms much longer than mine, and we smile at each other. Leo outlines a lavender splotch that begins on his arm and continues on mine. His finger is warm and meticulous in following the irregular shapes. I feel light-headed from the musty incense clouds floating in the air.

It's easy to feel small and insignificant in a majestic place, like you're a big nobody. But when Leo and I file into the pews, there's some irreverent jostling as Maddie and Gracelynn scramble to sit next to us with giant smiles.

"We heard you went out," Maddie whispers. "To a party."

"Shh!" Mrs. Johnson glares at our row, daring us to interrupt mass again.

Maddie and I have never talked before. In fact, she usually ignores me.

"Not really. And it was overrated," I whisper back to

her when Mrs. Johnson looks away.

It's hard to tell who is frowning more, Mrs. Johnson or Gracelynn. I stare at the tile floor and pretend I don't hear any more of Maddie's or Gracelynn's repeated "Psst! Lulu!"

From the row in front of me, Caroline and Genevieve peek back at me and cross their eyes, before turning so quickly, Mrs. Johnson can't catch them in the act.

After five more "Pssts!" Leo leans over me and shushes Maddie himself, leaving her sputtering. I laugh, and he gives me a wink.

When the service ends, our motley crew follows Mrs. Johnson and Father Coleman out the ornate gold doors and onto the lawn outside the church. Whatever reverence we could scrounge up has officially worn off, and the exhaustion from our six-hour bus ride has set in. Two St. A boys are basically walking zombies. Meanwhile, Caroline and Genevieve are popping chocolate-covered espresso beans and squirting eyedrops in their eyes to wash away the bleariness. Even Mrs. Johnson can't stop herself from yawning and putting her hand on her forehead every few minutes and closing her eyes. The only person *not* ready to collapse is Leo. He bounces on the tops of his feet and fluffs his hair up with his hands. He's got a University of Notre Dame brochure tucked in his back pocket and a pair of sunglasses dangling from a string around his neck. His backpack sits high on his shoulders, exuding first-day-of-school vibes.

He is a fresh celery stalk among us wilted broccoli heads.

From under a budding oak tree, Mrs. Johnson and Father Coleman make the day's announcements.

"Today, you'll be paired with a University of Notre Dame volunteer organization. You'll learn about the service opportunities available to college students." Mrs. Johnson waves her hand at Maddie. "Yes, today's hours will count toward your graduation requirement." Everyone around me lets out a collective sigh of relief.

I tune out. I've heard this spiel before. Community service hours are part of the honors program at St. Agnes. We have to complete fifty hours each year in order to graduate. "Siempre hay alguien que tiene menos que ti," Mami tells us. There's always someone who has less than you. Mami made sure Clara, Milagro, and I spent our middle school and elementary school weekends ladling chicken casseroles at soup kitchens and reading books to kids at the women and children's shelter in the next neighborhood over. It wasn't about remembering how lucky we were, she said. People aren't meant to be symbols of anything. It was about our moral obligation to help others.

As Mrs. Johnson runs down the list of volunteer assignments, the groans start pouring out. No one wants to help out at a food pantry or sort nails and wood scrap at a Habitat for Humanity site.

Father Coleman wrinkles his nose in disgust, but Mrs.

Johnson places a hand on his wrist to stop him from saying anything.

It's not totally out of the goodness of her heart that Mami pushes volunteering so much. Clara's volunteer hours are the reason she landed a full scholarship at the University of Iowa, more financial aid than any school on the East Coast offered her.

"Luz and Leo, you'll be heading to Green Leaf Growers."

"The nerds get to hang out at a weed dispensary? No fair!" one of the St. A boys interjects. I think his name is Hector.

I bristle. First of all, we are ALL nerds. (Except for Milagro.) That's the whole point of this trip. And second of all, there's no way we're working at a weed dispensary. I resist the urge to look up the medical marijuana ordinances in the state of Indiana.

"Excuse me?" Mrs. Johnson looks up from her clipboard. "The Green Leaf Growers is a *farming* organization," A few more St. A boys snicker and the vein over Mrs. Johnson's right eye comes alive, practically throbbing. "A working vegetable, fruit, and herb farm," she clarifies. It does nothing to quell their giggles. She takes a few seconds to find her place on her clipboard before she continues, "Amelia Brown . . ."

It's not as bad as growing weed (which is *not* legal in the state of Indiana, a quick google tells me), but I had been hoping for a volunteer job I'd done before. Even though I care about the environment and endangered species, I've never tried to grow anything. Mami loves fake flowers because she can't forget to water them. She's always joking about how our family is full of brown thumbs, literally and figuratively.

Leo strides up to Mrs. Johnson and grabs one of the tote bags by her feet. He shows me the contents: two thick work gloves, two matching trowels, and directions to Green Leaf Growers.

"Ready, partner?" he says, nudging me with a yellow glove that's big enough for both of my hands.

I gingerly slip it on over my fingers.

"Figures they'd make the brown kids work in the gardens." Leo shakes his head in mock disappointment.

I look up in shock, just in time to see him burst out into a huge grin. The curls on his head bounce slowly in the soft breeze as his shoulders are shaking with laughter at my surprise.

Leo stops abruptly, and I look up to see Father Coleman glaring at both of us. Or rather—just me, because I can't stop laughing.

Leo whips out his map of Notre Dame and holds it up over both of our faces, shielding us from Father Coleman's and Mrs. Johnson's judging eyes. The map is huge—tall and wide enough to wrap around both of us, like a science fair trifold.

"Look," Leo says, pointing to a spot on the map. "The Green Leaf Growers is only five blocks away, so we don't have to pile back on the bus with everyone else."

I nod, suddenly aware of how close Leo is. I haven't been this close to a boy ever, unless you count last summer, when the high school research interns occasionally shared microscopes to review our field samples. But I was infinitely more interested in bacterial multiplication than in any of the boys on my research team. Maybe it was because none of them looked at me the way Leo is now, like it's me and him against our chaperone overlords. When I smile up at him, I realize Caroline and Amelia were wrong. Leo isn't a nine; he's far and away a ten on a scale that should probably be redesigned, because it's not fair for the bar to be that high. I shake my head. These facts are irrelevant. I need to stay focused on Clara and Stanford.

When Mrs. Johnson calls out the last of the volunteer assignments, Leo lowers the map and we watch the St. A students shove each other back onto the bus. Milagro is the last to board and we scowl at each other. She looks at Leo curiously, then back at me. Her eyebrows furrow and she winks at me before scrambling onto the bus.

"Remember, we're all meeting back here for our next activity," Mrs. Johnson yells out from a bus window. The bus lurches forward and Mrs. Johnson smacks her head against the side of the window. Leo and I rub our foreheads in solidarity.

As the bus disappears, an invisible weight lifts off my shoulders. For the next few hours, I'm not the nerdy girl who bores people to death with her scientific facts. I look around. I'm also the girl without a partner—Leo has left me in the dust.

"I think this is it," Leo says. He stops at the entrance of a giant plastic monstrosity. The plastic arches loom over us. Everything in Indiana seems to be reaching for the big blue sky. I walk a few steps back and take in the entirety of the Green Leaf Growers. The building, if you can call it that, looks like a giant caterpillar. Two giant flaps serve as the doors, and the spine of the building is ribbed, with plastic arcs that extend for at least two hundred feet deep into the lot, covered in a thick white rubber material.

I push open a flap and Leo follows me.

"Hey, y'all! Welcome to aqua paradise!" A curly-haired woman in an electric-pink, zebra-striped caftan looks up from a raised flower bed and waves at us.

"Come closer, we won't bite!" a husky voice booms from behind a potted tree. I can see the hint of a long gray beard poking out beyond the tree bark.

"But the minnows might!" a woman chimes in. She's

juggling four water cans and has a clipboard tucked in her armpit.

"What is this place?" Leo whispers to me.

"I think we found plant heaven," I whisper back. A drop falls on his head and we both look up to find giant ferns dripping over us. He takes a few steps toward me, until we're huddled together, our tote bag squished between our shoulders. There's an overwhelming green that spreads out over everything, skinny vines winding around the plastic rafters, tall grass plants erupting out of potted planters, and rows and rows of plant beds exploding with leaves and colorful vegetables. I hear a click and then automatic water misters go off above us. The drops of water shimmer in the air, casting a soft yellow glow over everything. It's like we've stumbled into a fantasy world, one laced with the sweet scents of basil, mint, and fresh strawberries.

"Are y'all the high school volunteers?" the curly-haired woman asks. She stands up and wipes her hands clean, revealing a canvas apron over the silk caftan.

Leo and I nod.

"I'm Linda. And I need y'all to git yer butts over here. We've got rhododendrons that need pruning and weeding. All our college kids are on spring break, so we need all the hands we can get."

"Rota-what-ums?" Leo mutters to me under his breath.

"It's a flower, I think."

Linda leads us into another sectioned-off piece of the tent. She puts her finger to her lips and holds one flap of tarp in her hand before dramatically thrusting it open. "Voilà!"

Leo and I stare at rows of flower beds mounted on top of . . . fish tanks? Each one has a floating plant in it, and above that plant, deep purple lamps hover. It feels like we've stepped into a strange art exhibit or a disco party for earthworms. The purple light is nearly the same as the black lights at last night's party. It makes the whites of my sneakers glow, along with the stripes of Leo's shirt.

"Whoa. Cool." Leo squats and presses his face against the glass of the tank. "There are at least fifteen fish in here!"

Linda nods. "This is our aquaponics center. You're just in time for pruning." Linda walks us through the process of spotting unwanted plants that would disrupt the carefully maintained aquaponics cycle. "It's simple. The fish poop goes into the dirt, the dirt feeds the plants, and the plants feed people."

"Fish poop?" Leo's mouth is wide open.

"A complete life-cycle system," I mutter. "It's pretty cool."

"Exactly." Linda beams at me.

"Can we go back to talking about fish poop?" Leo interrupts.

"Poop goes into growing your veggies. Ever heard of fertilizer? I'll take fish poop over cow pies any day," I tell him.

Linda laughs. "The poop isn't the problem right now. These plants may seem harmless from the outside, but their roots will tear up the whole system. You gotta get them all out. Go on, try it."

I saddle up next to the tank and the fish scatter away.

"Don't worry about them," Linda tells us. "They're as hardy as a rock. Go on." She nods, gesturing with her pink manicure.

For a few seconds, all I hear are the whirls of the fans around me, and then a distinct *squish* as I plunge my hands into the thick, dark soil and pull out a scraggly green plant, careful not to tear too many of its spindly, floss-like roots. "Like this?"

"Yes, exactly right!" Linda beams again. "You're a natural. Y'all call me if you need any more help."

"Show-off," Leo says. He smiles and reaches over me to wrap his fingers around a tiny plant. "Watch out, you might actually turn into a plant person."

Leo and I fall into an easy rhythm: Scoop. Shake. Plop. Pat. Repeat. The hum of the generator, Linda's soft giggles to herself, and the scrapes and scruffs of the other volunteers' trowels fill up the silence.

"I had a fish once," Leo offers. "When it died, my sisters

and I threw an hour-long funeral for it. RIP Turkey."

I glance at Leo. "You named your fish Turkey?"

"I was six. I got him the week of Thanksgiving." Leo laughs. "What should we name these fish?" He taps on the glass, sending the fish scattering again.

"Mashed Potatoes and Yams?"

Leo smiles. "And Stuffing and Cranberry."

When we run out of sides, Leo asks me, "Do you like it here? Like as a college, I mean."

I shake my head automatically. "No way. Too many football fans, not enough microscopes. Do you?"

"No." Leo pauses for a long minute. "It's pretty far from everything I like. I don't mean the beach," he says quickly. "I know I mentioned Berkeley earlier, but it'd be weird to be a plane ride away from my family."

I think it sounds pretty nice, but I don't tell Leo that. "Is that what your parents think too?" I ask, dangling a green plant up in the air.

"No. Or I mean, that's not what they're worried about." Leo wrinkles his forehead in concentration as he tackles his next root. "They have a list of colleges in mind, most of them the highest ranked by some arbitrary system, *U.S. News* or College Board or whatever. That's the list they'll let me choose from. It's my choice, but they have some say too."

"Doesn't that feel stifling?" I ask Leo.

He looks at me, puzzled. "No? Or maybe it would, if the schools on their list sucked. I like most of them. My old high school was like four times the size of St. A's. It'd be nice to be back at a bigger school, with more options for electives and stuff." He taps on the glass at the fish. "Think of it this way. Some things are out of your control: the moon's gravitational pull, the timing of the tides, the strengths of currents, all that stuff. You could fight it, but you wouldn't get very far. Sometimes it's easier to ride the wave."

"So your parents are the ocean wave?" I tilt my head. I like where this is going.

He nods. "Oh yeah. An immigrant wave that started long before me and ends when my sisters and I all have graduate degrees." Leo stops for a second. "Just kidding. Kind of. They'd never admit it, but I know they're crossing their fingers that one of us turns out to be a doctor, just like my dad."

I shake my head. "I could never do that. I hate blood and guts. That was always Clara's dream, to become a doctor and help people. Or that's what she told us. You heard Robbie. I don't know what she wants to be anymore." I sink my fingers into the dirt and squeeze the soil in my hands.

"She sounds like me. I have no idea what I want to be when I grow up. Maybe it's a doctor. But maybe it's something else, like a civil engineer or a teacher. I don't know. But I'm not going to figure it out by fighting my parents over every decision—"

I interrupt. "What if their wave is leading you somewhere terrible? What if there's no way you're going to make it to shore?" I'm silent for a second, and then everything I didn't say on the bus comes pouring out. "I'm not sure my mom is sold on the whole 'college thing' anymore. Definitely not if it requires leaving the state of Maryland." I'm talking so fast, my words are running together. "To her, it's a weird American thing, to leave your family for toga parties and keg stands. She let one daughter get away and she's never doing it again. Now my mom won't even let me go away this summer, for this really cool internship. I had a secret plan to make it all work, but it was a bust."

"I find it hard to believe your plans are done for. You don't seem like someone who gives up too quickly," he says, gesturing to my two hands, which are wrapped around a particularly stubborn plant.

I don't know what to say to that. My cheeks start to flush.

"Anyway, I'm impressed. I can never keep a secret in my house. My little sisters are all up in my business. They're always convinced I'm hiding secrets, or that I have a girlfriend." After a few moments, Leo adds, "I don't. In case you were wondering."

"Don't what?"

"Have a girlfriend. And if I did, I wouldn't keep her a secret."

I nod. I know it's none of my business. It's just a fact, but it fuels my blushing even more. My mouth feels dry and I've suddenly lost the ability to talk.

Leo seizes on my silence. "Does this mean you can tell me about your secret plan?"

I sigh. "Sure, why not. It didn't work. I thought Robbie could help me convince my sister to talk to my mom about this summer, so she would let me go. But he didn't know anything and Clara wasn't any help either. I'm stuck in Baltimore." I yank until the plant finally loosens and the dirt flies up and smacks me in the face.

Oof. I puff out air and dirt particles blow off my face.

Leo laughs and uses his sweatshirt sleeve to dust my face off.

"That doesn't sound very fair at all." His voice is muffled. We're only inches apart, close enough for me to see the shadows cast by Leo's long lashes.

I keep looking up at him, our eyes meeting for a second too long. I feel that bit of happiness spreading across me when I see him smiling at me. He's the vision of optimism, and I just want a bit of it for me. I shake my head. "I don't think life is allowed to be fair."

"Maybe. But sometimes you just have to ride things out," Leo says. "Maybe it's not meant to be this summer. Give it a year, and that could be enough time for your mom to change her mind. Set the wave on a new course."

I have a sinking feeling in my stomach. Maybe Leo is right. Maybe I should just forget about Stanford. There's always next year.

"Helloooooooo, folks!"

Both of us jump apart and Linda claps her hands in glee. "Young love! It's beautiful."

I look at Linda, horrified, and Leo and I take two steps even farther away from each other. He's staring at anything but me, so I follow his lead and take a sudden interest in the ground. It's disappointing that staring at the same speck of dirt does not make your cheeks any less hot. Linda ignores us, inspecting our work with her zebra caftan trailing behind her.

"There are so many romantic spots on campus. Just the other day, I was reminiscing with Javier about the old pillow room."

Leo and I glance at each other, unsure if we want to know what happens in the pillow room.

"Notre Dame used to rent out one of the dorms as a hotel over the summer, but they stopped a few years ago. The janitors locked up the pillows and never went back for them. Find the room, and you'll be in the coziest place on campus." She stretches the *o* in cozy and dances out the door.

Leo and I can barely hold our smiles in, waiting until the plastic flap closes before we erupt into laughter, tumbling onto the green lawn outside as our giggles take over. We lie in the grass and stare up at a sky that's nothing like Baltimore, without gray buildings, a dusty cloud of pollution, or a cacophony of honks, yells, and street dancers. The world is silent until Leo mimics Linda and howls out, "So cooooozy," and it sets us off again. When we finally stride back onto campus, we look nothing like the clean and glamorous Notre Dame students, with their soft leather purses, candy-colored running shorts, and school pride ribbons tied around ponytails. My arms are aching and there are dirt specks all over my lumpy sweatshirt. Leo has a few leaves tucked into his pocket and a big smudge of dirt on his nose. The difference is even more staggering when we rejoin the rest of our classmates. (Of course, Milagro is nowhere in sight.)

"Hey, you guys stink," Caroline tells us while we wait for Mrs. Johnson to make her announcement.

I want to be offended, but she's right. I can't speak for Leo, but I *do* stink, like nature and bugs and things that are alive.

"Is that the kind of stuff that you do in your club?" Genevieve asks. She eyes our trowels and dirt-covered sneakers before peeking in Caroline's bag. "Did you bring snacks?"

"What?" I stare at her blankly. Leo nudges me.

"The sign-ups that you always post outside the locker

rooms. If we sign up, do we get to grow plants?" Genevieve tucks a pack of gummy worms in her shirt pocket.

I shake my head. "Not really. It's been more hands-off than that."

"That's too bad," Genevieve says, rolling up the sleeves of her denim shirt. "I was thinking it sounded cool."

Leo raises his eyebrows at me.

I perk up. "I mean, there are community gardens. We've never worked with them, but there's no reason we couldn't. I could talk to—"

"In your bags, you'll find a folder full of St. Agnes- and St. Anthony–approved club activities tonight," Mrs. Johnson announces, cutting off our chatter. "This is a mandatory activity for you AND your buddy." She tries to meet as many eyes as possible. "No wandering off campus and definitely no alcohol. Have I made myself clear?"

"Yes, ma'am," we murmur.

I tell Genevieve that I'll get back to her about plants, and she and Caroline march off with their St. A partners.

I reach in our bag and take out our folder. "Intramural flag football? Vegetarian Lovers United? International Cooking Club?" I read aloud and sigh. "None of these clubs look remotely interesting."

Leo shakes his head. "Isn't that what you said about gardening, like—oh, say, five hours ago?" He pulls the sheet out of my hand. "Why don't you let me do the picking."

I shrug. On the one hand, spontaneity is my worst enemy. On the other hand, I'm never going to go to this college, or maybe any college, so what does it even matter?

"My destiny is in your hands," I say to Leo. "Do with it what you want."

15
Milagro

IT WORKED! IT *freakin' worked!*

I throw my hands in the air and shimmy my hips like a dashboard hula-hooper hopped up on energy drinks. "YES!" I shout out to the world. A few strangers look up at me in confusion, their steps hastening to get past the lone girl standing in the Notre Dame grotto. But I don't care. Exactly thirty hours and forty-two minutes after I yelled at Pablo to get out of my house and then went radio silent, I got two interesting texts. I have read them approximately 2,274 times. I wanted to read them to Carmen, but she didn't answer my call, so I read them 500 more times on my own. I miss u. Do you still think about us? Unbeknownst to me, I was playing it cool and alluring, and it totally worked. Pablo finally remembered what a glittery catch I am and realized he never should have let me go.

I discovered the texts as Lucas and I walked into our assigned Habitat for Humanity site. It took all of my strength not to run around the lumberyard waving a power drill in one hand and throwing spare nails in the air with the other, yelling out "HALLELUJAH!" For the first hour of sorting nails, my fingers were itching to respond. I tried to imagine his elaborate "I'm sorry" production, one where he groveled for my forgiveness. He could unfurl a massive banner in the middle of a St. Anthony basketball game. The banner would be purple, my favorite color. The cheerleaders could make up a cheer too—maybe they'd find something that rhymes with *Milagro*. Then I thought about Pablo teaching the cheerleaders the cheer, which made me think about the mystery boobs on his phone, and then I wanted to dive into the extra-large barrels of paint that Lucas was stirring.

At the site, two girls with pixie cuts, impressive leather tool belts slung along their hips, and thick-soled black boots greeted us. They tossed power tools over their shoulders the way I might toss a feather boa around my neck. The girls were incredible: bossy and yelling out orders to everyone, all while keeping assembly lines of nail sifting, wood beam measuring, and hammering running at maximum efficiency. There was no way I was risking their wrath to send a text to Pablo. They put Lucas and me to work alongside white-haired senior volunteers, who introduced themselves as "H4H" regulars. They told us that the girls in charge were mechanical engineers at Notre Dame, and that every time they came to a Habitat for Humanity site, the girls were sporting a different hair color. I was too intimidated to ask them how they avoid hair breakage.

Lucas was quiet on the bus, saying he needed to read music, but then he stayed quiet for the first hour of volunteering too. It didn't help that the senior volunteers interrupted all of my attempts to recap last night's party, somehow always managing to steer the conversation back to their grandkids.

Finally, I couldn't take Lucas's silence. "Are you mad at me? I meant what I said on the bus this morning. I'm really sorry. I never would have invited Lulu if I thought she would break up the party or get anyone in trouble."

Lucas looked up, surprised. "Mad at you? No." He didn't elaborate. He kept his eyes firmly on the pile of hardware and nails that he was sorting.

It took two more prodding attempts before he would spill. "Fine. I'm meeting with Notre Dame's orchestra after this. Their director is supposed to be one of the best in the country. She could be teaching at a conservatory, but instead, she's here and I'm supposed to perform in front of her. I'm really dreading it. I just know I'm going to embarrass myself."

I wanted to sink into the ground, embarrassed by my selfishness. This whole time, it had never occurred to me to ask Lucas why he's on the trip. I tried to channel Carmen's best hype-lady talk. "Hey. Don't talk about my friend like that. You *can* compete—doesn't St. A's orchestra perform at the Meyerhoff Symphony Hall every year? Besides, you have an inside edge, thanks to all your reading, remember?"

Lucas gave me a half smile. "Thanks."

"This really matters to you?" I studied him, and I could tell his fingers were itching for piano keys so he could cram another practice session in.

"My future?" He snorted. "Yeah, it doesn't for you?"

"I don't know. I never really saw myself on any college campus. Doesn't really feel like something for me. I'm only here because of a fluke. Someone got sick and they gave her spot to me." I hated admitting this to him. "Maybe college is best left for the nerds. And unbelievably talented piano virtuosos like you," I quickly added.

"Now who's being mean to my friend?" Lucas said. "Fluke or not, I think you're selling yourself short. You seemed suspiciously into Vivaldi." He nodded to the girls bossing us around. "And don't let them hear you calling them nerds. They might pierce your nose in retaliation."

I took another admiring glance at the girls, who were setting up the studs for the house. "My mother would instantly disown me."

"LESS TALKING, MORE SORTING," the purple-haired girl yelled.

Lucas and I didn't dare talk after that, but we did trade sneaky smiles after we listened to the third potty-training saga from one of the senior center volunteers. At the end of our shift, the girls walked us around the site, pointing out the accomplishments of the day. It was wild to think I could have contributed to something as permanent as a house. Afterward, Lucas and Father Coleman took the shuttle to Notre Dame's music hall, and I waved my crossed fingers at him for good luck. I took a different shuttle back to campus, only I hopped off at Notre Dame's grotto instead of our dorms.

I stare up at the small white statue of the Virgin Mary, nestled on a stone perch that was cut into the hill behind the basilica. She's gazing up at the sky, oblivious to the hundreds of dancing candles lined up beneath her. Whenever something goes wrong, Tía Lochita always lights a candle for us at church—everything from bad haircuts and failing grades to a missed bill payment deserves a tiny tea light and a prayer of hope. I don't think Mary or Tía Lochita would approve of what's been troubling me, but I grab a matchstick and reach over the black railing to light a candle. According to the shiny brass plaque, the Virgin Mary statue has been here since 1986, when the grotto was built as a copy of the cave in France where Saint Bernadette saw an apparition of the Virgin Mary. Maybe it's the moss clinging to the rocks or the quiet trickles of water running down the wobbly stone blocks, but for the few minutes that I'm down here, I understand why Notre Dame students come here to pray. I linger, listening to the whispering of wind and the thud of my heart before I finally climb the steps out and sit on a bench in front of the grotto.

When I grab my phone, I have three missed calls from Tía Lochita. I should have known—she has a sixth sense for holy activity. I call her back, and Mami and Lochita crowd the screen. Their faces are extra pixelated, but nothing could hide the giant smiles on their faces.

I hold up my phone and show them the grotto. Tía Lochita oohs and aahs at the dancing candlelights, while Mami is considerably less impressed. "There's something like that in Baltimore. I'm sure of it." But before she can remember what it is, she's pulling out her own phone. "Hold on, Milagrito, the hotel is calling me. The chef did what?!" she yells, before drifting off the screen.

"Have you talked to your sister?" Tía Lochita asks me.

"Lulu? She's fine," I mumble. "She's loving the trip."

"No, I meant Clara. About, you know?" She raises her eyebrows at me and purses her lips, waiting for me to bite. The only thing Tía Lochita loves more than a secret is being begged to spill it. But I don't want to hear about Clara's latest accomplishment.

Tía Lochita whispers, "Your mother doesn't want you to know, but I don't think families should have secrets."

I hold back my laugh. Tía Lochita is a big chismosa like me. We would die without a steady stream of gossip. "What do you mean?" I ask instead.

"I told her Iowa was too far. Pobrecita. Her grades, you know? They were really bad." Tía Lochita sits back, waiting for me to react.

I am intrigued. What does "bad" even mean for Clara? She probably got her first A-minus. Before I can ask, Mami hops back on the screen.

"What are you talking about? Where's Lulu?"

Behind her, Tía Lochita zips her lips shut. Great. I tell Mami the briefest version of the truth. "She's fine. She's volunteering. I think she got sent to a greenhouse."

"Stay close to her, Milagro. Family is more important than anything else. It's like I always say—"

The last thing I need is a lecture, especially with Pablo's texts burning a hole in the pocket of my jean jacket. "I have to go, bye! I'll call you later!" I hang up the phone after we blow each other kisses.

I take a deep breath and dial Pablo's number. Each ring is excruciatingly painful, like plunging your hand down a stopped-up sink and not knowing whether you'll find a few noodles or a slimy sliver of raw chicken. When he picks up, I don't even give him a second to say hi before I blurt out, "Pablo! It's me. Milagro. Hi." Ugh. I want to kick myself right in my leopard-print yoga pants butt. So much for playing it cool.

"Hey. Did you get my text?" Pablo's voice sounds exactly the way it's always sounded, warm, deep, and slightly confused, like he needs me to show him the right answer. I will.

"That's why I'm calling." I hug the phone around my ear and wait for the desperation to pour out.

"Cool. So . . ." In the background, I hear what sounds like a ray gun, a *beep! Beep!*, an explosion, and a tinny animated voice screaming, "YOU GOT ME!"

My smile falls away. I bite my tongue, until I have to ask. "Are you playing video games?" I sit back down on the stone bench, bracing myself against the cool rock.

"Um . . . no?" His voice goes up at the end, the way Lulu's does when she's lying. "Do you want to get back together?" Another ray gun noise goes off.

"Are you seriously asking me while you're playing a video game?"

"I'm doing two of my favorite things at once." *Pew! Pew!* Gun noises go off again. "Oh crap!" Pablo yells. "Oops. Sorry. Not to you."

I want to reach through the phone and take hold of

Pablo's ray gun, wielding it in the air like a fierce warrior princess. Then maybe he'd find me interesting enough to give me his full attention. I hold my breath, hoping that if I don't say anything, Pablo will come to his senses.

"Um. Milagro? Are you still there?"

I zip my mouth shut.

"Hello?" Pablo sounds worried.

I grip the phone tighter in my hand. Yes! This is what *Cosmo* was talking about.

"If you don't want to talk to me, I'm going to go. We can talk after break."

My eyes snap open. "This isn't how this is supposed to go! You are doing it all wrong," I yell into the phone.

"Uhhhh. Tell me what to say? I'll do it."

"You're supposed to fight for me. You're supposed to try to win me back."

Pablo is silent on the phone. As the minutes stretch on, I decide I've had enough. "I have to go. Bye," I snarl. I hang up the phone and close my eyes. I want Lulu to build me a time machine so I can go back in time to ten minutes ago, when I still thought my plan had worked. Or maybe I want to go back to before I ever met Pablo, so I'd never have to dream about his hands on my knee or how happy Mami will be when I tell her that we broke up. Or maybe I could zoom to the distant future, when I've figured everything about my life out.

Instead, I kneel and cry harder than I ever have in my life. If the people walking past the grotto thought I was strange before, there's no telling what they think of the booger-covered girl whose heaves and wails could wake up the dead.

My cell phone buzzes, but it's only Clara.

When do you make it to San Francisco?

I text her back a date, but nothing more. I'm still annoyed she sent Robbie to watch out for Lulu. I'm tempted to ask her about Tía Lochita's gossip, but I'm too worn out from Pablo. I feel a tap on my shoulder. I look up and my eyes fall on Lulu's partner, who came to the party with us last night. I think his name is Kenneth or something? Something with a *K*. He's tall, with his shirt half tucked into his jeans. I've watched him let Caroline cut in front of him for the bus bathroom, and he gave Maddie's St. A partner an extra set of earplugs so he didn't have to listen to her and Gracelynn's impromptu Notre Dame fight song marathon. On top of being nice, he must get good grades, because Father Coleman looks out for him the same way Mrs. Johnson keeps tabs on Lulu. Neither of them want their star students to get in trouble.

Kenneth's face is frozen. "Are you okay?"

"Why?" I say, only it comes out all breathy, and a few tears trickle down my cheek. Then one last sob spills out, leaving my shoulders shaking.

Kenneth is inching away from me, his smile more of a grimace. I've broken the smiley-est guy on our trip. I'm ruining everyone around me. "Do you need to talk about it?" But nothing in his face says he wants to hear the saga about me or Pablo, or how I am going to be a virgin forever. I bet he'd spontaneously combust if I say the word *virgin* out loud.

"No! I am fine." I sniffle and wipe at my eyes. I try to smear the mascara residue off my fingers, but it only ends up leaving stains on my yoga pants.

He starts walking backward. "Okay, but if you need to talk?"

"Okay, fine, Kenneth. If you loved someone, you'd do anything to be with them, right? Like you'd at least stop playing your video games long enough to have a conversation with them, right?"

Kenneth's eyes are shifting left and right, looking anywhere but where I am.

"Um. My parents don't let me play video games? They say they're too violent. Also my name is Leo. Not Kenneth."

I start crying again. I put my hand over my mouth and try to rein it in, but words keep coming out. "I can't do anything right! I'm sorry, Leo."

"If I did have video games, I would not care about them as much as the people I cared about," Leo says. "People are more important than a screen. Unless you are a traffic controller. Or maybe an airline pilot? Although I think it's more about controls than screens in those circumstances . . ."

Oh my God, he and Lulu are perfect buddies for each other. My sobs subside. He's right, of course. "Thanks for the pep talk. And for checking on me. But I think I might need to cry a little more. And I'd prefer to do that in private."

"Um. Well. That's actually not why I came over to talk to you." He looks down at the ground and starts fiddling with his fingers. He's bouncing on the balls of his feet but not saying anything. He looks like he's ready to launch himself into space.

"Are you going to tell me?"

"It's about your sister. I kind of. I don't know. I want to do something nice for her. Since she's not having such a great time on the trip."

I perk up with excitement. When I saw the two of them together earlier today, I thought he had a crush on her! The rest of his words sink in and I feel gut punched. Lulu isn't having fun on this trip? Why wouldn't she tell me? The memories of last night come flashing back to me again—calling Robbie a bozo and telling Lulu she was a no-good snitch. Ignoring her on the bus, because she said she wished I was more like Clara. Instead of pining after

234

boys and throwing myself a pity party, I should be looking out for Lulu. In the museum of Worst Sisters, you'd find my portrait alongside Cinderella's stepsisters. I let out a brief sigh.

Leo interrupts my thoughts. "We have to go to a Notre Dame club meeting today, so I was thinking . . ."

"We do?! Since when?" I slide a hand over my forehead and lie down on the stone bench. "Why is Mrs. Johnson torturing us like this? Is it legal to make kids do so many activities?" I grab my phone and text Lucas to see if he knows about this.

"I have a plan, but I want to make sure that she'll like it," Leo continues, talking over my whining.

I clasp my hands together and pop back up. "Yes! A plan to win her heart?"

"What! No! Just a nice thing. As friends. You won't tell her, right?" Leo pleads. He blushes wildly.

I snort. "Like Lulu would believe anything that comes out of my mouth. I promise. Scout's honor." I raise my fingers up and wiggle them at Leo. He waits a few seconds before launching into his plan, waving his hands and jumping up in the air at the most exciting bits. When he finishes, I'm liquid butter, completely melted from the cuteness. Lulu is going to love it. And even better, Leo barely even needed my help. I only helped him nail the last details.

"Leo, you are seriously one rad dude. How do you have the most perfect timing? Now, and when we were going to the party, and when—"

He reddens and shakes his head. "Timing isn't real. This isn't a coincidence. Today, I came to find you. Anyway, you're not so bad yourself. If you're anything like Lulu, you're way too fascinating to be ignored. Whatever guy you're crying about isn't worth your time."

Leo jogs back to the dorms, leaving me alone on the stone bench. I glare at my phone and lie back down, letting my arms dangle off as I stare at the blue sky. My shot at love is as dead as the zombies in Pablo's video game, and there's not a single thing I can do about it.

16
Lulu

IN THE TIME since our volunteer hours ended, I've scrubbed the dirt and scraggly plant bits off myself and traded my Converse for a pair of strappy hiking sandals. I've paired my long-sleeved WWF shirt with my practical blue fleece the exact color of an April sky in Indiana. I'm almost out the door when my phone buzzes. I'm supposed to meet Leo in five minutes, but when I see Clara's name across my screen, I sink down on my mattress and tap "accept."

Clara's face fills the screen. She's got a coffee in one hand and what looks like a stack of papers in the other. There's a scarf wrapped around her neck, in a brilliant blue and pink; the colors are anything but muted. It's not very Clara-like at all. Her forehead is wrinkled and she reaches her finger out and taps the screen, as if she could tap me on the nose. "I know you're upset with me. I want to talk to you. Are you okay?" Seeing her face, I'm filled with long-ing for when Clara could fix every slight with a bear hug or a corny joke.

Except we're not on the same team anymore. "Why did you lie about Robbie?" I say flatly.

Clara shifts in her seat and bites her lip. "How's the trip going? Have you at least made any friends? On our trip, we stayed up so late and cleaned out an entire vending machine eating Twinkies and bags of chips."

"Why are you changing the subject? You could have told me you broke up. You didn't have to lie."

"Lulu. Tell me more about the trip. Stop fixating on me."

I roll my eyes. "Fine. I have made a few new friends. One might even be a good friend. I think. Technically he's my partner, but he's really cool. That's beside the point. I need to talk to you about this summer. This is really important to me." I can't tell if Clara is distracted by something in the room, or if she's deliberately avoiding eye contact with me. In the long pause, I realize it's not my imagination. Clara is looking anywhere but at her screen. "I'm sorry, Lulu. I have to go. I'll call you later. Be good. Try to focus more on today, and not what might happen this summer. It'll be better for you."

"Wait. But!"

Clara waves goodbye and my phone screen goes black. I

can't believe she won't talk to me. Our family has been out of sync for so long, maybe we'll never be able to recalibrate, Milagro, Mami, and me battling until there's nothing left of our house but a few scrap pages of graphing paper and smashed lipstick tubes. When I walk out of the dorm, the weather looks nothing like how I feel. Gone are the impossibly bright yet dismally gray skies of Pittsburgh, the chilly breeze that seemed to permeate even my thickest layers of clothing, and the reluctant, feeble sun. Everything is brighter, cleaner, and happier in South Bend, like the set of an antiseptic children's TV show. It looks like someone took an eraser to everything—the buildings, the preppy students, the tall sweeping trees—and scrubbed away the imperfections.

The campus shuttle buses that cruise by are big and white, the shiniest public transportation that I've ever seen. I wonder if it's for show, not a *real* bus, but then the bus driver waves at me. Actually, everyone waves at me, or at least cracks a smile, even though I'm a stranger to them. When I stand on the corner and squint, trying to read the name on the building, it only takes thirty seconds before someone approaches me and asks if I need help. I say yes to the random man, and he points me in the right direction.

I find Leo anxiously tapping his foot and checking his phone. I do a little hop and scurry over to meet him.

"There you are! Hurry, we're gonna be late!" Leo

239

nudges my elbow, pressing the soft fleece against my skin. He smiles at me, his eyes crinkling in the corners. A few locks of solid black curls gently flutter in the wind, the same dark color as his long lashes. I feel a shiver and cross my arms against my chest. Spring in Indiana is deceptively cold.

Leo and I race up marble stairs, his long legs gaining on mine. He's got a plastic grocery bag tucked in the crook of his elbow, and it jostles against his thighs with every step. He shoves open the green iron door to a big building and we creep inside, careful not to make noise as we walk down a long hallway. Giant portraits of old white dudes stare down at us, each one with a more elaborate white bouffant than the next. Their names are etched on gold nameplates under their paintings, along with how much they've donated to the school. My eyes bulge out when I see all the zeros. I don't know anyone who has that much money, let alone enough to give away.

Leo whips around the corner and we rush into a bustling marble-floored auditorium, with twenty folding tables set up. There's gold molding on the wall, and giant iron chandeliers with crystals dangling from rings. This room feels like it's meant for students who dress way fancier than my worn panda shirt, but as I glance around, I realize no one is dressed up. Maybe some of the boys are in wrinkled polos and button-downs, but they're neon colored, or Hawaiian printed, or have splotches on them. I can hear snippets of conversations about all-nighters at the library, lab reports, and missing their grandma's hundredth birthday. Leo points to a table, which has a folded piece of paper, "LUZ + LEO," resting on it. I smile when I see it.

There's a Bunsen burner on the table—I've never seen one out of a lab before. Next to the burner, there's a large box that's upside down. Leo unloads his grocery bag, laying each item on the table.

"Cheetos?!" I grab the bag. "What else did you bring?" I move to open the bag, and Leo reaches out, placing his hand on mine. Leo's hand is warm. Actually, it's really warm in this room. That must be why my cheeks feel so flushed.

"Wait, don't eat them yet!" Leo laughs. "I promise the wait will be worth it. Kind of." He sets out a jar of unidentifiable objects floating in a murky liquid, a wide tub of salt, a few limes, and a giant can of black beans.

The tables around us are unloading groceries too. I spy mangoes, countless spices, a can of SPAM, and even a jar of tiny eggs floating in pink liquid.

"What is this stuff?" I grab the jar and snap it open. "Olives?" I pop one in my mouth and purse my lips, squeezing my eyes shut. "Wow, these are sour." I offer the jar to Leo, but he waves it away.

"It was slim pickings," Leo says. His face is apologetic.

"I couldn't find any kind of oil, or any spices at the student center store. Everything food related came from the . . . um, how should I say this? Beverage section?"

I stare at the salt and limes, until it clicks. "Margarita supplies?"

"Exactly." Leo laughs. "And martinis." He points to the olive jar. "The sad thing is, I'm not so bad at cooking. Probably from all those years of trailing my grandmother around the kitchen. But even she'd be stumped by these ingredients. And no spices." He shakes his head mournfully. "Let's hope whatever is under that box includes—"

"LISTEN UP! JUDGES SPEAKING!"

I grab the limes and whisper to Leo, "These are my favorite foods in the whole world!"

I hear shushes coming from the middle of the room. "JUDGES SPEAKING," shout a group of girls in the middle of the room. They're wearing what Milagro would call a "signature look," dressed in black pants or loose-fitting black dresses, with bright lipstick and straight hair that's held back by a black headband.

"Hello, International Cooking Club members. You have twenty-five minutes to transform the items you brought into something delicious. There's just one catch: you're going to have to incorporate whatever is under your box."

Oh no. This is a cooking competition. While cooking could arguably fall under chemistry, my culinary expertise

242

begins and ends with the mac 'n' cheese that Clara and I are obsessed with. I do spend a lot of time in our kitchen, but unlike Leo, it's only because it's the best spot to eavesdrop on Mami and Tía Lochita's gossipy conversations.

Leo does a drum roll over the box as the rest of the room screams, "FIVE, FOUR, THREE, TWO, ONE!" I cross my fingers as he unveils the box and tosses it over his shoulder, yelping, "This is going to be disgusting!" We both stare at the contents: a pineapple, a roll of hamburger buns, and a small plastic container of black liquid are next to a potato masher, a small plastic knife, and a stack of yellow paper plates. I pry off the container lid and sniff the black liquid. "Definitely soy sauce," I say. I hand it to Leo, who sniffs and nods.

I turn the Bunsen burner on and put a frying pan over it, like a makeshift hot plate. Leo reaches for the jar of olives. "They're packed in oil. I figured it was better than nothing." He strains the olives and pours some of the oil into the pan.

"It's too bad we don't have cilantro. According to my mom, it makes everything better." I study our sad excuse for a pantry, poking the spindly spears of the pineapple. "Although, I don't think cilantro would help this meal very much."

"On the bright side, the mystery ingredients are all cafeteria kitchen leftovers, and the competition also doubles as a drive for Notre Dame's food pantry. That's what the black beans are for. So even if we mess up really badly—"

"Which we definitely will," I chime in.

"At least we're doing a good deed?"

I laugh. "Okay, what should we do with the Cheetos?"

"We could crush them?" Leo says.

I hold the Cheetos bag to my heart. "This is my favorite food on the whole planet. Second only to limes. It would be sacrilegious to pulverize them. I could never."

"Not even for charity?"

I wince and lay the bag down, pouring out the Cheetos and smashing them into a powder with the potato masher. Leo chops up the pineapple with a small plastic knife. It's not nearly sharp enough, so the fruit is raggedy as we drop it in the Cheetos dust before plopping it onto the frying pan.

The room erupts in smells, thanks to the different spices on the tables. For a literal hot second, there's a flash of fire in the back corner, and everyone gasps. One of the judges rushes over with a fire extinguisher, and the table is disqualified for being covered in foam.

Leo and I are tossing things in our pan, sprinkling the soy sauce and extra-crispy Cheetos crumbs over our pineapples. I try to cut shapes out of our hamburger buns, but it's impossible. We slice the limes and drizzle the juice over it too, creating a sticky mess. There are no rules, no instructions, and no way we're gonna place at this competition. We will be lucky if we are not dead last. While Leo and I are goofing off, daring each other to dip Cheetos in the soy sauce and trying to catch the Cheetos in our mouths, there are definitely people taking it seriously. The table on our left is deep-frying the contents of their box in egg roll form, while on my right, two girls with matching braids and bold red-and-blue-colored tracksuits are making pasta from scratch. Their hands are a blur as one whips together eggs on the bare folding table while the other rolls the dough out with an extra-long rolling pin.

"Taste." Leo shoves the spoon in my mouth.

I swallow. "It's kind of edible? Sweeter than I expected. Kind of like a fermented bottle of Tajín. One that never made it out of the factory." It takes half a second before I wince. "With a strong olive aftertaste. Not good."

He laughs when the timer rings. I can't believe a whole twenty-five minutes have gone by. It feels like we just started. We present our plate to the judges. The fried pineapple has started leaching fruit juice, which has turned orange, thanks to the soggy Cheetos breading.

"We present to you: fried pineapple sticks," Leo says. "Like mozzarella sticks, except nothing like them."

One judge hesitates as she brings the fork to her mouth, and then I wave her off. "You don't have to eat it. We're definitely not going to." The judges step back, obviously relieved. One of them grabs the can of beans and drops a ribbon on our table. "Thanks for participating."

Leo picks up the ribbon and reads out, "You tried."

"Say cheese!"

Leo and I both look up in surprise, as the judge snaps a photo, and then stare back down at our paper plate, which is getting soggier and soggier by the minute.

"Should we ask her for the pic for your food album?" I grin.

He shakes his head. "That'd be the biggest fall from grace, after yesterday's epic entry. My friends are all jealous of my trip now, thanks to you." His eyes lock with mine, both of us beaming.

There's a warmth that I feel spreading across my body, erasing nearly all the awful feelings lingering from my conversation with Clara. Nothing is fixed, but I'm feeling a tiny bit hopeful. Just now, things turned out okay, even if they weren't perfect.

The moment is broken by the judges, who yell for silence.

Leo glances at his watch and shakes his head. "Do you want to get out of here? We've got a few minutes before the next course starts."

"There's no way anything we cook could top that. Let's go!" I'm still giddy when we make it outside. The sun is starting to go down, brilliant pink and orange beams filling the sky with a Cheetos pineapple sunset.

Leo stretches his arms over his head. "I think if we get out early, we're supposed to meet Mrs. Johnson and Father Coleman at the dining hall."

I freeze. I don't want Mrs. Johnson to talk to me about Stanford. And maybe a small part of me doesn't want to stop hanging out with Leo. I make a split-second decision. "She'd never know if we ended early, right? I have two words for you. One: pillow. Two: room."

Leo's eyes light up. "Are you suggesting . . . BREAKING THE RULES?" he yells out to the empty pathways.

"Shhh!" I grab his arm. "I'm saying, let's just *think* about it, okay?"

Leo nods and points to his head. "Oh yes. I'm thinking about it very hard. Lemme check my phone to see where to go." He pulls out his phone. The screen is lit up with notifications, including one from MILAGRO ZAVALA.

"Is my sister texting you?" I blurt out. There's a buzzing in my ears as I try to come up with an explanation and fail miserably, my stomach dropping as I keep circling back to one reason.

"What? Oh. No. Um. Yes. But about the trip," Leo stutters, starting and stopping his sentences. He tries to shove his phone back in his pocket with enough force that his phone might have a denim burn. It flops out instead and bounces on the ground. Leo scoops it up and sighs with relief. "No cracks!"

But all I can see is Milagro's text on his screen. **Did you pick up Cheetos for me too?** My stomach sinks even lower. Milagro and Leo are texting. The tiniest part of me thought he planned the club meeting for me, but how could he, when there's a cooler version of me flitting around. I am a moth to Milagro's butterfly, a lowly earthworm to her shimmery cricket-ness. I think back to the wink Milagro gave me earlier. My insides are deflating as I realize it wasn't for me at all—it was for Leo.

"Actually, I think I'm going to go to do homework. We have an early morning tomorrow," I tell Leo.

"Are you sure?" Leo's eyes grow wide in confusion. "We don't have any homework?" He moves toward me and reaches into his pocket, probably to take out our field trip schedule.

"Maybe you can find someone else to break the rules with. There are a lot of Cheetos fans out there." I turn away from him and slink back to my dorm alone.

17
Milagro

"THERE YOU ARE, MILAGRO!" a voice booms out, somehow managing to rise above the low hum of the cafeteria. "I was looking everywhere for you!" The voice grows louder as it moves closer to me.

"Oh no," I mouth to Lucas. He and I scrunch down in the wooden bench, bringing our faces even closer to our extra-spicy curly fries. The neon sign across from him buzzes, announcing this place as Neptune Nuggets. I wish I could disappear to Neptune, or Mars, or any planet really, as long as it had no rules, no school, and most important: no Pablos. For now this place will do.

When I mentioned attending an official Notre Dame–sponsored club meeting to Lucas, we debated: What does "mandatory" *really* mean? Or "official"? Technically, Lucas had fulfilled that requirement when he met with the

249

orchestra. I was fine with skipping it. I can't help it if Notre Dame does not have clubs based around my interests, which at the moment are eating French fries and feeling sorry for myself.

Lucas is midway through filling me in on his orchestra practice audition (he aced it, of course) when Maddie and her best friend, Gracelynn, bound toward us and plop down at our table. Their St. Anthony buddies trail them and sit nearby, only they look like they'd rather be solving math problems than lingering in a greasy, fluorescent-lit basement café. "We were looking for you everywhere."

I look up and give them a limp wave. "Here we are?"

"What have you two been up to?" Gracelynn says.

Lucas and I glance at each other. Neither of us wants to mention the party.

"Who? Us? We . . . uh." My eyes grow wide, and I shove some French fries in my mouth. "We've been busy," I say, only it comes out more like "UHhhvah busshay."

At that moment, Lucas pulls his cell phone out. "Oh shoot, Jared's calling. I told him about the late-night crew you met, and he wants to hear more. Oh, and he says Craig wants to know the next time you're visiting." He snorts.

"Don't leave me?" I plead, but he walks outside with a big grin, already starting to laugh at whatever Jared is telling him.

"Craig who?" Gracelynn and Maddie stare at me,

tapping their French fries on their tray. They must have gossip radar hidden in the #2 pencils tucked behind their ears. Honors girls are so nosy.

I bite my lip. How to explain *Craig/Greg*, the dude of few words and many name potentials. "Um . . . nobody?"

Gracelynn taps her fingers on the plastic. "Tell us about *Craig*. What's he like?"

I purse my lips. The last time I saw Craig, he was snoozing in an alley, sitting next to a pile of dog poop. Last night was wild, wonderful, and weird, but only because of Kailee, the monsters, and the butterfly theater. But that's not the version of the story either of them wants to hear.

Maddie props her elbows on the table and leans closer to me. "What exactly did you guys . . . *do?*"

I stare at her blankly.

"You know. Like alone. Did you go back to his room? Did you make it to third base? Was there any clothing removal?" She's tossing questions at me like she's a tabloid reporter and I'm a scandalous movie star. All that's missing is a paparazzi camera and a giant microphone for her to shove in my face.

Gracelynn's mouth is open wide enough to catch a fly or two. I wonder if I should move my cup under her chin, to catch the inevitable drool.

I wish Lucas was here to save me, but this is a mess of my own making.

Maddie is leaning so close to the table, crispy French fry crumbs are getting tangled in the strands of her hair.

Craig/Greg and I exchanged about five words with each other, none of them in private. I don't know him, and I definitely don't know what he looks like in the dark.

"It was . . . fine?" I say, shrugging my hands.

"I heard the party was Lulu's idea."

I snort. "Yeah right. More like ending the party was her idea. She basically called the cops on us."

Maddie interrupts, "Your sister broke up the party?"

My stomach tightens. I don't know Maddie. I'd rather bungee jump off the Eiffel Tower than gossip with her, especially about my sister. It's not Lulu's fault I dragged both of us into the bowels of college cliché instead of keeping my promise to her. Curling up in an XL twin bed with Lulu and watching her corny shows would be miles better than this conversation. But Lulu is busy being wooed by Leo, thanks to my brilliant suggestions, so I must suffer alone. I make a mental note to text Leo and demand updates immediately.

Gracelynn clears her throat and taps her fingers on the table. Her French manicured nails make a clickety-clack noise that snaps me back to reality.

"You date that hot soccer guy, right? I've seen him pick you up from school sometimes." Maddie wrinkles her forehead in confusion. "Or I guess you *used* to date him?" she muses. I guess Hector has been spreading the news. Or maybe it's Pablo.

"My boyfriend says he's the best soccer player in the Catholic school league," Gracelynn chimes in.

"Basketball," I mumble. "They let Latinx athletes play other sports now."

"Who's the better kisser?" Maddie says, like we're the best of friends. She asks as if I've made a list of pros and cons, or a graph charting the strengths and weaknesses of Perfect Pablo and Greg the Lug.

"Um, both were . . . good? In different ways?" I'm lying my face off and getting more annoyed by the second. None of that mattered—in the end, neither boy cared about me. Who cares what Pablo kissed like, if he had one leg out the door and a pair of mystery boobs in wait the whole time?

Maddie smiles, pleased that I'm finally talking. "What's your secret? I mean, why *you*? No offense," she says.

I brace myself. Nothing good has ever come after the words *no offense*. No one ever says, "No offense, but you're beautiful." Or, "No offense, but I wish my eyebrows were as well shaped as yours." People cling to the words *no offense* like it's an insult eraser.

"You don't even look like the kind of girl that St. A boys would normally go after," Maddie says. "You're so . . . much. All the time." She waves her hand over my entire outfit, from my unruly curls to my painted lips and my shiny gold sneakers. "I don't mean to be rude. It's just a fact."

The kind of girl. Just a fact.

I stare at her. I'm too shocked to be sad, or mad, or any of the usual feelings. I'm not surprised that Maddie would feel this way, or that she'd say it out loud, but I can't believe she'd say it to my face. I need a way out of this conversation, and I need it fast. I lean in toward hers. "You want to know my secret?"

She nods and twirls a piece of her hair. If she had a notebook handy, she'd whip it out.

I crouch close enough that I can smell the canned strawberries in her shampoo. I'm close enough to inspect the tiny piece of kale that's stuck in her top left tooth and the chip in her lower right one. I lean in more and her eyes widen. I'm close enough to bite her nose off. Snap and chomp on it, like a rabid dog. She'd never see it coming.

I whisper, "The secret to driving boys wild is . . ."

Gracelynn is leaning in too, desperate to catch my words. She's practically lying on the table.

"The secret is . . . don't be as boring and as frigid as you."

Maddie makes an O shape with her lips. I want to plug her mouth shut with a curly fry. But I don't share my curly fries with anyone, especially not a devil with an outdated mani.

Gracelynn's eyes look frantically between me and Maddie.

Maddie's mouth shifts, the O growing bigger and bigger, until she bursts out laughing. "You're so funny, Milagro." She's cackling now, slapping the table for extra emphasis.

Gracelynn lets out a tiny sigh, and then she giggles too.

"I need to pee," I announce abruptly. I stand up and walk away from the table, holding in my fury until I've made it inside the bathroom. I count backward silently. *Ten. Nine. Eight. Seven. Six . . .* It's a meditation technique that Sister Hildie made us learn in gym class, during our yoga unit. I guess it comes in handy sometimes.

The walls of the bathroom are chalkboard black, full of scribbles and smudges and artistic graffiti. The turquoise floor tiles are crooked and there's a giant crack running down the mirror over the sink. The decor matches my insides perfectly. I sit on the toilet and contemplate flushing myself to the Pacific Ocean and living life as a mermaid. I don't even have to be pretty. I would commit to life as a sea witch if it meant never having to associate with the Maddies and Gracelynns of the world.

¡Regresa a mí! Aunque sea por solo un momento.

The trills of Gloria's saddest ballad radiate from deep inside my purse. I dig through my bag until I find my phone.

"¡Hola, chica!" Carmen squints at me from my tiny

phone screen. "Wait a second. Where are you?"

"I'm in the bathroom. In Indiana." I wrinkle my nose. "This trip sucks."

Carmen's skin is an even deeper brown, even though she's only been on the island for two days. She's got an orange bikini on, the color of a ripe tangerine, or maybe the sun on the hottest day of the year. She's sprawled on a blue towel and I can see bits of sand on her face and around her shoulders. "So what's your big news?"

My mind goes blank, until I remember the ecstatic texts I sent her only hours ago. "He said he wanted to get back together," I mumble, recounting our conversation to Carmen. "But he didn't mean it at all."

"Want my auntie to put a Santería curse on him?"

"No. He's not worth the energy." I look away from the screen and read the graffiti scrawled all over the wall. It's full of cheerful messages like FAKE IT TILL YOU MAKE IT and YOU ARE ENOUGH and NEVER TRUST A MAN IN A TWEED VEST.

"You're right. Anyway, if my abuelita even hears us contemplating curses, she's gonna sic an exorcism on both of us. Hey!" she chirps, when she sees me looking away.

I look back at Carmen. Her eyebrows are furrowed and her lips are pursed. If she could reach through the phone, I know I'd be in the middle of one her epic feel-better-forever hugs.

"Come on, don't cry. You know we're gonna find out whoever left those boobs on his phone and teach them a lesson."

"As a vegetarian, aren't you morally obligated to be a pacifist?"

"What's more natural than restoring the food chain? Don't forget, Milagro. We're the sharks. Pablo is a minnow. He was lucky to swim alongside you."

In the background, I hear a warbly voice call out, "¡Qué! ¿Tiburón? Did someone say shark?"

A foot appears on the screen, next to Carmen's shoulder. It's tan, wrinkled, and sporting some electric-yellow nail polish and a small silver toe ring. Carmen looks away from the phone and up at the sky.

"Carmen! Sharks!" the voice cries out.

"No, Abuelita. No sharks. It was a joke." She sighs and looks back at me. "I gotta go. Just remember. We aren't the minnows. We've got too many teeth to let a pathetic boy mess us up."

I nod slowly.

"Okay, now smile. Show me your shark teeth," Carmen says.

For the first time today, I'm grinning. Carmen is a hype-lady genius.

Carmen gives me a "WOO!" and a fist pump.

I blow her a kiss and wave goodbye. Carmen is right. If

I'm going to survive the next four days on this trip, I might as well make it an Oscar-winning performance. I stand up and scribble Carmen's words on the bathroom wall.

SHOW YOUR SHARK TEETH.

Pablo is going to regret messing with a shark. If Maddie and Gracelynn want stories, then I will give the performance of a lifetime—even if it couldn't be further from the truth. I shove the door open and stride out of the bathroom, ready to tell all. I toss my curls over my shoulder and clear my throat.

Maddie and Gracelynn stare up at me.

"So what do you guys want to know?"

18
Lulu

THERE ARE AT least two hundred things I would rather do than eat brunch with Milagro. For example, I could reread the Greenpeace Charter. Or I could eat with Amelia, Caroline, and Genevieve, who invited me to picnic outside while Caroline did a dramatic reading of the smuttiest lines from her favorite romance novels. That actually sounded like fun, but I'm reaching new levels of desperation, and Milagro is my last hope for getting through to Clara. Maybe with the two of us combined, we can figure out a plan to salvage my summer dreams. Last night, between pacing my room anxiously and not practicing for my Stanford interview, I asked Milagro to meet me for breakfast in the dining hall, but she texted that she might "die if she eats another dining hall meal," and to meet me at Bitter Ends Bakery instead.

The flickering neon HOT COFFEE sign in the window doesn't inspire much confidence. I push open the wooden door and a bell tinkles. The barista looks up and smiles before returning his focus to the elaborate machine in front of him. It's humming and vibrating, with all kinds of steam and foam whizzing out of it, expertly caught in mugs that seem impossibly small. Next to the espresso machine is a glass case overflowing with enormous pastries. Delicate, flaky croissants piled high and tumbling over into blueberry muffin territory, which is bordered by crispy and buttery apple fritter land. I hope I'm the only one who can hear my stomach growling.

In the back corner, a girl huddles over a textbook. She's wearing long gold earrings and her blonde hair is tucked into a braid that winds around her head, like the world's most elegant milkmaid. She's sitting next to a skinny boy who could be an old-timey train conductor, or a lumberjack, or maybe both. He's sporting green plaid and a handlebar mustache that twists up at the end. Of course Milagro has picked the trendiest café in South Bend. And of course, she's late to meet me. Fifteen minutes later, the bell tinkles again and Milagro walks in. She's in a St. Agnes sweatshirt too, only her sleeves are rolled up to show off her bangles and bracelets. Her dark jeans are cuffed right above her velvet green loafers. When she opens the door, the sun streams around her, picking up on the shimmery stuff on her cheeks. No wonder Leo has a crush on her. I stare at my feet. It's not fair that hermit crabs and snails have the ability to curl up and hide from the world when things don't go their way.

Milagro saunters up to the counter and orders a coffee. She looks at me and I shake my head. I don't have money for extras. She waves her hand at me. "It's my treat, since I dragged you here."

I bite my lip and study the pastry display again, finally pointing to the smallest muffin on the top shelf.

Milagro announces, "We'll take that muffin, and two croissants, two egg-in-a-nests, and a slice of your pie."

I widen my eyes. "Are you sure we need all that?" I'm calculating how much it'll cost, and it's a lot.

Milagro grins triumphantly at me. "I won the Never Have I Ever pool. I'm swimming in cash." I heard Milagro, Maddie, and Gracelynn stay up late last night, giggling until the early morning hours. "Plus, I owe you. Broken promises and all. Go save us a seat." She nods to the tables in the back.

I'm surprised Milagro even remembers our pinky promise on the bus, especially since she broke it the first chance she got. I push this aside. I need to stay focused. Clara. Stanford. This summer, and college too.

When Milagro reappears with our feast, I blurt out, "Have you talked to Clara?"

"So tell me about Leo," Milagro says at the same time. "You've been spending a lot of time with him."

"Who? What?" I shift in my seat. "I barely know the guy." I push aside memories of yesterday's laughing in the grass and our celebratory hug after we messed up our pineapple so badly. He's just my partner, and he's only hanging out with me because he has to, I remind myself, for the millionth time in the last twelve hours.

Milagro tilts her head at me and frowns. "I thought that's why you wanted to meet up? He is cute." She points a croissant at me. "Don't you think so?"

It's an absurd question. I don't think he's cute—I think he's hundreds of miles beyond it, squarely in the thermosphere, a whopping three layers of atmosphere above me. It's why he and Milagro make sense together. As far as I'm concerned, they can pursue their romance far, far away from me, preferably at least two time zones. "I wanted to talk to you about Clara," I say firmly.

"Definitely do *not* talk to Clara about boys." Milagro's lips are now smeared with blueberry skins and sugary crumbs. "Anyway, what's Leo's deal? He doesn't seem as big of a nerd as the rest of the St. A dudes," Milagro muses.

"Can you stop thinking about dating for just one second?! Did you know that she broke up with Robbie?"

She snorts. "Talking about Robbie isn't talking about dating? Good one."

"They broke up in January. Months ago."

"Thank God. He was so boring. Nothing like Leo." She winks too, enough to see the sliver of purple eye shadow swiped across her lid. Her eyes narrow. "Wait a minute. Then why were you hanging out with Robbie? I thought Clara sent him to look after you."

I frown and look away. "No. That's exactly my point. They aren't talking anymore. I wanted to find out if Robbie knew anything about Clara's fight with Mami, and he was no help."

"I can't believe you were desperate enough to contact that lug."

I cover my face with my hands. "You don't get it. Remember Friday? When Mami made me promise I would stay home this summer? That means no Stanford this summer, and at the rate she's going, maybe ever."

"What's so good about Stanford anyway?" Milagro says, scraping off a bit of icing with her spoon and licking it off.

"Do you really want to know?" I pry my hands off my face.

She shrugs. "Sure. Try me."

"I don't even know where to begin." Now my hands are in the air as I get more animated. "Well, for starters, there's the wildlife conservancy program, which doesn't even exist anywhere else in the world. Then there's the guaranteed research for every student who's interested, even the first years. How long do you have? I could come up with reasons all day."

Milagro gives me a small smile. "It sounds perfect for you. You've wanted to do this since you were six years old and poring over the algae in the pool pumps at Mami's work."

"Remember when the assistant manager threatened to push me in the pool if I told the guests what I was doing?"

"Mami said that if he touched you, she'd throw him in the deep fryer and turn him into chicharrón." She snorts. "But really, this program does seem made for you."

"I know." I take a big sigh and stare at the ground. "That's why I had to find Robbie. I'm tired of waiting for things to work out, and I thought he'd know something. I want to fix things between Clara and Mami. No, I *need* to."

"Santa Clara? You know she's a Goody Two-shoes. She probably blames him for her bad grades. Or maybe Clara met someone cuter than Robbie. Like Leo." She nods encouragingly. "He's funny too, right?"

"What bad grades? What are you talking about?"

Milagro hesitates for a second, and then she raises her voice. "I'm trying to talk about *Leo*."

This conversation is suddenly making me queasy. "Just date him already, if you think he's so cute. I have more important things to talk about, like my future." Milkmaid girl glances over her shoulder at me and the barista gives me a look for raising my voice. "I need to figure out—"

"Why would I date him when it's so obvious that he has a crush on you?" Milagro cuts me off. She reaches for a muffin.

"Leo doesn't have a crush on me." My messy bun is ready to blast off into space from how hard I'm shaking my head. "He has a crush on you. He was texting with *you*."

"About YOU," Milagro yells over me. She tosses the muffin wrapper at me, showering crumbs all over my nose. "I texted him about you. I thought you were supposed to be the smart one."

"But. But." I'm stammering, unable to get a single coherent thought out. There's no way that Leo has a crush on me. No one has ever had a crush on me. I reject Milagro's hypothesis.

"C'mon, the guy is following you around."

"He's my partner. It's in the rules!"

Milagro scoffs. "He told me you were fascinating. No one else's partner is out here saying stuff like that. Some boyfriends don't even say stuff like that." She's quiet for a minute, and then she brightens. "Do you like him? And if so, what are you going to do about it?" She turns her steely gaze on me.

I cross my arms and shift in my seat, staring at the empty plate in front of me and mulling the word *fascinating* over in my mind. Stalagmites are fascinating. So are several species of snails. I don't think this adds up to having a crush on me, even if there's a tiny spark in me that desperately wants it to be true. Then I shake my head. I can't get distracted. "I need to figure out Clara first," I say stubbornly.

"Just for one minute, can you stop worrying about stuff that isn't supposed to happen for months from now? Clara isn't thinking about us right now." Milagro shrugs. "So she didn't tell us about Robbie. She was going to tell us eventually—you can't keep a secret that big forever. Are you really going to let your heart grow dusty cobwebs while other people figure their shit out?" Milagro stares at me, holding my gaze firmly.

My mind is whirling. "But . . ."

"Emergency response management!" Milagro says. "Put out urgent fires first. Leo is an urgent fire. A hot, hot, hot one!" She giggles.

I want to smack her with my slice of toast, but her words remind me: "Oh crap. I wanted to go to this class. It's led by this cool ecologist who studies recycling management in challenging terrains. But they're for juniors and seniors." I slump down in my seat. "They don't want some high school sophomore crashing their class."

"Do you want to go to this school?" She wrinkles her nose as she looks out the window.

I shake my head. "No. I don't."

"So if you're never going to see these people again, who cares what they think?" Milagro says, still gazing out the window.

I take in Milagro's shiny hair, coordinated outfit, and sparkly pink lips. That's easy for Milagro to say. She's built an armor against the world, protecting her from what people say and do. How she's done it is a complete mystery to me. Impressing People 101 is a course I'll fail every time.

She looks up when I don't say anything. "Tell you what. I'll come with you for moral support. Afterward, you have to promise me that you'll talk to Leo."

I nod.

"Wahoo!" She throws her hands in the air. "Let me send a pic to Mami to mark this joyous occasion. She whips out her phone before I can say no and snaps a photo, one with my eyebrows furrowed with worry, while Milagro is grinning with wild abandon. *Miss you*, she captions the photo, before sending it off to Mami and looking back up at me. "It's just school. And then your feelings. You can do this."

I take a deep breath. "I can do this."

Thirty slides deep in the International Environmental Law and Policy course and I'm rethinking Milagro's words. This isn't "just" school—this is a marathon of information. My hands can barely keep up with the stream of facts pouring out of the frumpy, disheveled professor standing at the lectern. His words-per-minute rate is remarkable, eclipsed only by how fast he hits his clicker and moves on to the next slide. My fingers are scrambling, racing across the page to write it all down. I'm breathing hard, like I ran a mile instead of sitting through a thirty-minute lecture. I look up midway through slide number fifty and spot Milagro doodling away in her notebook, endless loops and stars and at least one hundred balloons.

When the professor takes a rare break to cough into his handkerchief, the two boys sitting a few rows in front of me shake out their hands in the precious few seconds before the professor begins again. Even as my fingers start cramping in new and extremely painful ways, my brain is thrilled, overflowing with new information about environmental cropping and waste management techniques that could revolutionize our consumption of plastic.

"Psst. Lulu. Can I borrow your water bottle?" Milagro whispers to me.

"Shhh!" I whisper back to her.

"Just one sip. I'm parched over here." She squeezes my knee and I yelp.

The professor stops mid–bullet point. He looks up from his computer to stare into the giant lecture hall until his eyes meet mine. "Excuse me, miss. Do you have something to add about trucking routes? Or a question, perhaps?"

Everybody whips around to stare.

My whole body is on fire. My face is the temperature of a fried egg.

"Um. Er. Um." If I ever regain control of my limbs, I'm going to murder Milagro.

"I do." Milagro stands up.

"You do?" the professor asks. "Go on, then."

Milagro clears her throat. I make a mental note to investigate legal emancipation from your siblings.

"Yes. I was wondering how autonomous transportation might improve driving patterns and allow for expanded habitat protection?" My mouth drops open. Milagro was actually paying attention to the slides? When did she start caring about this kind of stuff?

"What an astute question! What did you say your name is again?" The professor peers at Milagro, smiling at her like she's a budding scientist and not an academic delinquent. It's the kind of smile that teachers reserve for me. What is happening? Have I entered an alternate universe?!

"Milagro." She sits back down and picks up her pen, as if she was taking notes the whole time.

"Autonomous vehicles are a fascinating new field," the professor lectures, before tying Milagro's question back to his next slide and returning to his normal drone.

Milagro smiles at me and winks again before reaching into my tote and taking a long sip from my water bottle.

I want to be annoyed, but all I have is awe. Everything comes easily to her—scoring a spot on this trip, scamming her way through this class, even winning over the ice queen honors girls. She is the ultimate adaptable species.

When class ends, the professor calls Milagro's name. She scampers to the front and then waves at me to follow her. I take my time, trudging down the stairs.

"This is my sister Lulu. She's the real brilliant one in the family." She points to me. "You should read her research on the endangered biosystems in the Chesapeake Bay."

I stare at Milagro. "You've read my research?"

"Is that right?" the professor says. "Your parents must be so proud to have two young budding scientists in the family."

I'm blushing and stammering, not sure where to look. Milagro finally breaks the silence. "Thanks! Excuse us. We've got some fires to put out." She grabs my hand and drags me out of the room.

"Maybe your interview skills do need some work," she laughs. "We can practice later."

"I could take a tip or two from you." I shake my head at Milagro. "When did you pick up sub-Saharan recycling knowledge?"

She crosses her eyes at me. "Sometimes I listen to your documentaries. They're not all so boring."

"You were amazing in there," I tell her. "Like you

belonged in there with the other college kids."

"Yeah right. The important thing is that if I could hang in there, you could too."

"You were more than hanging! I wish Mrs. Johnson could have seen it. Her eyes would have popped out. She might even have canceled your detention."

Milagro looks taken aback. "Detention. Right. That's why I'm here," she says quietly, staring at the floor, before brightening. "Time for you to uphold your end of the bargain." She points to the door. "Go find Leo. Tell him how you feel. Afterward, we can sort out the Clara stuff. I know! Why don't you take him to the grotto?"

I shake my head. "I know just the place." I whip out my phone to text Leo.

Milagro's smile is huge, spreading ear to ear. She shows me her crossed fingers. "You've got this."

I'm waiting for Leo outside his classroom. When the class ends, students stream out as fast as they can, but there are no bouncing high school students in sight. I peer around the door and find Leo deep in conversation with the professor. I duck back out, leaning against the wall and sliding down to the ground as they wrap up. When Milagro said I had to talk to Leo, she didn't say how. I'm just supposed to blurt my feelings out?! I stare at my fingers, like the answers might be etched on the palms of my hands.

"What are you doing here?" I look up to find scuffed-up sneakers standing next to me, attached to a confused Leo. "Did you finish your mountains of homework?"

"Homework can wait. I have something better." I grin. "I researched Linda's story at Green Leaf Growers."

"Wait. Are you talking about what I think you're talking about?" He stoops down, his face a few inches away from mine. I can feel my heart beating faster as I stare up at Leo's deep brown eyes and the hint of soft peach in his cheeks. The shadows of his lashes dance across the top of his cheekbones.

Leo's joy is contagious, spreading over my body like a glowing tan. I'm contaminated with happiness. I give Leo a half smile and slide my phone in my pocket. "One campus secret coming up."

"Let's go!" He hops up and sticks out his hand to pull me up from the ground. His hand is warm in mine. When he pulls it away, the cool breeze feels extra chilly where his fingers used to be. On our walk, Leo tells me about the class he visited. He saw designs for buildings halfway around the world. He tells me about the math involved in material transportation and I ask him about sustainable sourcing, about bricks and raw wood and carbon fiber fittings. I'm brimming with happiness and there's nothing else I'd rather be talking about.

I lead us back to the dorm room where we're staying.

"Here?" he asks, puzzled.

"I know. We're not going to your room. Or my room. I mean. We could. But. It's not. Er." I'm flailing now.

Leo laughs.

On the elevator, I punch the thirtieth-floor button. "Trust me," I tell him. The elevator zooms up and my ears start popping from the rapid shift in altitude. Leo closes his eyes and hums. I study him, taking in every dark tight curl in his hair, the twelve stripes on his shirt, and the tiny freckle near his eye, and my stomach flip-flops again. I bite my lip and try to keep myself together.

We stumble out of the elevator and I lead him down the hallway. I stop abruptly in front of a nondescript door. "Prepare to be amazed . . . I hope," I tell him, showing him my crossed fingers.

The door is painted gray and it says "UTILITY CLOSET" across the front of it. "Are you sure this is the right door?" he asks.

I tuck my scraggly frizzies behind my ears before I swing the door open. Our jaws drop. My eyebrows practically fly off my face.

Linda was right. This room is the definition of cozy. The room is carpeted—wall to wall—with giant white pillows, reaching as high as my waist. The pillows are crammed into the room, so many that they're spilling out of the door, a lava river of muddy gray fluff. The pillows are overstuffed, or at least they were at some point. They look like floppy versions of the kind you'd find in a hotel. I lean forward and poke one in front of me. It's not as firm as the ones from Mami's hotel.

"Whoa," I whisper.

"We found the pillow room," Leo says, his voice full of glee. He's practically hopping, he's so excited. He slips his shoes off and lines them up along the hallway wall. He takes a look at me and nods before taking three giant steps back. With a running leap, he blasts off into the room. He bounces up and sinks down, until all I see are the bottoms of his black socks.

"Lulu! Come in!" Leo's mouth is muffled by the pillows, but I can still hear his laughter spilling out of the lava of fluff.

I fold my arms across my chest and look both ways down the hallway. What if someone catches us? Then I think, *What would Milagro do?* I snort. I know exactly what she would do. I slip my Converse off and copy Leo, a running start and a graceful leap into the pillow pile. Only my legs get tangled up and my leap becomes a face-forward plummet into the depths of fluff.

"Oof!"

My face collides with Leo's chest. His shirt is soft on my cheek, a million times softer than the pillows that surround us. He smells like fresh laundry, pine trees, and a hint of pancakes. When his hand reaches up and grazes the top of my head, he stops at my messy bun, like we've always done this. I remember my promise to Milagro and chicken out, rolling away into the depths of the pillows.

"Why'd you go?" Leo tosses a pillow at me. It just misses my face, but my inner competitiveness is roaring. I grab the corner of a pillow and heave it toward Leo. It bounces off his chest, where my head was lying a few minutes ago.

"Hey!"

I gulp.

A pillow sails through the air and plops on my head.

"You're on, Zavala!"

The pillows start falling around me. I wrap my fingers around the corner of the closest pillow and toss one back at him. The fight is on. All I can hear is my gasping breath and our giggles as pillows soar above our heads. Our bodies ride the sea of fluff, occasionally colliding before a hit to the face or the chest sets us apart again. Every time I start to lose my footing and slip down into the gray pillow abyss, Leo's hand finds me. His fingers curl around mine and he yanks me upright, long enough to throw a pillow at the top of my bun and set me off again.

It's like the pillow fights I used to have with Clara and Milagro, back when Mami's bed felt like a giant lagoon and Clara and Milagro weren't mysteries to me.

"Truce!" I yell out, in between the giggles. "I'm officially calling a truce, please!"

Leo gives me a gentle push and we stumble out of the room and back into the hallway.

"I can't believe this place is actually real," Leo gasps.

"Me either."

"Hey, what is that?" He points to my arm.

"Oh shoot." I glance down and the world goes wobbly and out of focus, the dark gray of the carpet swimming with the white walls. A drum kit has taken residence in my ears and the pounding gets louder as I look at the cut on my shoulder. It's a tiny battle wound, a trickle of blood. "I should probably mention that I'm squeamish about—" I put my hand on the wall to brace myself. "Blood."

Leo springs into action. "Let's go to my room. It's just a few floors down."

"But the rules . . ." My voice trails off.

"I think that Mrs. Johnson would make an exception for this," he says. He pumps his arm in the air. "Finally, the safety kit my mom forced me to pack comes in handy."

"Okay," I say weakly, my stomach already churning.

Leo places his hand on my lower back, anchoring me to the ground that feels wobbly beneath my feet. He steers us toward the elevator and then his room. The hallway is eerily quiet, except for Leo's cheerful running dialogue about the Notre Dame baseball game and how all the St. A

276

boys left together hours ago, so they could get good seats in the students' section.

Leo uses his card to swipe the door open. I sit on Leo's bed and count to ten backward before starting on the alphabet. Anything to stop my brain from thinking about the blood.

Leo sits next to me, wiping up my arm with a small white towel. "These weird sinks come in handy after all," he says, pointing to the sink in the corner of his dorm room. "This whole dorm used to be seminarian housing, for priests. Then Notre Dame added more students and turned it into dorms." His voice is quiet. He hums as he wipes my arm with a paper towel.

"Look at me. Don't look at your arm," Leo says as he presses his thumb down on the edges of a Band-Aid. I take a shallow breath of air.

His face is so close to mine, I can count his dark lashes. Seconds pass as I study the different shades of brown in his eyes, amber, mahogany, really the entire *Swietenia* genus of trees. I want to conduct a color study on all the shades.

I can practically hear Milagro in my head, urging me to just tell him already. I turn my face away and study the messy piles of papers on his desk instead. One catches my eye. It's a familiar maroon-and-gold brochure, with a giant tree on the impressive letterhead.

Goose bumps spring up my arms. I shift away from

him and toward the desk. "What is this?" I ask. I'm no longer pale or a weak shell of myself. My face is getting hotter and hotter, and the walls of Leo's small dorm room are shrinking.

"What?" Leo asks.

I snatch it up from the desk and open it up. *Dear Leo, we'd like to invite you to interview for Stanford University's prestigious summer scholars program . . .*

It's the same letter I have. *One person per state is chosen. It's an honor to be nominated.*

"Is this why you've been being so nice to me?" My voice gets tight and loud at the same time. "Why didn't you tell me?" I'm clenching my teeth now, trying to stop more words from coming out of my mouth.

But Leo sits silently, looking between my face and the paper in my hand, like I'm a living Ping-Pong match.

Yesterday's conversation flashes back to me, when Leo told me that maybe it was for the best that Stanford wasn't going to work out. *Wait out the wave,* he said. *There's always next year.*

I snap my head up. "Is that why you told me not to worry about the interview? And to skip the program this summer?"

"What are you talking about?" he says, and his shoulders are creeping up to his ears.

"The summer program that I've been telling you about.

278

It's this one. Only ONE STUDENT can go," I say. I jab my finger at Leo's letter.

"I didn't know?" Leo sits up straight. "That's cool that you got an invite too. It's usually just St. Anthony boys. It's okay, I'm—"

"No, it's *not* okay." I'm so sick of people telling me the way things should be: Mami making up rules about college, Clara deciding she's over our family. Milagro deciding we're the best of sisters one day and strangers the next. Now Leo, revealing that he's been my competition all along.

"I'm leaving." I stand up, grab the Band-Aid wrappers, and shove them in my pocket.

"But Lulu, wait."

"Good luck with your interview," I say.

The last thing I see is Leo's face. It's the first time I haven't seen him with a smile.

I charge down the stairs, my feet flying over the steps so fast, I'm catching air. When I make it to the girls' bathroom, I throw myself into the stall and slam the door. My feet are tucked up over the toilet seat and my hands are wrapped around my knees. I hug myself, hoping that if I concentrate hard enough, I can forget about summer at Stanford or any college at all.

Clang!

The door of the bathroom swings open and I hear a

high-pitched giggle that sends shivers down my throat.

Oh no. Not now.

"I know. She's so freakin' cool." From the crack in the stall, I can see Maddie lean over the sink to grimace at herself in the mirror. She starts poking at her teeth.

"How do we get invited to college parties?" Gracelynn asks, tightening the Notre Dame ribbon around her ponytail.

"Do you think she'd let us come next time?"

"She invited her *sister* to the last party. What a waste of an invite," Maddie says. She's got her pinky finger over her incisor tooth and she's chipping away at whatever is jabbed between them.

The pit in my stomach that appeared when Gracelynn and Maddie started talking is now a swirling vortex. I take a deep breath and close my eyes, imagining myself anywhere but in this dingy stall.

"And she actually called the cops? What a freak," Gracelynn says.

For the millionth time, Robbie isn't the cops! But there's no correcting history. Brutus didn't have a historian on his side. I don't have one either. I imagine a world where I'm bold enough to storm out and defend my honor. I slink farther down, my chin resting on the top of my chest.

"Can you believe Lulu actually walked in on her and Pablo? Talk about embarrassing."

Milagro told them about that? I'm biting my lip so hard, I'm surprised it's not bleeding. I grip my knees tighter. I don't know if I'm angrier at her for pretending to care at all about me, or me for falling for it.

"Seriously. It's so tragic how she's so obsessed with her club and that stupid Stanford program. Everyone thinks so."

Everyone? My mind is racing, thinking back over my conversations with Caroline, Genevieve, and Amelia. Was that all just an elaborate joke? My whole body fills with hot shame as I hear Gracelynn's and Maddie's giggles.

Gracelynn and Maddie leave the bathroom in a cloud of perfume, leaving behind the stench of raspberries, cucumber melon, and coldhearted betrayal.

This trip was supposed to be a chance to imagine my life on my own terms. I'm tired of waiting around for people to change their minds—Mami, Clara—or reveal their true colors, like Leo and Milagro. I need to do something drastic, so that they'll all realize I'm serious. I need to take charge of my life, and there's only one way to do that.

I'm going to find Clara.

19
Milagro

FRY ME UP and serve me on a hoagie with a side of fries, because I am one hot fish! There's an extra pep in my step and a gold sheen in my sneakers from going to class with Lulu.

It was exhilarating. Not because of the professor—he was a total bore, even if his jaunty hat reminded me of *Newsies*. And definitely not the subject matter—I would happily go the rest of my life without exploring the intricacies of plastic containment in the sub-Saharan desert. High school has been a slow-motion word vomit of facts crammed in my brain, dumped on an exam, and immediately discarded for more interesting things like lipstick primer. Going to that class made me realize that there has never been any original thought required of me, unless you count figuring out the fastest way to get my homework over with.

Thinking on the spot, and actually getting it right? That's like fireworks in my brain, or the way you feel after the first bite of a salted chocolate bar, or the shock of cold when you cannonball into a pool. I look at the photo I sent to Mami, of Lulu's deeply furrowed brows and my wild grin, astounded at the absurdity of going to class with Lulu. Even after going to class, it still feels absurd to think I could fit in there, especially when I think about the hours that Clara spent doubled over an SAT prep book, or that Lulu spends willingly in the library. But Lulu said it could be me, and she's hardly ever wrong about things.

I resolve to ask her if there are college classes about stuff that's actually interesting, classes that I could use in real life. While I wait for her to come back from hanging out with Leo, I'm lurking in the dorm, avoiding everyone who isn't related to me.

This whole trip, the St. A girls have been complaining about sharing a bathroom in the dorms. I don't get it. I've never *not* shared a bathroom. At home, mornings have always been a four-way fight for the shower, full of careful negotiations, strategic maneuvering, and occasional sabotage (via the dishwasher or washing machine). I'd happily replace our tiny bathroom with the massive industrial shower that I'm standing in. Having my pick of ten shower stalls is a dream come true.

As the water pours over me, I try to block out the

late-night stories that I told Maddie and Gracelynn, about Craig/Greg and Pablo, and all the things we never did. It was so easy to lie and tell embarrassing stories about Pablo, but the more it made them laugh, the emptier I felt inside. Earlier this morning, I told Lulu not to care about what other people think, and yet I've been spinning in circles, trying to impress an audience I don't even like. I tried to tell them about the late-night musical theater and costume designing, but Maddie steered the conversation right back to hookups and boys. It's all they want to hear from me. It's all anyone really wants to hear from me.

Before Pablo, Mami was too busy working or keeping track of Clara's and Lulu's commitments to Model UN clubs or volunteer hours to remember I existed. Before Pablo, I'd never done anything worth noting. Even Clara is the same. Our conversations—when she's not on my case about grades—are always about me and Pablo. Where do we go out, and are things serious, and so on. Sometimes I want to shake the computer screen, until she realizes that I'm a whole person, not a plus-one to a studly boy.

I wrench the shower knob closed and wrap the thin, dorm-issued towel around my body. My flip-flops leave a trail of drips down the hallway. I've got my Ziploc bag of shower essentials clutched to my chest. I knock on Lulu's door to see if she's back from hanging out with Leo.

The door creaks open and a familiar bird's nest of hair

pops out. Lulu and I lock eyes. I burst into a smile. "Lulu! Tell me everything!"

Lulu's mouth is a straight line across her face. I can practically hear her teeth grinding. Her eyebrows are furrowed and I don't think the pink in her cheeks is from a newfound appreciation for blush.

"Lulu?" I take a few steps toward her. "Are you okay?"

Lulu shifts and I realize that her giant hiking bag is slung over her back. The straps are digging into the shoulders of her worn St. Agnes sweatshirt. "I don't want to talk to you." She shoves past me and slams the door shut behind her.

She moves like a turtle, her arms and legs working furiously, to little effect. I'm holding my breath, hoping she doesn't tumble over. With her khaki bucket hat pulled tight over her forehead and her giant sunglasses, she's ready for a safari, or an undercover sting. "Stepping out for a hunt? Gonna go catch some poachers?" A giggle escapes, I can't help it.

Lulu whips around faster than seems physically possible when you're sporting fifty pounds on your shoulders. "I know what you told Maddie and Gracelynn." I flash back to my stories of Pablo's horrific BO and how his parents spoon-feed him oatmeal in the morning, since that's the only way he'll eat his breakfast. I snort. That can't be it.

There's an anger in her eyes that I've never seen before.

Her frizzies are standing straight out around her face, tiny lightning bolts radiating from her scalp. Her fists grip both her backpack straps and her eyes are flashing. She looks fierce and determined, like Joan of Arc in the stained-glass windows of the St. Agnes chapel.

I stop mid-giggle. "Lulu? What are you talking about?"

"Are you too stupid to understand? Let me spell it out for you. Leave. Me. Alone."

All I can hear is the word *stupid*, over and over again. My mouth is hanging open. Lulu might as well have ripped off my towel.

Stupid. Stupid. Stupid.

In a flash, Lulu becomes the conductor to the mean chorus in my head, the one I hear every time I mess up— which is A LOT.

Stupid Milagro. You'll never amount to anything. Didn't your mami raise you better? Mal criada. Why can't you be more like Clara?

I swallow. My mouth is sticky and I'm not sure what to say back. I don't know what I've done wrong. I don't know why Lulu is so mad.

Lulu doesn't notice. "Sorry I'm such an embarrassment to you."

I pull my towel closer around me. I've got chills and an eerie sense that whatever comes out of Lulu's mouth next, she won't be able to take it back. I want to stop her, to push the words back into her chapped lips. But Lulu can't be stopped.

"Actually, I'm not sorry. I'm not sorry about any of the bad stuff that happened to you. I'm not sorry that your loser boyfriend turned out to be just as loserish as I predicted." She stomps toward the elevators and jabs the button so hard, I'm afraid she's going to crack it in half. "And I'm not sorry for being right all the time. The only thing I'm sorry about is having you for a sister." The last part comes out in a huff of hot air. The transformation is complete. She is a dragon, and I am ashes, burned to a crisp.

No. If she's going to start a fire, then I'll burn the whole building down. "Maybe if you stopped judging everyone from behind your giant book, you'd realize that *I'm* the only one that's honest with you. All Clara has done is lie. She's lied to you about Robbie; who knows what else she's lying about." This goes way beyond a bad mood. Whatever happened to Lulu, whatever pushed her to be this mad—I don't care.

"With a sister like you, who needs enemies," Lulu snarls. "You don't know anything about me or Clara. I'll take my chances on my own."

The ding of the elevator breaks her glare. She hops on and jabs a button. Her tears are the last thing I see before the door shuts in my face.

Lulu leaves me dripping on the floor, staring at the

chipped polish on my left toe. I don't remember the day she stopped being my sister and became a cagey and angry wild beast, like the ones she wants to save. I don't know what her natural environment is or what she needs to thrive. Everything and everyone that gets in her way— including me—is collateral damage.

When I walk back down the hallway, I notice Lulu's door is wide open. It must not have latched shut, from when she slammed it. I wince, remembering the echoing thud, reverberating to the very bottom of my heels. The knob is cool on my hand as I pull it toward me. I glance in as I close it.

My heart stops. Something is very, very wrong.

The desk where she'd carefully set up her tower of books, laid out her notebooks, spaced out all her pens?

Empty.

The chipped wooden desk is as barren as the shiny blue mattress that lies next to it. The sheets have been stripped and folded carefully, with corners that would make Mami proud. There isn't a stray sweatshirt hanging over the desk chair, or an extra pair of Chucks peeking out from the closet. I step into the room and I fling open the closet doors. They're empty too. There's no evidence that there was ever a student here, much less someone as messy as Lulu.

I have a bad feeling in the pit of my stomach. It's the

same feeling I had before Clara clicked her college acceptance letter open, or when Tía Lochita didn't answer our phone calls and it turned out she had slipped on a patch of black ice.

I messed up. Mrs. Johnson must have scheduled a mandatory activity that involves packing up your whole room for funsies. Or I got the time wrong. We must be leaving for San Francisco *now*, instead of early tomorrow morning. I'm careful to leave the door to Lulu's room open. I race back to my room, my flip-flops slapping against the linoleum tiles and my towel flapping in the wind, giving the empty hallway a free show. I reach into my bag and pull out the shiny orange folder that we received at the beginning of the trip. I've barely looked at it. I rip through it, tossing the emergency contact information and pamphlets about alcohol poisoning and Ultimate Frisbee championships over my shoulder, until I find the pastel-green sheet of paper that has our itinerary printed on it. My finger races down the page until I make it to Monday.

These are the activities listed: a baseball game, a charity hot dog eating competition, and an evening tour of South Bend's Italian neighborhood. None of them involve packing up your things and vacating the premises. I throw the paper on the ground and grab whatever clothing I find. Then I grab my phone too, before running back to Lulu's room.

Lulu, where did you go?

But my text goes unanswered. Back in Lulu's room, I channel my best TV detective. I square my shoulders, tie my hair into the tightest ponytail possible, and dive under her bed. I look behind her desk and even in her trash can for clues. Her room has been wiped clean.

I sit down on her bed and call her over and over again, each ring more agonizing than my failed phone call with Pablo. Lulu's corny message—"It's Lulu. Make like a tree and leaf me a message!"—taunts me each time. My texts to her (**Seriously, where did you go? Why did you pack up? WHERE ARE YOU?**) don't get a text back. For the second time this week, I'm hunched over my phone, waiting for a response that doesn't seem likely to come.

Time is moving slower than ever. I've left Central Standard Time and moved straight into Lulu Time. I can hear my heart pounding and I wonder if my breath has always been this loud and ragged.

I don't *think* Lulu is in danger. I think that she's done something creatively bad. There has to be a way to undo it, to get her to turn around or reveal wherever she's hiding. I start scrolling through my phone, to find Leo's number.

Think, Milagro, think.

A knock at the door breaks my concentration.

A high-pitched voice calls out, "Have you seen . . ."

I look up. "Lulu?!"

Mrs. Johnson steps into the room and stares at me. The neutral look on her face slides right off and another one takes its place, firmly in "disgust" territory. She's the epitome of "turn that frown upside down," only it's reversed for me, the Milagro special.

"Milagro Zavala." Her eyes narrow. Even though Mrs. Johnson is stumbling over the *A*'s in my name, somehow butchering my last name beyond recognition, she still sounds like Mami before she goes on a tirade. All she's missing is my middle name.

"I was looking for your sister. She's supposed to meet me to practice her interview, but I need to speak with you too."

My stomach tightens. No good can come from those seven words. Definitely not when there's a pointer finger out, waggling in my face.

"Are you aware that you have missed nearly every required session on this trip? You were a no-show at the information session *and* the tour at Monongahela University." Her voice reaches a new level of screech as she continues. "Then you skipped the mandatory club meeting."

Am I aware? Yes. I did it, after all. Even though I hate rhetorical questions, this will not be my hill to die on. Not when Lulu is MIA. "Mrs. Johnson. I need to . . . I can . . . listen," I stutter.

"No more excuses, Milagro." She shakes her head. "Haven't we taught you better? The St. Agnes mission teaches young women that they can accomplish anything." She thrusts her fist in the air. "But I can't force you to try."

I realize Mrs. Johnson is right. We *should* focus on me. We should focus on anything that isn't Lulu related, until I figure out where she went.

Mrs. Johnson is on a roll. She won't be deterred. "I'm very disappointed in you. This was supposed to be an opportunity for you to see what's out there. Instead, you've spent the trip sulking."

I nod emphatically, like a bobblehead. "You're right."

"I am?" Mrs. Johnson stares at me, her mouth wide open.

"Yes. I have been very, very unappreciative of what I've been given. And I've let St. Agnes down." I stand up and tuck my phone in my pocket.

Mrs. Johnson takes a step back from me, like I'm a ghost, a banshee, or an otherworldly creature.

"Do you think there's a way I can make this up?" I reach out my hand to Mrs. Johnson. Her eyes are wide open and bewildered and she shakes my hand limply. "Maybe I can go to an extra class, or write some kind of paper about it?" I guide her out of the room, back into the hallway. "Or maybe there's some community service I should do?" I ask sweetly.

She pulls her elbow away. "That would be a good start." Her mind is whirling. "Or maybe you could help out in the dining hall. It's the only place that can guarantee full supervision."

I cross my eyes. Wherever Lulu is, I hope she appreciates what I'm about to do. "Sure, Mrs. Johnson. Whatever you want!"

There are three important things to know about the University of Notre Dame's Wilkerson Dining Center.

There is a mandatory hairnet policy that I'd like to report to the United Nations as a human rights violation.

The dining staff get unlimited soft-serve ice cream. (I've tried all five flavors; peanut butter is the best.)

No one has seen Lulu in the last four hours, not even Leo.

This is all I can think about as I cut hundreds of apple pie slices to faceless University of Notre Dame students.

"She ran out of my room. I don't know where she went," Leo told me earlier, when I asked him to meet me outside, by the dining center's dumpsters.

"Can you text her?!" I begged. "Here, I'll do it for you." I reached my hand out for his phone.

His eyes grew wide at my desperation, but he stood firm. "I haven't heard from her since after class. I have to

go join the South Bend tour group, or I'll get in trouble."
He gave me a small shrug. "She's probably waiting to go on
the tour."

Twenty minutes later, Leo texts: No sign of her. I covered
for her. Should I tell Mrs. Johnson?

I feel sick. No! I'll figure it out, I type back.

"FOR THE TENTH TIME, PUT YOUR PHONE
AWAY!" our cafeteria overlord shouts. I jump in the air
and slide my phone back in my pocket sheepishly.

The line cooks point to the sink, and I trudge over to
wash my hands again.

"Can I just say"—Lucas slams his ladle down from
the stove next to the sink—"this is really messed up." He
crosses his arms over his giant white apron, full of smears
of mystery meat loaf and stiff stains of mashed potatoes
on it.

I blush and my whole body turns hot. I get why Lucas is
mad at me. How was I supposed to know that when I vol-
unteered myself for dining hall duty, Mrs. Johnson would
make him join me?

"Everyone else gets to tour South Bend, while we're
playing cafeteria workers? Why would you sign us up for
this?" Lucas stares at me. "I thought we were friends." His
hairnet is sliding off his blond curls, making a break for the
white collar of his polo.

I want to bury my face in my hands and explain everything, but I can't tell Lucas about Lulu yet. Not until I have a plan.

Ding!

"Lucas, I—"

"I can't believe I'm stuck in the kitchen, *again*. This is what every shift at Double T Diner is like, but at least I'm getting paid for those hours," Lucas says.

My heart is racing. I pull my phone out of my pocket again.

"Milagro. Put it away! I don't want to get in trouble AGAIN because of you."

I went to visit Clara on the bus. I'm almost there. You can't stop me. I'll text you when I make it.

Lulu is on a bus?!

BOUND FOR IOWA?!

"I have to go," I tell Lucas.

"I'm not covering for you," Lucas says, shaking his head angrily, his hairnet now dangerously close to falling into a bubbling pot of tomato soup.

I want to smash my fists over each delicate slice of apple pie in front of me. Why would Lulu go visit Clara *now*? I rack my brain, going over our last conversation together in the café. I remember the way that Lulu's face lit up when she talked about her nerdy summer program at Stanford. What could have been so important that she'd wreck everything? I think about Lulu and her messy bun on a bus, tucked away in a book while faceless thieves ransack her backpack or convince her to give up her belongings. This big world is full of creeps who could hurt Lulu in more ways than I want to imagine. My message back to Lulu fills the whole screen with question marks.

I rip my hairnet off and turn to Lucas. "I'm sorry. I'm really, really sorry. I promise, I'll make it up to you."

"Milagro!" Lucas shouts after me. "I'm serious!"

My curls stream behind me as I run to the dorms, where I know I'll find Mrs. Johnson. My hand is poised over Mrs. Johnson's door, ready to knock, when my phone vibrates in my pocket. I want to sing with relief. Lulu must have been playing a prank this whole time. She's down the hall, and I'm a sucker. She even got Leo in on it.

But when I glance at the screen, my shoulders slump all over again. Lulu isn't calling me—it's Pablo. A photo of him fills the screen, his gorgeous smile wide enough to reach either side of my phone. It's unprompted and random, the first sign that he gives a flying fig about me. But when I stare at the phone, all I can think about is Lulu. Whether she's scared, or worse, in trouble and all alone. And so I silence my phone and pound my fist against the door.

As my knuckles rasp against the wood, I imagine a world where I can fling my stupid lanyard off an ocean and begin a new life as an only child. Carmen can sell her godly dulce de leche cupcakes and we'll be the ultimate power BFFs. I'll bleach my hair pink and never waste another thought on little sisters who single-handedly ruin everything by disappearing into the night. Instead, I open my big mouth.

"Mrs. Johnson? I need to talk to you. Lulu is gone and it's all my fault."

📍 IOWA CITY

Caroline, Gracelynn, or Maddie. My face burns, flooding with hot shame all over again, and then I remind myself that I will never hear those shrieks again because I am almost certainly expelled from St. Agnes. It's hard to imagine that a college like Stanford will want me for their summer program, let alone four years of college. I spend the next six hours stuck between wondering if I've made the hugest mistake of my life and convincing myself that this is what I had to do, in order to earn myself any sort of future that isn't staying at home with Mami for the rest of my life. The flames are burning and I need to see them through.

When I finally make it to the University of Iowa, everything feels monumental. Here are the ornate black gates where Clara crossed from being an ordinary Zavala girl to a bona fide college student. When the gates are pulled open, their wrought iron welcomes everyone, even a lumpy girl like me, with city instincts and a lifelong dream of hibernating in a library. Here is the green bench where Clara sits and watches the leaves turn color, and then fall off, and grow back again. Here is the tall glass building where Clara took her first biology course. This is the bike rack where Clara told us that her roommate's pricey bike got stolen, even though she assured us, "Iowa City is totally safe. There are more cows than people here!" Here's the doughnut shop where Clara decided that red velvet doughnuts were the best on the planet. (She's wrong. There is nothing

302

better than powdered sugar jelly-filled fried dough.)

I stand up a little straighter, emboldened by my new-found freedom. At University of Iowa, no one knows Clara's sister is a socially awkward runaway. For all they know, I'm a certified genius, an aspiring juggler, or a champion water skier. Every step I take toward the black iron gates is a step I take toward becoming the Lulu I've always wanted to be—starting with getting Clara to 'fess up about why she and Mami aren't talking, then convincing her to make things right. There's no way I can make it to Stanford now, but this isn't about next summer. This is about the rest of my life.

If there was a quiz on the landscape and architectural design choices of the University of Iowa's college campus, I would ace it. I'm taking mental notes on everything, from the sloped hill where students are reading to the glossy windows and slanted walls of the humanities building. Everything in Iowa City feels special because it belongs to Clara, even parts she never mentioned. There is a sandwich shop with a line that winds around the block, where anxious students check their mail and gossip about last night's power outage. Harried professors run to catch a bus before the giant storm clouds burst open. A nursery school class of tiny humans carefully hold hands as they totter across the lawn that marks the entrance to the University of Iowa.

The wind swirls around me, lifting my frizziest hair strands away from my face. There's a heavy weight in the air, and I can smell the rain. I pull my windbreaker tighter around my body and hitch my bag up even higher. I walk over to a security guard, clad in blue with leather patches on his elbows. He smiles at me, leaning out of his small guard box to point me to the Sanders First Year Residence Hall, where Clara lives. I'm the first person in my family to see it in person. When Clara moved, there wasn't enough money for all of us to fly with her. She told Mami it wasn't worth taking the vacation days off just so she could turn around and go home.

I take a deep breath and tap a girl in front of the dorm. "Excuse me?"

She looks up at me, taking in my giant backpack and my worn St. Agnes sweatshirt. She doesn't say anything.

"Can you sign me in? I want to surprise my sister and she—"

The girl shrugs. "Yeah, whatever. Just pass me your ID."

"What? Really?" I blurt out. I want to take the words back as soon as I say them.

She shrugs. "You wanna surprise your sister. I get it. It's not like you're some thief . . ." She stares me up and down, her eyes scrutinizing mine. "Or are you?"

"No! I promise I'm not." I grab my wallet and wriggle out my school ID. "I'm just a kid." She studies it and nods, before sauntering up to the guard, telling her she has a guest to sign in.

"I'm surprising her," I mumble, more to myself than anyone else. "Clara wants me to be here."

I wave goodbye to my Good Samaritan and push the elevator button. While I wait, I check my phone, reading Clara's words over and over again.

Hanging out in my dorm room. No plans today. I hadn't told her I was coming, but everyone likes surprises.

A small crowd of students gathers around me. There's a boy standing next to me, with giant headphones that float in his hair. He's listening to angry cymbals, but then the song switches to the familiar piano chords of Mami's favorite ballad. It feels like a giant sign from the universe, not that I believe in that. When the elevator finally arrives, we all pile on, pushing the buttons for our respective floors. I hit the fifteenth-floor button.

"Penthouse dorm room. A fancy floor for a fancy lady," Mami said when Clara announced her room assignment. It was July, the summer before Clara left, and 100 degrees outside, but Mami wasn't going to let a little humidity stop her from baking empanadas. "Maybe they put all the honors students at the top. The higher the floor, the closer to God," she laughed, before smacking Milagro's hand away from the bowl of meat stuffing. "Isn't that what they say?"

305

"My roommate is from Washington," Clara said to us, ignoring Mami. "Her name is Darcy." I pulled up a map of the state on my phone and brought it over to the table, where Milagro and Clara were sitting. The three of us stared at the square state.

"What . . . do they have there?" Milagro asked, her nose wrinkling up. We didn't know anyone from Washington, or even from California. The West Coast might as well be Timbuktu. "If she wants to go to Iowa, it can't be so great."

"Maybe Washington IS great. Maybe it's the best state in America, but she doesn't know how to appreciate it and she's making a BIG mistake by turning her back on it and leaving. Did you ever think about that?" Mami interrupted. I shrug the memory away. I don't understand why it can't be both. I can love home, and the dream of somewhere else too. I don't want to choose.

As the elevator rises, I keep waiting for someone to stop me, to point at me and scream, "Imposter!" I hold my breath and mouth the words to Mami's favorite prayer, feverishly wishing that these college students won't suddenly turn and demand to see my ID. By the tenth floor, I'm alone. When the doors finally open on the fifteenth floor, I'm bouncing on the tips of my toes. My quest is almost over.

I step out onto the floor and turn to find a giant window. It offers a view of campus—everything from the big black gates that mark the entrance to the low hedges that dot the outskirts. But even more impressive is what's beyond the edges of the small-town campus. Long green hills for miles, rising and falling until they meet the horizon. There's nothing here to remind me of home. If you handed me a glass helmet and an oxygen tank and told me we were on the moon, I'd believe you. Maybe the flip side of being removed from the world is that you feel like the rest of the world stops existing. It makes today's mission even more important. I have to remind Clara that we exist.

I turn away from the window and begin my hunt for Clara's room. I'm moving slowly, even though I know from our first video call that it's the door all the way at the end, closest to the girls' bathroom.

"I don't even have to walk that far to take a shower!" Clara told us, and she showed us too, walking her laptop over to the entrance of the bathroom. She was wearing a pink robe that I'd never seen before and her hair was half up, with a few tendrils over her right eye.

We could hear someone call out, "Sup, Z!" and Milagro and I looked at each other in wonder. Clara had made friends already?

"Sounds like your room might smell like poop," Mami

said, wriggling her head in between mine and Milagro's. "Better light that prayer candle that I sent you. Pray the smell away," she said, doubling over laughing.

"Ew, Mami! Get away," Milagro said, elbowing Mami's head out of the way so Clara could finish her dorm tour. But Mami kept laughing at her joke, laughing so hard, she had to wipe the tears away. She kept wiping those tears up long after she stopped laughing.

As I walk down the hallway, I can't help but peek in the dorm rooms. Everything is exactly like we saw through our scratched computer screen. There's a giant poster of a Corona bottle on a beach on the first door and someone has taped a "GO IOWANS" sign over it, along with a reminder that SPF saves lives. That has to be where the swimmer boys live. Clara says they're aspiring doctors, just like her. For the first few weeks of school, they even studied together. Next door to them, I can see—and smell—clouds of smoke pouring out from under the door. It smells like parks in Baltimore, if you're hanging out in them after dark. Clara says they only talk about abolishing the electoral college. She spent the first day of school trading brownie and cookie recipes with them, only to realize that they weren't talking about the same kind of baking. Milagro and I smiled at each other when she told us this story. This was classic Clara.

When I make it to Clara's door, I'm relieved that it's

closed. It gives me a few minutes to pull myself together and explain what the hell I'm doing in Iowa, far away from Mrs. Johnson, Milagro, and everyone I know. I practice my best smile, trying to remember how to look normal. Once I read a study that found smiles are more believable if you show your teeth. Predators don't show their teeth to be liked. Only humans do. Nature doesn't always make sense, but I practice my grimacing all the same.

I take a deep breath, then knock on the door.

No one answers. I knock on the door again, and then three more times. Maybe Clara fell asleep, or maybe she ran out to grab a packet of ramen. She swears that the shrimp flavor packets can chase away the worst strains of the common cold. But there's no answer. I knock three more times, harder this time.

"Okay, okay!" I hear from inside the door. "I'm coming, sheesh, hold your horses."

The door swings open. I have my arms out, ready to give Clara my best wiggling jazz hands. My mouth is wide open, midway to "Surprise!"

"You're not Clara!" I blurt out instead.

"Um. Excuse me? You're the one that knocked on my door," the girl says. "The door that belongs to *my* room."

I take in this girl's square rimless glasses and her braces with blue bands. Clara had mentioned her roommate was "eccentric," but she hadn't gone into too much detail. This had to be Darcy. "I'm looking for my sister," I say, my voice tilting up at the end, as if it were a question and not a weeklong quest. I look down at my hands. "Clara? She said she was in her room."

"Clara? Why?" She studies my face, taking in my St. Agnes sweatshirt, my messy hair, and my oversized backpack. "Wait a second. Are you . . ." She scrunches her face up. Her eyes get all squinty and she's got her lips pursed, shifting them from right to left as she racks her brain for the answer. Then her eyes bug open and she shouts, "Lulu! You're Lulu!"

I nod, and she pumps her fist.

"Yes! I knew it!" A smile spreads across her face. Then her shoulders slump. "But what are you doing here?" she asks, twirling a piece of blonde hair in her fingers.

"It's a long story," I mumble. I tuck my hands in my back pockets and pray my cheeks won't blush. I stare at the ground and mumble, "Did Clara step out?"

Darcy's eyes widen. "But Clara doesn't . . ." Her voice trails off. "Don't you know?"

"Know what?" I say. Everything feels hot, and I reach into my pocket to grab my phone, to show her Clara's messages to me. "Clara said she was in her dorm room. Give me a sec, I'll show you." I set my giant hiking bag down in the doorway while Darcy stares at me.

My shoulders are aching from the weight of my

backpack, and I'm breathing heavily, as if I ran up all fifteen flights of stairs. The longer I stand there, the more I realize that I don't hear Clara moving around inside the room. My mouth is dry and I know something is wrong, yet I insist on stretching my hand out to show Darcy the texts from Clara. Darcy ignores my phone and gestures me inside.

I take a few steps in, until I'm fully in Darcy's half of the room. I know it's hers because there's a poster of a sunset on the beach over her bed, with that cursed phrase: *Live, Laugh, Love!* Her bed is made and she's got throw pillows with messages on them too: *Never stop dreaming* and *Dance like no one's watching* and *Follow your heart.* I wonder if Darcy ever feels overwhelmed by all these commands. On her desk, there's a framed photograph of a waterfall, and that's got writing on it too. Nature wasn't majestic enough for Darcy; she needs *Live like you're dying* written over the rushing water. I wonder if I should tell her about the failed attempts to jump the Niagara Falls, and how barrels are very poor vehicles for traveling rushing water, and one should not in fact live like they are dying, because what's so bad about living like you're living?

Clara and Darcy's room is L-shaped, and Darcy lives in the first half. You have to walk through hers to get to Clara's side. She takes a few steps forward and turns the corner of the room, walking me over. I follow her lead, and then I'm staring at nothing.

The room is completely, utterly empty. There's a bare blue mattress on a wobbly bed frame, and next to it is an empty wooden desk. Gone are the string hot pepper lights, which Clara swore perfectly matched her orange sheets. I think back to how she'd spent weeks running her fingers over all the rugs at Bed Bath & Beyond, until she'd finally settled on a yellow furry floor mat. It's nowhere to be found. All I can see is cold gray tile, covered in dust. It's like Clara never lived here.

"But. But. Where is Clara's stuff? She didn't tell me she switched dorm rooms."

"She's not . . . She didn't." Darcy sighs. "I told her this was a bad idea from the start. Um . . . here, why don't you sit down," she says, pointing to the slick blue mattress.

I can already feel my stomach start to clench. No good news ever begins with taking a seat. Why is that a thing people do? Like bad news will be suddenly better because my butt is touching a hard surface? "No, thanks. I'd rather stand."

"Um. Okay," Darcy says, tucking her hair behind her ears. She looks behind her, at her poster, like she's gathering courage. "So." She takes a deep breath. "Clara left. More than a month ago?" she says. "Right when the semester started."

I frown. "What do you mean left?" I say. "She's been

texting me this whole time. All of us. She said she was right here, just a few hours ago."

"She said she needed to take time off school. She came back from break and cleared her stuff out." Her eyes grow wide as she realizes that this is news to me. "Do you need a minute?"

"No," I tell her. "I'm fine. I knew that Clara was gone. This was a joke," I say. "Ha ha, you fell for it!"

"Okay," Darcy says, her eyebrows furrowed. "Does Clara know about this joke?" she says, trailing me as I scamper out of Clara's half of the room. Or what used to be Clara's half. "Is she on campus with you?"

"Oh yeah, sure. Gotta go, bye!" I say, taking the longest steps possible, until I'm out of Darcy's room too and back in the hallway.

"Um, do you, like, need directions or something?" Darcy calls out from her doorway. "Let me lock my computer. I can help you get somewhere?"

"Sorry, I'm in a rush! Got a very important date. Meeting. Something." My words spill out, pure word association, only nothing I'm saying makes any sense. It doesn't matter, because there's no way Darcy can hear me. I'm already in front of the elevators, jamming my finger over the button, until my finger is bright red.

When I walk out of the building, the college magic is gone and I'm sagging under the weight of carrying my whole world on my back. Everything is horribly, utterly, disappointingly ordinary. And the magic is never coming back, because I've broken every rule. My fire raged out of control and I am the ashes. There will be no regrowth, no stronger season.

I text Clara back.

I know the truth. I'm never talking to you again.

📍 SAN FRANCISCO

21
Milagro

WHEN I TOLD Mrs. Johnson that Lulu was gone, she took off for Lulu's room, as if I might have been lying for fun. Once inside, she took her cardigan off, folded it on the desk in Lulu's former dorm room, closed her eyes, and took two deep breaths. When she opened her eyes again, she didn't say a single word. She grabbed me by the wrist and deposited me in my room. Mrs. Johnson must have sent out an alert to every University of Notre Dame class-room, storefront, and greasy food hideaway. One by one, each St. Agnes girl appeared in the hallway, grumbling as she dropped her cell phone off in the box outside Mrs. Johnson's room. All activities were canceled. All phones were confiscated until further notice, mine included. Mrs. Johnson wanted to know if Lulu was trying to reach me, without me playing interference.

After two hours of imprisonment, Mrs. Johnson announced to the hall that she had "some calls" to make. She appointed Amelia Brown as hall monitor. We were allowed bathroom breaks every two hours, accompanied by Amelia and no one else. A sad dinner of soggy tuna fish sandwiches and celery sticks was dropped off outside our doors. No one knew *why* we were stuck in our dorms, only that something very bad had happened.

The St. A girls formed two factions. At one end, Caroline, Amelia, and Genevieve were brainstorming why we were in lockdown. "Maybe there's an ax murderer on campus" and "Maybe Mrs. Johnson and Father Coleman are finally gonna get it on" were their two reigning theories. I shrugged and looked away when they asked me where Lulu was. At the other end, Maddie comforted a teary Gracelynn, quietly patting her back.

"Her grandma is really sick," Maddie told me when Gracelynn went to the bathroom. "She hates being out of touch with her family."

"I hope your grandmother is okay," I told Gracelynn before disappearing into my room. I stared at the white cinder-block walls of my room for five hours. My room smelled like wet towels and moldy shoes, the perfect setting for replaying my conversation with Lulu, trying to pinpoint where we went so wrong. I should have known this was important to her. I should have done something to stop her from leaving. I spent the whole night tossing and turning, dreaming of giant red vans snatching Lulu, Greyhound buses falling off the freeway, and spotted leopards pouncing on her giant backpack and dragging her back to their lair. At 6:00 a.m., I woke up to a sharp rap at my door. A thin-lipped Mrs. Johnson told me campus security had found Lulu in the University of Iowa's library. They had escorted her to the airport, and she would be landing in San Francisco a few hours after us. Mrs. Johnson would take her to her Stanford interview. I heaved a sigh of relief. Lulu was okay. Her future was secure, even if mine wasn't. I could feel every emotion sliding through my body. Who runs away to a library? Where the hell was Clara?! How in trouble was I? Mrs. Johnson had no time for my emotional journey.

"I left voice mails for your mother. Pack up your things. The bus leaves in an hour" was all she could muster.

The bus was silent. Everyone was too afraid to bring on the wrath of the newly emboldened Mrs. Johnson. Even Father Coleman seemed scared of her. He let her do the announcements—a few barked orders about carry-on bags and personal items—without any interruption or bragging about his boys. The boys were unusually quiet, each of them shooting furtive glances at me, but not because of what I looked like, or what I was hinting I could do. The St. A boys had been primed on Lulu's indiscretion. Each

319

one was jittery, bursting with a secret they couldn't wait to share with their St. Agnes partner. I figured Lucas would hammer a million questions my way, but when I sat next to him, he pulled me in for a hug and said simply, "I'm still mad at you. But I'm also really sorry about your sister." It was a small kindness that I didn't deserve.

Mrs. Johnson was the first to go through the security line at the airport, and that's when I found my opportunity. I muscled my way through my classmates, until I was just a few people behind Leo. I nodded toward the bathrooms next to our gate, and he nodded back. At the water fountain, I hurled question after question at him. *When did Lulu get this idea? Why would she want to go? How did she get the money? Why didn't you stop her?* Our water bottles were overflowing, spilling onto the tops of my pink-glitter-painted toes and Leo's beat-up sneakers.

Leo didn't have any answers. "I don't think she wants to talk to me," he said quietly. He capped his water bottle and took two steps back. I followed him to our gate and we sat next to each other while we waited. We didn't have our phones, a fact that Maddie kept insisting was "illegal property seizure and against our civil liberties. My dad's a lawyer."

"We all know," Amelia told her, rolling her eyes.

Maddie scowled at her and returned to whispering to Gracelynn.

Somewhere between the drizzly runway and where our jumbo jet soared off into the clouds, my worry turned to anger. Maybe it was the distance.

"Forty-two thousand feet," Leo told me when I asked. I wasn't really expecting an answer. Who knows how high a plane flies off the top of their head?

While we were in the air, anything could happen to Lulu and I wouldn't know until I landed. It was rude and inconsiderate of her to put all of us—especially me—through this emotional trauma. She was being moody, immature, and making bad decisions. She was acting like *me*.

Five hours is a really long flight. It's long enough for Mrs. Johnson to lecture me about Lulu's disappearance, and how I have jeopardized her entire future. She goes on and on about this summer program, and how Lulu is extraordinary. *Nothing like you.* She doesn't say it, but I can read the subtext. There will never be college in my future, because no St. Agnes teacher will ever write a recommendation letter for me. I'm probably already expelled—all Mrs. Johnson needs is Sister May's stamp of approval. That Notre Dame class with Lulu will be the first and only college course that I'll ever attend. I wish I had known that. Maybe I would have stuck around longer, or taken this whole trip more seriously. Lulu once told me that my natural environment had to involve boys, or I'd go extinct, like the dodo birds or the manatees. Now there will be nothing to challenge her theory. I thump my knees against the back of the seat in front of me, earning me the stink eye from a lady in a three-piece suit and red-rimmed glasses. I glare until she looks away. It's not my fault she can't afford first-class seats and has to sit with peasants like me.

The plane's aisle lights flash twice. The pilot's voice fills the air. "Folks, we are going to hit some turbulence. For your safety, please stay seated."

I tune him out and lean my head out the aisle. Mrs. Johnson clutches the two seats in front of her while kneeling to make her announcement, before thinking better of it. Her face is ashen, a gray that almost matches her beige cardigan. Her posture is nothing like a few hours ago, when she was a dictator. She's wobbly in the aisle as she makes a beeline for the bathroom, leaning too hard on the seats. With every turn and bump of the turbulence, she veers off into the opposite direction. Father Coleman's eyes dart between Mrs. Johnson's mouth and the thin plastic bag that hangs in the left pocket of her pants, until she reaches her destination.

When we land, Mrs. Johnson's purse erupts in a series of shrill beeps, bings, and the melodic tunes of the "Macarena" as all of our phones go off at once.

Bing! Bing! Bing! Bing! Bing! Bing!

My phone's alert is the loudest and most obnoxious, just like me. The messages have to be from Mami, who finally found service at the retreat center. I picture her standing under a Virgin Mary statue, jumping in the air with her phone in the hopes of getting an update from Mrs. Johnson. At baggage check, Mrs. Johnson returns our phones to us, one by one.

When she hands my phone to me, her eyes bore into mine. "A phone is a privilege. Do not make me regret this." I nod meekly. When I look at the screen, my stomach drops, the way Mrs. Johnson must have felt for the whole plane ride, like the ground is shaking below you and one missed step means your guts could be hurled onto an innocent bystander.

I have seventeen missed messages, all from Clara. Clara, who wasn't with Lulu when they found her. Clara, who hasn't talked to Mami in two months or called me of her own volition in months. I'm furious with Clara, angrier than I've ever been with anyone. What could possibly have been more important than meeting Lulu on campus? I slide my head into my crewneck St. Agnes sweatshirt, but my phone keeps buzzing in my hand as more messages pour in.

Do you know where Lulu is?

Where is Lulu?

Call me when you see this.

Call me.

Milagro!

I really messed up and I need your help. Can you do it for Lulu?

I don't know how to begin with the number of ways I have failed Lulu. I don't know what prompted Lulu to run away to Clara. She must have been hoping Clara would fix everything for her, the way Clara used to when we lived together. But Clara let her down. Just like me.

I press my phone to my head and text Clara back.

Let's talk after Piedmont College. Maybe in two hours? I'll try to sneak away.

Clara doesn't message me back on the van ride from the airport to Piedmont College. In fact, I don't get any texts from anyone in my family. The whole ride, Mrs. Johnson sits next to me with her shoulders hunched, her teeth gritted, and her thumb poised over her email app, refreshing it over and over again. When we hop off the van onto Piedmont's campus, she tells me, "Lulu made her flight. I thought you should know." She takes a deep breath. "I'll escort her from the airport myself. She'll be back with us in just a few hours." I want to hug Mrs. Johnson, but I settle for a meek nod instead. "Oh, and Milagro? Piedmont College is an art school. I always thought you would like it here. You know, before everything happened."

My mouth hangs open. "You did?"

She motions to the auditorium. "Go join your class-mates."

"Raise your hand if you speak more than one language."

Among the St. Agnes and St. Anthony group, only I raise my hand. My eyes widen as I take in the rest of Piedmont College's auditorium, full of hundreds of students. There are at least sixty hands up.

The admissions officer leading the information session tries another question. "Raise your hand if you came from out of state."

At that, everyone in our group raises their hands, but then again, so does almost everyone in the auditorium. The admissions officer nods his head approvingly and crosses his arms over his structured gray blazer, his thumbs pointing up to his pink-striped bow tie, which pops against his dark brown skin. Between his shiny leather loafers and his neatly trimmed gray beard, he looks like he belongs in a Distinguished Gentleman Catalog, or a fancy library somewhere, reading a book full of words I don't know. I can't help but smile when I notice that the stripes in his bow tie match his pocket square.

"Raise your hand if you're visiting from out of the country," he continues, his deep voice waking up everyone from their midday grogginess.

I expect the auditorium to be stumped, except there are five separate families who came all the way out to this tiny art school for a tour. I've never even left the country. What would it be like to study with people who don't know every embarrassing thing you ever did, beginning from the time you were six years old?

Mrs. Johnson leaves the information session early to go pick up Lulu. She doesn't look at me. She only gives laser eyes to Father Coleman, who sits up in his seat and salutes her exit, like a colonel in the military. I stare at my phone, torn about whether to text Lulu or not. Her interview is a few hours away and I don't want to mess her up. Whatever I did was enough to send her packing, only to be let down by her other sister. When I told Mrs. Johnson that I tricked Lulu into going to Iowa and seeking comfort in the arms of our older sister, it was both true and also couldn't be further from the truth. I put my phone away in my pocket.

My classmates around me are falling asleep. Two rows in front of me, three of the St. Anthony boys are watching a basketball game on someone's phone and one row in front of me, I spot Lucas rapid-fire texting with Jared. Within minutes, even Father Coleman is scrolling through the headlines on CNN. He's too busy reading to notice Caroline, Amelia, and Genevieve sneaking out of the auditorium. I'm the only one who is captivated by everything this fancy admissions man is saying. Maybe it's because the session doesn't start off with bragging about the stats of the students or how many sports trophies the school has earned. There's no extended monologue about the buildings on campus or alums who graduated decades ago. Instead, he talks about this idea that people are concentric circles, made up of more than their major, or what they want to be, or what they do on the weekends. When he stares out at us and says we have potential to be more than one thing, and that we are extraordinary before we get to campus, not *because* we're on campus, I want to believe him.

He talks about how college doesn't have to be a stale manufacturing line: input a premed student, output a doctor. According to him, the biochemistry and psychology majors *need* the studio art and philosophy majors to make new breakthroughs in their fields, and vice versa. One isn't better than the other, and they are definitively worse when they are sequestered.

All my life, I've thought of art school as a destination for rich kids. The kind of place you go if you want to take your clothes off and paint random splotches on a wall and call it "experimental art," or spend a summer in Paris eating croissants and talking about dead philosophers whose ideas should have gone extinct with the dinosaurs. At Piedmont, the creative majors pair their studio time with practical courses in business, entrepreneurship, and communications. No one told me you don't have to choose a lane. My paths can merge.

After the session, Father Coleman walks me over to Katori Hall. "Mrs. Johnson will pick you up from this doorway in an hour and a half." His eyes bore into mine. "Don't even think about any funny business. The rest of the group will be walking the Golden Gate Bridge while you're attending another college course to make up for your actions. I hope you use this as a real learning experience."

I nod solemnly. After Lulu's stunt, I'm lucky to not be attached by a leash and dragged around with Father Coleman or Mrs. Johnson. Both of them decided that tourist sightseeing would be an unfair reward considering my actions, so they decided to let Piedmont College babysit me.

The lecture hall is massive and *old*. It's full of dark wooden seats, the kind that you have to push down if you want to sit in them. Each seat comes with a tiny desk that you lift up from the side and pull down across your lap. The classroom is big enough to require stairs to make it down to where the professor stands. I pick a seat in the last row possible, as far away from the front as I can get. I can't stop flipping through the pages in my notebook, even though they're all blank. As the students file into the class, they fill up the first two rows, making me look even more like a clueless creep.

One of the students walks to the front of the classroom and sets down an iced coffee and a pile of papers. She's wearing a psychedelic-print button-down shirt that she's tucked into her purple pencil skirt. Her skin is caramel brown and her oversized cat-eye glasses are bright yellow. I watch as she writes the date on the board, along with "IDE-ATE" and "SCAMPER." The words might as well be in German, because they mean nothing to me. I squirm in my chair, crossing and uncrossing my arms. I finally understand why Mrs. Johnson left me here. She wants to torture me.

The student looks up at the room and claps her hands. "All right, let's go ahead and get started."

Wait. She's the *teacher?* She doesn't look anything like the blazer-clad professor from Notre Dame, with a paunchy belly and thinning hair. I thought college professors were all old and stuffy—and *white*.

"I see we have a new student," she says, pointing straight at me.

Thirty pairs of eyes whip around and stare. My mouth freezes in a perfect O. I can feel my lipstick cracking at the corners.

"Why don't you come on down," she says, pointing to a seat a few rows in front of her. "We won't bite, I promise."

I want to say no, but that would require talking. I nod

shyly and make my way down the stairs. *One foot in front of the other,* I chant in my head. I don't want to spill down the steps like dominoes. I make it to the second row and sit next to a girl with a neon-green backpack and ancient Doc Martens. She gives me a quick smile and turns her attention back to the professor.

Professor Psychedelic begins her lecture with the history of color theory, and I'm already dreaming of coffee. I rest my fingers on my arm, ready to pinch myself to stay awake. I've got a bag of gum in my pocket too, just in case pinching doesn't work. But it turns out that color theory is a fancy way to study colors, and Professor P is interested in the design implications. She walks us through several apps, pointing out button colors and text colors that make us pay attention, keep us hooked, wanting more. It's stuff I've never thought about before, millions of decisions that are silent but powerful.

As the lecture goes on, I'm filling up my notebook, racing to get all the facts down. My hand actually *hurts* from taking notes, something that has never, ever happened to me before.

When Professor P clicks to the last slide, a tiny bit of disappointment sinks in. For the last hour, I've been lost in colors and how the brain works, far away from a reality where every member of my family is mad at each other. Everyone around me is packing up, so I duck down and shove my notebook back into my bag too.

"Are you coming?" my seatmate says, over my head. "I'm pumped. I haven't seen the new exhibits yet."

I pop my head back up. "Exhibits?"

"In Piedmont's gallery. We're ending class early today, so we can see the new exhibits and design something inspired by the color palettes. If you go right after class, Professor Ekowanjo usually treats us to coffee afterward."

"Like with her own money?"

The girl laughs. "Yeah! She knows we're broke college students."

I bite my lip, remembering Father Coleman's stern warning. I don't want to risk his wrath, or prolong whatever punishment Mrs. Johnson has cooking up. "I can't."

"Next time!" she says, and then scrambles up the stairs to join the rest of the students.

After a few minutes, I'm the only one left in the giant lecture hall. It's quiet enough to pretend I'm a regular student here, not a high school kid held against her will. Mrs. Johnson has always said that college is a place to "find yourself." I always thought that was stupid advice. What's there to find out? But it turns out there are hidden pockets for me to find. I could be the kind of person interested in big ideas and niche topics. The more I learn about *me*, the more I want to stake a claim, point to something and say I did this. I made this. Me.

Creak.

I glance up. The door of the lecture hall slowly opens. I straighten up and pull my belongings closer to me. Class isn't supposed to be over for another forty-five minutes, but maybe someone forgot a book, or is looking for a quiet space to study.

The lights are bright, so I'm squinting and trying to make out if it's a student or a professor. As the person steps down the stairs, out of the lights, my mouth drops open. I rub my eyes twice, to make sure I haven't gone fully delusional. But when I take my hands off my face, there's no mistaking the person coming down the stairs.

It's Clara.

22
Lulu

IN THE RIDE from the University of Iowa to the Des Moines airport, Clara texted ten times.

"Don't you want to get that?" the campus security guard said, his eyebrows furrowed in the rearview mirror. I stared out the van window and shoved my phone deeper into my pocket. Clara called fifteen times before my flight landed in San Francisco. I silenced those too. When I landed in the San Francisco airport, Mrs. Johnson's strict instructions were to stay quarantined in the viewing galley and not speak to anyone. I'm still ignoring Clara's calls and messages, choosing to pull apart an enormous Cinnabon rather than talk to her. I've spent what feels like centuries watching airplanes take off and land again, each one guided in and out of the runway by neon-clad airline workers. Sometimes the wind snatches the light sticks out of their hands and they whoop and jump up to catch them. They pile hundreds of suitcases on rolling dollies, loading luggage on and off conveyor belt ramps. Do they get tired of doing the same thing, over and over again? Maybe there's solace in accepting a process that never changes or disappoints.

All I wanted was a glimpse at a life outside of Baltimore. Believing things could change is like picking a fight with gravity, or wishing the glaciers would stop melting. I have no control. My life is no different than the suitcases on the runway. Picked up and shipped around, tossed in one direction and another, no real will of their own. I pull out my notebook, ignoring the smears of icing that my cinnamon bun left behind. I flip through my pages of notes, running my fingers over all the stats. I rub my thumb over where Leo's green pen fact-checked me. My cinnamon roll feels more like a rotten apple in my stomach.

I lean my head against the cold metal chair and sigh, letting my icing-covered fingers dangle by my sides. I don't know what's going to happen now that Clara has apparently dropped out of college and I am certainly expelled from the only place I love more than the library. When I dial Mami's number, it doesn't even ring. It goes straight to voice mail. She's probably on her way home from the retreat, and there's no way Mrs. Johnson hasn't gotten to her first. I will never be allowed to leave the house ever again. I will need a chaperone for the rest of my life.

I hear a very familiar *tap tap tap tap* across the linoleum tile. When I look up, Mrs. Johnson is marching toward me, her arms pumping at her sides as she races across the wide center aisle of the airport, dashing around travelers before she reaches me. She doubles over, gasping for air, and holds a finger up to me, the universal sign for "please be quiet." The excuses that have been swimming around in my brain disappear. I don't know how to say "Sorry, I ran away so my sister could fix things, but it turns out she's a pathological liar and I'm all alone in the world." As I wait for her to expel me from St. Agnes and end my life as I know it, all I can think about is Mami. I can practically feel her arms wrapped tight around me and Milagro, thanking us for coming back home. I can imagine weeks of sleepless nights on the couch, blaming herself for Clara's selfishness. I'll never be able to leave now. Maybe it's for the best.

Mrs. Johnson gasps and says, "You Zavala girls don't make things easy."

"I'm sorry, Mrs. Johnson. I don't know what to say." My head is hanging low and I'm whispering. "I know I'm expelled. I'm so sorry." My fingers brush against the tops of my jeans, rubbing over the threads of denim. I try to focus on the rough fabric, rather than the mountain of trouble that is about to collapse on me.

"We're lucky your flight landed with enough time to

get you to Stanford." Mrs. Johnson glances down at her papers in her hands and waves at me to stand up. "But we need to move." She grabs my giant mountaineer backpack and slings it over her purple cardigan. She nearly bowls over from the weight, before straightening up and resuming her purposeful strides. She walks a few feet and turns around. "Let's go, Luz. We don't want to be late."

"What?" I chase after her. "The Stanford interview? That's still happening? But aren't I expelled? And in big trouble?"

Mrs. Johnson calls over her shoulder. "Of course the interview is still happening. Milagro told me everything. I know that it wasn't your fault that you went to Iowa. She told you that you had to go." Mrs. Johnson's voice is muffled by my backpack. "You could have told us that she's been bullying you."

I stop walking.

She whirls around, nearly knocking out a businessman on his phone. "This can't be easy to hear, but she's going to be in a lot of trouble for leading you astray. She will be facing immediate expulsion when we land back in Baltimore." Mrs. Johnson shakes her head. "I told Sister May that good grades don't mean everything. Even with her high GPA, Milagro doesn't have the attitude of an honors student. But you don't need to worry about that. We're so happy that you made it to San Francisco in one piece."

"Milagro what?" My mouth drops open. "What do you mean that Milagro doesn't have the attitude?" My shoulders feel bare without my backpack slung across them.

"Sister May thought this trip would knock some sense into her." Mrs. Johnson glances at her watch and speeds up her pace. "Technically she had the GPA to qualify for the trip, after taking everyone's vacation schedule into account. But there's more to being an honors student than good grades."

"But. But . . . ," I stutter. "Milagro told me that she was on this trip because of detention. She didn't mention . . ."

Mrs. Johnson starts speed walking again. "Luz, your sister is a troubled young woman. She has a serious problem with the truth. But right now, you need to focus on your interview. This could mean big things for you. And your future."

Mrs. Johnson says this like my family and my future can't possibly be linked. Vertebrate or invertebrate. Mammals or fish. To pick one is to reject the other. Two points on a graph, never meant to cross.

She gestures her hand out to me, waving me along. "Come on, Luz. Let's go."

Outside the airport, the sky is a brilliant blue shade that I thought only existed in Milagro's nail polish collection and Mami's oilskin tablecloths. There isn't a single cloud in the sky. The air is cool enough to keep my giant sweatshirt on. I should be leaping in the air with glee. I'm still Lulu the Genius, the girl with all the answers. Except for one: Why would Milagro cover for me? My cheeks burn when I remember all the words I yelled at her. I called her stupid when I didn't mean it. Even if she did tell Maddie and Gracelynn about the embarrassing things I've done this week, it doesn't mean they weren't the truth. Back at the café, she just wanted to help me with Leo, in her Milagro way. And now she's still helping me, lying to protect me. While I'm jumping to conclusions and expecting the worst, overcome with emotions. We're not so different—Milagro and me—only I never would have made the sacrifice that she did.

Mrs. Johnson and I climb into a brand-new airport shuttle. We're the only people, aside from a bus driver, who ignores us for talk radio. She's got her eyes closed and she's taking measured breaths, but judging by the tight grip on her bag, I can tell she's not asleep.

"Mrs. Johnson?" I whisper. "Shouldn't there be someone else coming with us? A St. Anthony boy? Leo Joseph?"

"No, he canceled weeks ago. Father Coleman is very disappointed." Even though her eyes are closed, she can't mask her glee. "He said they send a student to Stanford every year, but his gentlemen will have to wait until next year." She has a smug grin on her face. "The spot is yours, Luz. I can feel it."

I lean back in my seat and stare at the ceiling. How could I have gotten everything so, so wrong?

When our airport shuttle bus rolls onto Stanford's campus, I'm convinced our driver has made a colossal mistake. The entrance looks like an exclusive resort, only everyone is wearing oversized sweatshirts and backpacks instead of tiny bikinis and Hawaiian-print shirts. There are palm trees everywhere—at least two hundred varieties, according to their website. I always imagined they'd be crammed in a tiny community garden on campus, not scattered all over for everyone to enjoy. The tall palms wave their leaves in the breeze as students hop in and out of the shade. There are boys on skateboards and girls on skinny bikes, a team of sweaty, shirtless runners darting around slowpokes like me and Mrs. Johnson.

By the time we reach the giant wooden doors of the Archer Williamson Environmental Research Center, I'm wishing I was back in the San Francisco hanger loft, watching the airplanes with my cinnamon bun. Mrs. Johnson is wrong. I'm not a world-renowned scientist or a prize-winning chess player. I haven't started a company or saved the world, and neither has anyone in my family. While Mrs. Johnson announces our arrival to the secretary, I shrug a few times and hop in place. I swing my fists by my sides, trying to pump myself up like a Parma wallaby. The secretary peers over her glasses at me and I quickly correct myself, pulling myself to a standstill.

Mrs. Johnson gives me a gentle shove when the secretary calls my name. I walk up reluctantly, following him into a hallway and stepping into an office. The door closes quietly behind me. I'm staring at the ground and the tiniest bit of dirt right below my left ankle. I can't even keep myself clean—how can I possibly have a conversation with an expert biologist? This was all a big mistake. I tense up, wondering if it's too late to double back out the door, hop in the van, and fly myself back to Baltimore. I'll take whatever punishment Mami has for me, as long as it saves me from embarrassing myself in front of this distinguished professor.

"Luz Zavala?"

I look up. A man with frazzled hair and deep-set wrinkles stares back at me. He's got a streak of brilliant blue in his white hair, which is pulled tight to the bottom of his head into a ponytail that trails down his wrinkled blazer. My eyes widen. He looks like he wandered off the stage of an eighties cover band performance, not like he's responsible for single-handedly revolutionizing our nation's recycling program.

"Please, sit." He gestures to the chair across the desk from him. "My name is Professor Randall. Let me tell you a little about the Stanford Summer Scholars Program." I nod and tuck my hands under my thighs. Professor Randall's eyebrows go up when he talks, reaching nearly the top of his scalp while he describes the research and programming available to the summer scholars. I can't stop staring at the space between his eyebrows and his scalp. His deep-set wrinkles would make a bulldog jealous.

Professor Randall peers over me. "I hear you want to study environmental science," he says.

My stomach churns and there's an awkward silence where I stare at anything but him—the gadgets on his desk, the gleaming awards behind him on his shelf, the framed diplomas on his walls. The silence lingers on.

Oh. He meant that as a question, not a statement.

"Yes?" I clear my throat and repeat myself, this time a little louder. "Yes. I do. I want to study marine biology." Relieved to have survived the first question, I sink into my seat. My feet barely touch the green fuzzy carpet below them.

His mustache twitches and then he breaks out into a grin. "Is that so? Are you familiar with—"

I brace myself for a trick question, an easy way to weed out the true scientists from the diligent but hopelessly uncreative note takers. Any second now, he's going to realize I'm a phony.

"Phosphorus management?"

I perk up. "Yes! Last year, I visited the Chesapeake Bay Waste Management site to talk to scientists about how they distinguish legacy phosphorus from the phosphorus in stormwater and farmland drainage."

Professor Randall nods. "Go on."

I bite my lip, not fully convinced that I could tell this professor anything new. I think about Milagro sitting on our bed, holding a compact mirror in one hand and a shiny tube of lipstick in the other. "I may not be the first to wear red lipstick, but I can be the most memorable," she always says. Back in Indiana, she told me the program was perfect for me. She was so confident in the café, her eyes were sparkling. For once, I choose to believe Milagro. I open my mouth and start to talk.

For the next hour, Professor Randall and I trade insights and questions about pollution and watershed activity. The minutes stream by so fast, the way a dam processes more water than you can even imagine. I'm swimming with the big fish, and I'm not even sinking. When Mrs. Johnson pokes her head in and says it's time to rejoin my classmates, Professor Randall begs her for special permission so we can go see his labs. His tour is way better than the one at MonU. I'm actually meeting people doing work, instead of oohing and aahing over unused lab equipment. Dr. Randall's students are bent over five monitors, each one loaded with a harder math problem than the next, or puzzling over an iPad with a simulator running. I snap a photo for Leo, until I remember that I yelled at him. He must hate me. Meanwhile, my feelings for him haven't changed. My shoulders slump, and I tuck my phone back in my pocket.

At the end of the second hour, when Mrs. Johnson insists that I have to go, Dr. Randall walks us both out of the research center. He shakes my hand and says, "Good luck with the rest of your studies, Luz. Stanford would be lucky to have you." He nods to Mrs. Johnson and turns back into his office.

Even though I'm cool as a cucumber, I want to explode with joy. I feel like cartwheeling across campus or having a dance party in the quad. But my resident party maker isn't here. She's in trouble, because of what I did. And I'm left with no one to celebrate with.

Mrs. Johnson listens to the news on the way back, but I can't focus on trade agreements between political leaders. I need to figure out a peace treaty of my own. It's time to make things right with Milagro.

23
Milagro

"WHAT ARE YOU doing here?!" My mouth drops open. I rub my eyes to make sure that I'm not dreaming. Clara—or some version of her—is coming down the stairs toward me. My eyes bug out. I feel like Mami whenever I come home a few minutes after curfew, her eyes scanning my body to see if she can spot a difference.

Clara's natural curls are out in full force, piled high into a messy bun on top of her head. Her hair is high enough to show off what I think is a shaved undercut. I squint, but it's hard to know for sure under the yellow lights of the lecture hall. Clara's clone has a sparkly nose piercing that glints like a tiny sequin on her nose. "¡Qué sucio!" I can hear Mami exclaiming when she finds out. She's wearing a knit crop top that rises and falls, exposing her belly button

344

with each long step she takes down the stairs. I don't know this stranger.

"You're here! You're here!" Clara's Clone yelps. "I can't believe it!" She races up to me and wraps her arms around me tight. I might as well be a mannequin, for all the words I can muster. The only parts of Clara that are familiar are her warm brown eyes, long sweeping lashes, and the scent of cucumber in her hair. Clara's top slides off her shoulder and I spot the hint of black ink, a new tattoo. Santa Clara is the patron saint of cliché rebellion. Except the more I look at her, the more I realize it's not cliché. Clara's triple ear piercings have a set of prayer hands and a tiny cross, and she's wearing her cross necklace, tucked under her shirt. She's the same. I think.

I look down at my own worn sweatshirt and jeans and back at Clara. How did I become the boring sister?

"Milagro. Aren't you going to say something?" She looks me up and down before talking right over me, like she always does. "You must have so many questions. I know it's probably confusing, but—"

"You're supposed to be in Iowa. *Studying.*" I stand up and pull my books together. "Why are you *here*?" I point to the auditorium around me. "Or even in this state! We are really, really far from Iowa. Which is where Lulu went, to find YOU." I'm angry, way more angry than when I saw

Mystery Boobs on Pablo's phone. This feels more hurtful, because it's not just me who Clara lied to. It's Lulu too. I jab my finger at Clara. "Except you're here. And you never told us. You're a liar. Go back to Iowa."

She lets out a barking laugh, loud and echoey through the auditorium. "God no. I never want to go back." She shudders.

My jaw drops open again. This, more than the multiple piercings or the suspicious absence of a bra, seems like the most radical change of all. Santa Clara is breaking the first commandment—thou shalt not take the Lord's name in vain.

"How did you even find me?" We're sitting in the lobby of the lecture hall, waiting for Mrs. Johnson to come collect me, her prisoner. I take a sip of my lemonade, staring at Clara. I still can't believe she's here.

Clara looks at me, surprised. "You texted me you were here, remember? And Lulu sent me the itinerary months ago."

"But what are you doing here?" I wave my arms around Piedmont. "Not here, but in San Francisco?"

"It wasn't for me." Clara shakes her head, staring at the hulking chocolate chip cookie in her hand.

"What wasn't for you?" I reach over and grab it, taking a big bite.

"College. Iowa. Biology. All of it. It was nothing like home." She sighs and tucks her hands under her thighs.

"Oh yeah. Sure. You missed us so much, you ran away to another state. One where we don't live." I roll my eyes. Nowhere in her halting speech has there been a good enough explanation for how she ended up in San Francisco.

She leans down and talks to the green linoleum floor in front of her. "The first few weeks of college, all I could think about was Mami's escabeche, and whether someone was unplugging her curling iron, and if Lulu was remembering her bus pass. But you guys seemed so fine. Better than fine."

"Yeah," I say dryly. "Imagine that, I can be responsible."

"And then I flunked my first test."

"You?!" My mouth drops wide open.

"Perfect me." She crosses her arms over her chest. "And then I flunked another one. And not just bio. Chem and calculus too. I got so behind on everything, before I knew it, my GPA was a pathetic 1.5. I was on academic probation and at risk of suspension, all while you, Lulu, and Mami were thriving without me."

I suck my breath in. None of us has ever failed a class before.

"I almost lost my scholarship. I almost lost everything." Clara's head hangs low and her voice gets soft. "I didn't know how to tell Mami, but it turns out the school told

347

her. We got in a huge fight. She wanted me to go back and get better grades, but I was done."

"That fight over winter break?"

Clara nods.

"Mami wanted you to go back?" My voice is incredulous. "After all her talk of Ms. College? And how Baltimore was better?"

"She said I was giving up too easily, but she doesn't understand that I wasn't giving up on my dream. I was giving myself space to find another one. After winter break, I went back to Iowa and withdrew from the semester. That week, I heard from Father Alfonzo, and it felt like a sign that I was doing the right thing. I used to volunteer with him at St. Agnes. He told me that there was a volunteer organization in San Francisco that needed Spanish translators. They let me stay at the monastery in exchange for volunteering. It was only supposed to be for a week, but there's always work available." She bites her lip and looks down at her hands. "No one has asked me to leave, so I've been here for six weeks."

I rake my fingers through my curls, trying to imagine how Clara could have lied to us for so long. "But all of our video calls. You were in the library!" I think about all the conversations I had with Clara on the bus, in my room, in the lobby of St. Agnes while I waited for Pablo to pick me up.

"There are college libraries in San Francisco too." Clara

looks up at me, brown eyes full of tears.

"Did Mami know too? She was so mad at you." My mind is whirling, remembering the frosty silence between the two of them. "Have you been lying to her all this time too?"

"Mami knows everything," Clara says with a sigh.

"What!" I yelp. "She never told us." I start to chip away at the faded nail polish on my nails. "She never said a word."

"She said I had to tell you myself. She wouldn't do it for me." At this, Clara doubles over and cries, her shoulders shaking and her sniffles echoing in the lobby of the building.

It's not something I'm proud of, but deep down, I've wished for this moment. One tiny beat when Clara reveals she's just as human as we are. But seeing Clara actually break down in front of me is awful. I don't feel a single ounce of satisfaction; I just feel sad. I gently rub her back. Her shirt is soft under my palm. Clara sits back up, wiping at her eyes and tugging her shirt down. "Once I started, it snowballed. It was too hard to tell the truth. I convinced myself it would be easier to explain in person. I knew Lulu would be here eventually, because of the trip. Then when you joined, my plan seemed perfect."

"But why wait for so long?"

"I guess I was embarrassed. But it was more than that. I wanted you and Lulu to experience the college trip without me and my baggage. I didn't want you to believe college wasn't possible for you, just because I failed at it."

She gestures to the auditorium in front of us. "There's this whole big world outside of Baltimore. You and Lulu deserve to see it. You'd both be great at it. Better than me."

"You mean Lulu would be great at it," I say pointedly. "You only ever talk to me about Pablo. You never talk to me about *anything* but boys."

Clara puts her hand on her forehead. "Ughhh. Of course I mean you too! I didn't talk to you about anything because I was so sure you'd know I was lying. Your bullshit detector is one of the things that I envy the most about you. That and your honesty."

My phone buzzes and I snooze it. "You're really jealous of me?"

"Wait. It could be Lulu." Clara reaches over me and unlocks my phone. "See?" She holds the screen in front of my face. "It's Mrs. Johnson. She says they're running late. You're supposed to take a cab straight to the dorms."

"How do you know my passcode?"

"I'm your big sister. Of course I know your code." Clara stands up. "C'mon. We have to go."

"We? I'm already in big trouble." I point to her nose. "And don't you have somewhere cooler to be? Like a rave or some kind of underground tattoo party? Is that thing even real?"

Clara's checks redden and she ignores my question. Her voice is firmer. "I need to fix things with Lulu."

My shoulders hunch up toward my ears and my gut clenches as I remember Lulu's words. "No way. Lulu is furious with me. I can't imagine how mad she's going to be at you. Do this another time."

Clara shakes her head. "If I've learned anything from this year, it's that you have to confront secrets head-on, or they'll slowly destroy everything you care about."

I shudder. "Okay, but do I have to be there when Lulu finds out? She's going to go ballistic."

She laughs, this time for real, her cheeks reaching up toward the sky. "Don't worry. I'll do all the hard work." She reaches her hand out and I take it. Her chipped black nail polish—something I never would have picked out for her in a million years—seems as natural on her as the tiny scar that's always been on her pinky.

Clara leads us out the door. "You have to come back to try the matcha tea. It's out-of-this-world good," she calls over her shoulder.

I go cross-eyed and utter the word *matcha* under my breath. Underneath her new, rebellious veneer, Clara is still the snooty tea drinker I remember. I clench my fingers, my nails digging tiny half-moons into my palms as I'm flooded with homesickness. Not for how things used to be—New Clara is already a serious improvement from Old Clara—but for my actual home. I miss Mami's nosy "¿Qué estás tipeando?" when I'm lost in my phone screen and no longer responding to her. I want Tía Lochita's salty hot cachangas with a layer of strawberry jam to balance out the fried perfection, and Lulu's documentaries blaring at full volume. I'm ready to go home.

Our cab winds through the city, all while Clara charms our driver, a gray-haired sixty-year-old San Francisco native. They chat in a mixture of English and Spanglish. I've got my nose pressed against the window, watching as hundreds of stores and restaurants stream past me. There are sign-posts advertising foods I've never heard of before, busy runners darting in and out of traffic, and bikers with thick muscular calves zooming past us. I'm too entranced to join Clara's debates with the driver over who makes the best pollo a la brasa in the city, whether Cuban flan is better than Peruvian flan, and where to find discounted Inca Kola. Midway through our journey to the dorms, Clara asks him, "Can we make a quick stop at this address?"

"Clara. I can't get in more trouble!" I hiss at her.

"It's just one quick stop. We'll be back before Mrs. Johnson is." She leans over and tells the driver, "Just give us five minutes."

"Are you sure we're in the right place?" I ask when our car pulls up to a store with multicolored donkey piñatas hanging from the faded yellow-striped awning. I run my fingers over the delicate tissue fringes, which dangle a few inches above my head.

"Just get in here, will you?" She ducks into the door.

The clerks of "JUANITA'S JOYERÍA Y FIESTA SUPPLIES" shout when I walk into the store. "¡Qué bonita! ¡Qué buena suerte, esos rulos." The ladies gesture to my curls and smile at me. "Debes cuidarlos," one of them tells me. She points to the avocado bowl by the register. I shake my head. "No gracias." I remember Carmen's abuelita's wild hair remedies. I'm not putting avocado gunk in my curls. The clerks shrug and turn back to each other, pointing to the small television in the corner that's playing some dating television show. They jeer the men, calling them names I've never even heard. I'm giggling to myself watching them, while Clara is marching up and down the aisles of the dusty store. I've never heard Spanish like this in the wild. Aside from the very respectful and curse-free Spanish of Mami's and Tía Lochita's houses, or the front seat of Carmen's abuelita's aging station wagon, my world is always in English, all the time.

"We'll take that 'CONGRATULATIONS' balloon arrangement." Clara reappears by my side and points to a banner of gold-foil letters as big as my torso. They hang above the counter, casting a shadow over all of us.

"¿Cuál es la ocasión?" one of the ladies asks us, in between snaps of her pink bubble gum.

"My sister aced her interview. She's going to her dream school this summer."

The store clerks clap and move in with hugs, wrapping their arms around me. "¡Qué excelente! Tu madre debe de estar tan orgullosa."

"Not me!" I squirm out of their embrace and give Clara the stink eye. "What are you doing? You don't even know how it went. I don't want to be a part of this!"

Clara's eyes turn serious. She's got her arms rigid against her sides as she says, "You and I both know there's no known—or unknown—universe where Lulu didn't ace that interview. Take this." She shoves streamers and paper confetti of sparkly little alligators. "It's as close to nature themed as we can get."

Clara had been so confident in the store. Her head tall, she bossed the clerk around, asking for a little extra air in the balloons, telling me to tie my shoes, slipping the cab driver a $20 bill for waiting for us. All that confidence disappeared the second we broke into Lulu's dorm room. Now Clara is pacing up and down the room and squeezing her elbows, muttering to herself, and undoing and redoing her ponytail. Every two minutes, she fidgets with the balloons, adjusting the letters and creating an awful squeaking noise with the Mylar. After the seventh time, I threaten to pop all the balloons if she doesn't stop. It's hard to imagine she ever had the guts to pull off a cross-country move, let alone keep it a secret.

"Clara. Is it real?" I point to the septum piercing in her nose. "Do you like it?"

She balls her hands into fists and shakes them by her side. "I'm just trying new things, okay?"

"So it's not real?" I ask from my perch on Lulu's dorm bed.

"It's a clip-on, okay?!" Clara is exasperated enough to stop her pacing. "I can take it out whenever I want." She glares at me.

I twirl a curl in my hair. "Maybe you should take . . ."

The doorknob turns. Clara and I both lock eyes. We've got our fingers crossed in front of us, and then Clara makes a last-minute mad dash to the closet. There's no time to drag her out. The door creaks open and the *Congratulations* letters make a break for it, an *A* and an *L* zooming toward Lulu's head. She reaches up and grabs it, pulling it close to her and studying the letters. I hold my breath.

"For me?" she says, hugging the balloon close to her chest.

I'm staring at her, searching for clues that might reveal how her interview went, but her clothes are just as practical and wrinkly as any other day. Lulu could win the lottery, accept a Nobel Peace Prize, or pull off a bank heist, and she'd do it all in her St. Agnes sweatshirt. "Of course!"

I tell her, before rushing in for a hug and wrapping my arms around her. I bury my head in her frizzy hair, inhaling Lulu's familiar scent of laundry and freshly sharpened pencils. "I'm sorry. I should have known how important this was to you. You didn't have to disappear. Don't ever do that again!"

Lulu burrows into me, hugging me back. "Mrs. Johnson told me you took the blame for me. You didn't have to do that." Lulu's voice is muffled.

"Of course I did. You were meant for that program. I meant it. And you're meant for all of this." I gesture to the whole room. "College, dorm life, all of it."

"It could be you too." She pulls away from me and smiles. "Not just me. Mrs. Johnson told me you're on this trip for good grades, not detention. It could be both of us. I tried to tell her that I went to Iowa on my own. Not because you bullied me." Lulu frowns. "I think she's starting to believe me. I'm going to work on it."

I feel a glimmer of hope in me, one I'm trying desperately to ignore. I know that no matter what Lulu says, there's no way I'm *not* expelled from St. Agnes. I hug her tighter, and then I remember and jump away. "Wait! What about your interview?"

Lulu steps away. Her wild, wide grin gives everything away. "It was so cool." She points her fingers to her head and mimes small explosions. "They have the coolest tech.

I talked to a research scientist." She hugs her arms and says shyly, "They really liked me."

I clap my hands for her. "I'm so freakin' excited for you!"

"Surprise!" Clara leaps out from the closet and shouts. She tosses the tiny alligators in the air. They rain down around us, falling in our hair and the insides of Lulu's sweatshirt hoodie. The room is silent as Lulu and I stare at Clara's jazz hands, wide-open eyes, and smile that's frozen in place, like a jack-o'-lantern.

Lulu freezes and pulls away. An avalanche of emotion wipes every ounce of joy off her face. Lulu's mouth is a straight line across her face. She's looking at the flickering fluorescent bulbs, the scuff marks on her sneakers, the detailing on my tote bag, anything but Clara.

"Lulu. I'm so sorry. I can explain everything." Clara is smiling and her eyes look so hopeful. "I'm so happy for your interview." She takes a step toward Lulu, then thinks better of it, falling back to her spot against the wall.

"What is *she* doing here?" Lulu points at Clara and looks at me. "Did you know she dropped out of college too? Or am I the only clueless one?" She scowls.

I shake my head and raise my hands up. "I swear, I didn't know until two hours ago."

"I can explain," Clara pleads. She waves her hands at Lulu. "If you'll just hear me out, I can explain everything. Please."

"Explain what? Why you've been lying to us this whole time? Why you've abandoned us for who knows where? Why you've got that gross nose ring when it is only going to impede your breathing pattern?" Lulu makes a fake retching noise and takes a step back, closer to the door.

I snort. Clara and Lulu both turn and glare. "Sorry! Ignore me." I sink back onto the bed.

"You have every right to be mad. It was wrong of me to lie. I should have told you the truth. But I can explain. It was something I had to do."

Lulu sneers. "Wow. That must be nice. But what about us? Did you ever think about us? About Mami? About everything you left behind? People didn't stop needing you, just because you went to go 'find' yourself." Lulu's quote fingers are out in full force. I don't envy Clara. I expect her to crumple in front of Lulu's angry words, to double over and cry the way she did at Piedmont College.

"Lulu, if you could just—" I interject, fashioning myself the peacemaker in this dormitory war.

"No, Milagro." Clara stands up taller and puts a hand up in my direction. "She has a right to be mad. I hurt you, and I can't force an apology before you're ready." She looks at Lulu. "You're right."

"I am?" Lulu stares back at Clara in disbelief. "Yes. I am." She clears her throat. "And I'm not ready. To forgive you." She's got one hand on the doorknob and seems ready to bolt.

"I accept that," Clara says. "I'm ready to work hard to make it up to you. But even when you're mad at me, I'm still your older sister." She twists one of the studs in her ears as she waits for Lulu's response.

My jaw is on the ground. Who is this woo-woo version of Clara, standing up for herself, while still owning up for her mistakes? Usually Clara is a sea of apologies, taking the blame for things that are out of her control.

We jump at the knock at the door.

Mrs. Johnson pokes her head in. "Milagro? Are you in here?"

I wave my hand. "The prisoner is present and accounted for."

"Clara? Is that you? You're not—" Mrs. Johnson falters. "What are you—? When did you—?" Mrs. Johnson seems totally incapable of complete sentences.

I grin. Finally, someone else is getting in trouble instead of me.

"Only current St. Agnes students are allowed in the dorms" is all Mrs. Johnson can come up with. She crosses her arms and stares at Clara's nose ring.

"There must be an exception for family," Clara says. She states it like a fact. There is no question mark in her voice. She squares her shoulders and stares down Mrs. Johnson.

"Well . . . technically there's no rule that family isn't allowed," Mrs. Johnson says. "But." She looks at the three of us and sighs. "I suppose you can stay here. Milagro, you are not to move from this hallway." Her eyes fall on Lulu. "You either, Luz," she says slowly, still processing that St. Agnes's star student broke *a lot* of rules. Almost as many as me.

I salute Mrs. Johnson. "You got it, Mrs. J."

"I can take it from here." Clara waves to Mrs. Johnson.

Mrs. Johnson looks at the three of us and bites her lip.

"Milagro, you're okay with this?" I flash Mrs. Johnson two thumbs-up. Mrs. Johnson turns to Lulu. "And this is okay with you too?"

Clara and I hold our breath as we wait for Lulu to decide our fate.

Lulu gives the tiniest nod. "It's okay with me."

Mrs. Johnson shrugs and puts her hands in the air. "I know better than to get between the Zavala sisters. Lulu, make sure you check in before the next activity." She closes the door.

Clara, Lulu, and I look at each other.

"So are you going to tell me how you ended up in San Francisco or what?" Lulu asks Clara. "And is that thing real?" She points to Clara's nose.

"Why does everyone keep asking me that?!"

I pull Lulu next to me and toss her a limp pillow. "You're gonna want to sit down for this story. Trust me, it's a good one."

Lulu sighs and then nods at Clara. "I'm ready to hear it."

24
Lulu

EVERYONE LIED TO me. That's the moral of Clara's sob story, delivered in the dimly lit room that Mrs. Johnson has cornered us in. Clara's eyes are wide and hopeful, but I refuse to give her the smile she's looking for. "I still don't understand." I can feel my fingernails leaving imprints in my palm. "You could have told me. You didn't have to lie for months."

Clara rubs her eyes as if she's trying not to cry. The room is deathly silent except for the hum of fluorescent lights and the angry buzzing of a fly battering against the window. There is nothing to say. We used to be fused together, but whatever bonds connected Clara to me and Milagro are broken. We are repelling atoms, toxic and dangerously unstable.

"Darcy told me you planned to leave all winter break. The whole time you were home, you were planning it."

"You talked to Darcy?"

"Who is Darcy?" Milagro scrunches her eyes before turning to Clara, who seems to shrink in front of us.

"Her roommate." I jut my finger out at Clara. "We could have figured it out. Now I'll never have the same chances as you." My voice is loud and accusatory.

"You will, Lulu! You already have big opportunities waiting for you."

"I won't. Mami told me I have to stay home this summer," I say stubbornly, my eyes welling up with hot tears.

"She's saying that because she's scared. She blames herself for me dropping out. She thinks she didn't prepare me well enough, that she was a bad mother for letting me go in the first place. She's convinced she sent me away, and she doesn't want it to happen to you. But it wouldn't. It has nothing to do with you. Or her. I got to school and realized I don't want to be a doctor."

"You don't?"

"No, or maybe I do, but not anytime soon. I don't know what I want. Not to be in school for a minute. I needed a reset, and Mami wanted me to keep at it. She's not anti-college—she's anti us giving up." Clara stares at me. "You can be mad at me. I deserve it," she says quietly. "But you didn't come to Iowa for me."

I nod stubbornly. "Yes, I did. Fire management. I burned everything I had to the ground so I could see you. To fix things with Mami."

Milagro's eyes are as big as satellite dishes, oscillating between us, waiting for a punch or a slap. But this isn't reality TV. I'm not performing for anyone. This is about Clara, not me.

"No. You burned things to the ground because you were running away from hard stuff. Like the interview. Like I ran away from Iowa." Clara reaches out her hand and holds mine. Her hand is soft. It still feels startling to feel her next to me, after two months of talking through screens and scattered text messages. I didn't realize just how much I missed having her around. "You were scared."

I pull my arm away and cover my whole face with my hands, whispering through my fingers, "I don't want to fail."

Clara pats my back, her hand making small circles between my shoulder blades, like she used to at home when I was upset. "Don't make my mistakes, Lulu. Don't be so afraid of failing, you don't even try."

"You can't mess up if you don't try," I mumble. Clara sits down on the other side of me and squeezes me as tightly as Mami does.

"Trying is good, Lulu. You should never stop trying."

She tilts my chin up toward her and wipes away the tears that have started to form. "There's no shame in being the world's best try-er." Clara's brown eyes stare straight at me, and I look up at the big sister who I've missed for so long. I lean into Clara and her arms envelop me again.

"Oof!"

"It's a Zavala sandwich," Milagro exclaims as she crushes us together. "Served piping hot and with extra lime." She squeezes my shoulders tight.

The sound of her giggles makes me wiggle my elbows and break free. I turn to Milagro. "I'm still a little mad at you. I heard Maddie and Gracelynn in the bathroom. It was messed up that you were talking about me to them." I stare at the worn blue carpet and rub my toe over the tiny green alligator confetti, littered all over the floor. "Caroline and Amelia and Leo are all probably laughing about me."

"What are you talking about?"

"You know. When you were saying all the things I care about were so stupid? My club. This summer."

Milagro crosses her arms. "I would never say that, especially not to them. Sheesh, I'm not a monster. Maddie and Gracelynn were probably still annoyed that Genevieve and Caroline kept interrupting our Never Have I Ever game to ask me about your club. FYI, those girls want to be your friends, if you would just give them the time of day. Anyway, what happened between you and Leo?"

"Who is Leo?" Clara asks.

"They do?" I look at Milagro in surprise before I remember her question. "I yelled at him and then I ran out of the room."

"Did he do something to you?" Milagro's voice is loud and sharp.

I shake my head vehemently. "But I did. I really wrecked things between us."

"Hello!" Clara says to both of us. "Would someone please tell me who Leo is?"

I sink down into the mattress, falling flat on my back. I let gravity slowly pull me down. "Someone who hates my guts." I'm sliding off the bed and melting into the floor. "Someone who never wants to talk to me again."

"You have to try," Clara says, leaning over me. "That's all you can do."

I slap my hands over my face. "But what if it's too late to fix things?"

"He'd be a dummy to say no." Milagro hops off the bed and beelines for my bag. "But what will you wear?! This is an emergency!"

Clara and I laugh as Milagro tosses T-shirts and fuzzy socks over her shoulder and mutters to herself.

"I have to try?" I look up to Clara.

She nods firmly. "You have to try."

* * *

Two hours later, I'm on a very high hill, sitting cross-legged on a green park bench and double-fisting sandwiches. The hill and the snacks were picked out by Clara, while my jeans and favorite fleece were selected by Milagro, after intense deliberations and weather calculations. Over the last two hours, I've cycled through every major natural disaster that could prevent me from making things right with Leo. Tsunamis seem extraordinarily unlikely. Equally as unlikely are monsoons or a sudden snow squall. A powerful earthquake, on the other hand, is always around the corner. I lean over and check the steel bolts of my bench.

It's taking all my willpower not to squeeze the foil-wrapped packages in my fists until the contents explode out of the top, like salsa volcanoes. Instead, I focus on all of San Francisco spread out before me, underneath a maddeningly wide sky that melds into the water. The sky is a deep blue, like the most mysterious bottom layers of the ocean. I want a sign that things will be okay, that Leo won't hate my guts. But there are no guarantees when it comes to things that matter. Except this guarantee: I have to tell him I'm sorry. And I have to beg for his forgiveness. This plan seemed easier when our reconciliation was just a scenario in my head. Milagro and Clara all but whipped out pom-poms as they came up with girl-power aphorisms like "You got this!" and "He'll obviously forgive you." I most definitely do not have this, and when it comes to

Leo sits silently, absorbing this information. "Did you fix things with Clara?"

"I didn't. Not in Iowa, anyway. It turns out that was a really bad idea, because she wasn't even there. She hasn't been at school for weeks." I shake my head. "Then she found me, here."

"Like in San Francisco?" Leo raises his eyebrows and his jaw drops open.

"She's been here for a while, all while pretending to be in Iowa." I shrug and look away from Leo. "It's still sinking in that she's really here."

"I didn't know you were applying to the Stanford program. I tried to tell you that I wasn't going," Leo says quietly. "Father Coleman gave me that packet because he wanted me to change my mind." He watches the toddler fall flat on his bottom and let out a shriek. The dog comes bounding over. "He doesn't know that I got into a different program this summer, at MIT."

My eyes widen. "Wow."

Leo bites his lip. "I didn't tell him because I didn't want him to make a big deal about it. I haven't told anyone, really. Aside from my family, of course." He looks up at me. "It's for high school juniors only, not like the Stanford program. But you could apply next year."

"Um. Sure." I redden, filled with embarrassment all

over again. "And you didn't know because I never told you. It was a momentary lapse in sanity. And even if I had told you, you should do whatever you want. Even if it's something I want too. Here, take this." I hand a foil package over to him. "It's a sandwich peace offering. And congratulations too, a torta ahogada. A sandwich that's drowning in chile de árbol salsa. Kind of like me, except I'm drowning in remorse."

He studies it, raising the torta in front of his face. "It's certainly unconventional. I don't think it would fly under the Geneva convention, but I accept your offer." He reaches his hand out to shake mine.

"Wait. That's not it."

His hand hangs limply in the air. I take a deep breath. "You saw the real me, full of big facts and rushing to conclusions—wrong ones, majorly wrong ones—and you didn't laugh or point out any of my mistakes. I was a bad friend to you, and you were my friend anyway. So." I clear my throat. "I want us to be friends again," I tell him. Only my voice cracks because it's not entirely true. My body, forever a traitor, is the ultimate lie detector machine. "Or, you know. More than friends. If you wanted."

"Like lab partners?" Leo says. He sits up a little straighter.

My ears are hot and there's a pounding louder than any church bells. Seismic waves of mortification are flowing out of my chest. I want to melt away into the ground. Another social miscue, a classic Lulu blunder.

Leo sets his torta down. His smile returns in its blinding glory, his eyes crinkled in the corners and his eyebrows raised at me. He leans over. I am drawn like a moth to a flame, transverse orientation, navigation systems failing. He places his hand on my chin, soft and firm. He turns my chin toward him, so that his big brown eyes are only inches away from mine. Everything around us fades away. I'm in the center of a hurricane—why can't I stop thinking about natural disasters?—and all I can do is count the long lashes that line his deep-set eyes. My brain is short-circuiting and yet my lips are parting, without me even doing anything, until the space between us is no more. His lips are on mine and we are kissing. This is a fact. But to call it *kissing* would be a tragedy of language. It doesn't capture the explosions happening in all my nerve endings. A simple "kiss" can't possibly account for his fingers in my hair, or his thumb just underneath the tiny diamond-studded earrings I've worn since I was a baby. Or me, one hand on his denim jacket, the other reaching for more.

Kissing him is a sunrise, glowing hot orange and pink where there was once moody blues. I can feel a light I didn't know was in me peeking over the horizon. Every molecule reacting. It's tentative at first, and then we're greedy, kissing each other harder. Our sandwiches are long forgotten on the bench. We are flashes of reds and oranges and then we are on fire, carbon atoms full of potential.

There's nothing scripted about it. There are no rules we have to follow. I'm not thinking about Clara or Milagro or even an endangered species. All I'm thinking is that I never want it to end.

Leo's phone rings and breaks the spell. We pull apart and stare at each other. My lips are parted and puffy and his eyes are wide open, taking in all of me.

"Wow," he says.

"Wow," I say back.

25
Milagro

WHEN CLARA LEAVES, we are two mascara-smeared monsters with red-rimmed eyes and chocolate smudges on our faces, thanks to three vending machine runs. I make Clara promise to call Mami, and she pinky swears that she will when she's "ready." I roll my eyes at her asterisk, but it's better than nothing.

Lulu returns a few hours later, after her rendezvous with Leo. There's a sparkle in her brown eyes and she can't stop herself from grinning. I grill her until she swears she will never talk to me again if I ask her another question.

"We have to do it, you know."

"I really don't want to," Lulu says. "I'm going to be in such big trouble."

I take a deep breath and call Mami.

The first part of our call is bad—really bad. There is a

lot of yelling, threatening to sue Mrs. Johnson for letting Lulu out of her sight, and lengthy descriptions of what our punishment (extreme house arrest) will look like as soon as we're back in Baltimore.

When Mami finally runs out of angry steam, Lulu asks her why she didn't tell us about Clara.

Mami is quiet. "I wanted you three to be honest with each other. And to figure things out together. I know you don't believe me, but sisters have to stick together. You're all you have in the world."

I squeeze Lulu's hand. I can't tell if she accepts Mami's explanation. Lulu changes the subject, giving us a play-by-play of her interview. The three of us pretend that their Friday-morning promise didn't happen—maybe Clara is right. Some things are better sorted out in person. While Lulu talks, my phone occasionally chirps with a message from Pablo.

"Do you want to get that?" Lulu mouths to me, pointing to his name on the screen. I hit ignore every time. When Lulu finishes, I recap the class I attended at Piedmont and the paid internships that their students can do. I tell her how Lulu helped me look up different art schools, even a few close to home.

"I think . . ." I hesitate. "I think I could do it. Differently than Clara or Lulu, but I think I could."

Now it's Lulu's turn to squeeze my hand. Mami is

silent. I immediately want to take back my words. Maybe she's still thinking that if Clara couldn't hack it, there's no way I can. When I hear a sniffle, I brace myself for the worst.

"Ay, Milagro. I never doubted you. Not for a minute." My smile grows as Mami's voice gets even firmer. "You're brilliant. Don't even try to deny it. There's no question that you could handle college. I just hope that college can handle *you*."

I laugh, but Mami is dead serious. "Don't doubt for a second that you're not as driven or wildly talented as your sisters." She pauses and then breaks out into a wide smile, her eyes still shining. "After all, you all take after me. Son hijas de su madre."

Lulu, Mami, and I burst into giggles. After that, Mami fills us in on the hotel drama that she missed this week, everything from the sous chef and the hostess getting caught making out in the elevator to the lobby piano man quitting in a huff after one too many Frank Sinatra requests. I sit up straight. "Wait. What if I can fix this for you? It would be a huge favor for me. Not that I deserve it," I add quickly. By this point, Mami is yawning, and time zone differences have finally gotten the best of her. She hears me out and gives me a tentative yes, before laughing at my impromptu dance party and then kissing us goodbye.

After Lulu goes back to her room, I begin my vigil,

which has evolved into a six-hour stakeout. I've discovered that when I crouch down on the ground in front of my door, press my face to the crumbly gray carpet, and squint, I can just make out the tiny crack of Mrs. Johnson's heavy wooden door. I know every whorl, dent, and graffiti inscription even better than I know my own closet door at home. As soon as the light in Mrs. Johnson's room goes out for good, I make my move.

I race down the hallway, bounding past half-cracked doors and Lulu and a few of the St. Agnes girls. Caroline is coaching Genevieve on a witty text to send to some coffee shop girl, while Lulu and Amelia debate the physics of a lacrosse ball. Maddie and Gracelynn are nowhere in sight. I hope they finally found their party. I burst onto the stairwell and slowly make my way through each hallway, until five floors later, I find the one with St. Anthony boys crowded around a TV. Sports noises are blaring and their faces are bathed in the blue glow of the giant flat screen. They barely look at me when they point out Lucas's room down the hall. "Father Coleman has been knocked out for ages," one of them tosses out, and the other shushes him.

I knock on Lucas's door, and it swings open. Lucas looks up from his cracked flip phone. "What are you doing here?" His room is immaculate, complete with hospital corners on his floppy mattress and a pile of folded clothes resting on top of his bag. The only thing out of place is me.

"Take this." I stretch my hand out to him and hand him a postcard. "It's a huge apology. The start of one. And a thank-you for putting up with me on this trip. I was the worst partner ever."

Lucas turns the postcard over and glances at the glossy Baltimore skyline with Mami's hotel logo stamped on it. "Thanks, but I don't need a hotel room in Baltimore." He tosses the postcard back at me. It lands at my feet, and I scoop down to pick it up.

"No, but they need you."

His head snaps up.

"I owe you big-time. You should have been able to enjoy the whole trip without getting dragged into my family drama." I hold my finger up to him to stop his retort. "I know you're a piano virtuoso. And I know you're on a full scholarship at St. Anthony, like me. Or like I was, anyway." I point to his phone. "No one has one of those for fun. I happen to know the manager of this hotel. They need a piano player, especially one who doesn't drink on the job. It's kind of boring, hanging out in the lobby and playing show tunes during their cocktail hour. But their rates are *really* good, and even better: you're already hired."

He raises an eyebrow at me. "Your apology is a job?"

I shrug. "I could get on my knees and beg. You'd deserve it. But something tells me this job is better than flipping pancakes at a diner."

He takes the postcard back from me. "I could be persuaded. I do like an excuse to wear a tux," he muses.

"Plus, sometimes celebs stay there?"

"Really?"

"Just the mayor . . . when he needs a break from his wife." I wiggle my eyebrows at Lucas, the way he did on our first day as partners.

He raises them back. "You seem pretty cheerful for someone who got expelled. Or is that just a rumor?"

My stomach tightens. Clara and I practiced my apologies to Sister May and Mrs. Johnson a million times. She vetoed pleading temporary insanity and instead drafted long apologies for me, sentences full of "accept responsibility" and "reaching my potential" and "extreme emotional duress." "I'm negotiating the terms of my detention," I finally tell Lucas.

"Father Coleman said I was absolved of all wrongdoing. Something about you taking the blame for everything that's gone wrong on this trip."

I shrug. "What can I say? Drama just seems to find me."

"So what's in the box?"

"Oh. This is part two of my apology. Would you like a cupcake?"

He peers into the cardboard box that I'm holding. Two dozen cupcakes spell out the words *I'm really sorry* in electric-pink frosting. Lucas snorts. "You really ordered those for me?"

"Don't be mad, but I didn't. Pablo sent them to me." I wrinkle my nose. "He had them delivered to the dorm as an act of contrition. I guess my stories haven't made it back to him yet. The cupcakes look really tasty, but I can't eat them. They're all yours."

He laughs and reaches for the box. "You're something else, Milagro."

I smile at him. "I know."

Back in my room, I delete seventeen texts from Pablo. During my stakeout, he finally discovered how to ask me questions, like Why aren't you responding to me? and Do you really want to give up on us? I'm ignoring all of them, choosing instead to lie flat on my back and stare at my ceiling, anything but go back to whatever we had. I think about me and Pablo in my bedroom, in the moments before Lulu stormed in. I was unsure and Pablo was impatient, pushing me to figure out my feelings *fast*. This past year, I have played the adoring girlfriend, content to sit on the sidelines and let Pablo make all the calls. That's not how I want things to be, ever.

I used to think that falling in love was like finding your missing piece. Pablo was everything I wasn't: richer, faster talking, so sure he could do anything. I thought if I stuck around him long enough, that might right rub off on me. But love isn't like that at all.

It's like sitting in a room while the sun is setting and it's getting darker and darker, but your eyes are adjusting so fast, you don't even notice. The darkness settles around you. It feels normal, like a familiar friend. It tricks you and makes you think you've always lived this way. Falling in love is someone walking into that room, flipping the light switch. It's a spotlight that shines on all the parts of you, even the parts you forgot about, and maybe some you didn't know existed. Every part of you is exposed. You're bathed in the glow. There's no hiding who you are—or who you can be.

This trip, the wild cross-country college hopping, fighting and making up with Lulu, finding Clara—it was all a giant light switch. Only I'm the one who flicked it on. Pablo didn't know me and he never cared to know me. I'll probably never find out who Mystery Boobs was, but it doesn't matter. I don't need answers, or a feeble light from a boy who can't linger long enough to see me. From now on, I'm shining a light on myself. I'm discovering the parts of me that make me laugh and dance and run down the street to show people what I can do. Any other guy who comes along is gonna have to love me even more than I love myself.

BALTIMORE

26
Lulu

TWENTY-FIVE YEARS AGO, Mami tottered off a plane at Dulles International Airport in an impractical set of red heels, waited in customs for more than an hour, and then heaved four overstuffed suitcases into Tía Lochita's sputtering car. Counting all the layovers, it took Mami nearly twelve hours to travel two continents, abandon the only home she'd ever known, and stake her claim on the American Dream. I've never asked her, but now I wonder if when she boarded the plane, did she know all that awaited her? Did tears stream down her face as she said a silent goodbye to everything she had ever known?

There are no tears on my face today. I'm glued to the plane window, my nose pressed up against the glass as I take in every rugged mountain range and jagged river and water estuary. All of them are leading me back to home, to Mami. And to Leo, who promised me a date at Frank's Chicken Stop Shop the moment he lands. When we finally touch down before the gentle sloping arches of Dulles Airport, Mrs. Johnson has abandoned all pretenses of chaperoning. In her eyes, the trip is over, has been since we took off from San Francisco at 6:45 a.m. Father Coleman isn't even around to take over—the St. Anthony boys got to take a later flight. Mrs. Johnson shrugs at the flight attendant, who frowns at her and then sighs before repeating for the fifth time, "The seat belt sign is STILL lit, if everyone would PLEASE stay in their seats until we've reached our gate."

All around me, St. Agnes girls are mumbling how they wish the trip would never end, leaning across each other to take last-minute selfies, and texting their parents that the flight is stuck at the gate.

Even though I'm banished to the exit aisle with Mrs. Johnson (just in case I decide to make another break for it, I guess), I'm not ready for this trip to end either.

Genevieve and Caroline lean over my seat. "Don't forget to tell us when you get those gardens going."

I smile back at them. "I won't."

I click my seat belt buckle open and reach up to grab my bag. When I shuffle off the plane, someone grabs my shoulder and yanks on my hand.

"Wait up for me!" Milagro shouts. "I don't want to lose you again!"

I roll my eyes. "I'm right *here*. I'm not going anywhere."

"Promise," Milagro says. Her eyes are poking me for secrets. When she's satisfied I'm not going to leave, not even she can resist a small smile at the role reversal that we've found ourselves in. This is new for us, but if this trip has taught me anything, it's that new doesn't have to be bad, or even scary.

"Promise," I say, for the ninth time today. My grin spreads across my face.

When we emerge by baggage claim, Mami shrieks and gallops toward us. She pulls both of us into a giant hug, all while Milagro complains that Mami will ruin her hair.

I push her away so I can get a good look at her outfit.

She's decked out in my Stanford sweatshirt, and somehow Tía Lochita has gotten one too, even if she keeps calling it "Es-stanford."

Tía Lochita smooths the sweatshirt out and twirls around for Milagro and me. "Mira, hija. Do you like it? Maroon brings out the highlights in my hair."

"Or maybe the cañas," Mami says, before doubling over laughing.

"But it's so far away," I say, my voice cracking. "It's okay?"

Mami wraps her arms around me and whispers in my ear, "I'm so proud of you. And still mad, of course. I've done a lot of praying about it. You can go wherever you want, but only after you've served your house arrest."

When she stands back up, Mrs. Johnson is there, her mouth in a tight line. "Mrs. Zavala? I need to talk to you about your daughters."

Milagro stares at Mrs. Johnson and the color slowly fades from her face. Tía Lochita mouths "¿Quién es?" to me, but I have something important to do.

"Um. Mrs. Johnson?" I tug on her cardigan.

"Not now, Lulu." She turns to Mami. "Your daughter Milagro has violated every single rule on this trip."

I pull out my folder. "Um. Excuse me, Mrs. Johnson. Milagro was a late addition to the trip, so she probably didn't sign the conduct forms, right?" I point to the crumpled honor code form that I signed months ago.

Mrs. Johnson's brows are furrowed and her lips barely move. Mami has to lean in to hear her utter a very quiet, "What's your point?"

"If she didn't sign the forms, then technically she didn't break any of the rules."

Mrs. Johnson's voice grows louder as she sputters. "But . . . That's not . . . We have a St. Agnes code of conduct . . ." She sighs, realizing she isn't going to win this one. "I'll need to talk this over with Sister May. I'll get back to you," she tells Mami.

Milagro smiles sweetly at her and waves goodbye. She grabs her suitcase and nods toward the door.

"Wait," Mami says. "We're waiting for one more person. We have a few more hours."

My stomach drops. "Clara?"

Mami nods. "She's coming home."

On the car ride home, we're squished into Tía Lochita's ancient car. I've got Clara's elbow in my side and Milagro's legs draped over my right knee. It's even more uncomfortable than the bus we left behind in Indiana, but I wouldn't change it for the world.

I don't know if I'll get the internship, if Clara is going to be okay, or if Milagro will really be able to weasel her way out of trouble. But I've decided that uncertainty is not a bad thing. It's like feelings, or maybe the weather: unpredictable, but still very real and valid. The trick is paying attention to the feelings that matter. The warning signs, the moments of joy and disappointment. The butterflies I feel when Leo's hand slips into mine and holds on, or when he tells me an animal trivia fact that reminds him of me. The satisfaction when I nail six *Jeopardy!* questions in a row or I hit print on my lab report.

I've spent most of my life writing weather reports of other people's feelings. I've been charting moods and whims in the hope of understanding what my life is supposed to be. No more. After today, I'm that drought, earthquake, torrential downpour, whatever I want to be. Maybe it's here in Baltimore, or somewhere as far away as San Francisco, or Hong Kong, or if Leo's dreams come true, a colony on Mars.

I'm a hurricane of feelings, hopes, and dreams, and I'm setting myself free.

Acknowledgments

Thank you so much, Taylor Haggerty, for believing in this book and championing it fiercely, all while radiating so much energy, excitement, and absolute confidence. I knew we were a perfect match during our earliest calls, but hearing you refer to the submissions process as "my party" confirmed it a million times over. Thank you to Jasmine Brown, everyone at Root Literary, and Alice Lawson at Gersh, for keeping my party going.

Thank you to my incredible editor, Alessandra Balzer, for your brilliant vision, thoughtful edit letters, and unrelenting enthusiasm for Lulu and Milagro. You saw the best version of my story and built me a bridge (laden with the kindest Word comments) to get me there. I am so grateful.

This book would not exist without so many wildly talented HarperCollins folks. Thank you to Shannon Cox, Nellie Kurtzman, Aubrey Churchward, Andrea Pappenheimer, Kerry Moynagh, and Kathy Faber for shouting to the world about my book. A huge thank-you to Patty Rosati, Mimi Rankin, and Katie Dutton for working hard to get this story into the hands of some of the best people in the world, teachers and librarians.

Thank you to Corina Lupp and Alison Donalty for a cover that makes my heart sing. And to Iliana Galvez, thank you for creating a work of art that makes me grin so wildly whenever I see it. Thank you to Lindsay Wagner, Lana Barnes, Vivian Lee, and Jessica Berg for looking out for my typos and logistical leaps. And a special, extra-hearty thank-you to Caitlin Johnson, because assistants truly make the world go round.

The idea for this book was born in 212 Hamilton Hall. Thank you to all my former coworkers, but especially Diane, Dominique, and Joy, for teaching me how to consider the entirety of a student's story, and not just what exists on paper. To the unforgettable Peter Johnson, who changed so many students lives, including my own, your legacy lives on. I love you all madly.

To my earliest readers: Alexa, Kamilla, Rhoda, Tara, Leah, Mercedes, Sophronia, Sophie, and Vanessa. This book exists (with an ending!), because you kept texting me about it. How lucky I am to have friends who believe in my dreams. I love you all so much.

I am forever thankful to Crystal Maldonado, Lilliam Rivera, Adam Silvera, and Natalia Sylvester for your time, consideration, and kind, enthusiastic words about my book. There aren't enough exclamation marks in the world to convey my gratitude!!!

Thank you to Angie Cruz. I am forever grateful you took a chance and shone your light on me. Your generous cheerleading, mentorship, and support has changed my life. Thank you to the University of Pittsburgh faculty, including Irina Reyn, Bill Lychack, and Erin Anderson, for teaching me how to polish a story and share it with the world. To my Pittsburgh family, especially Alfredo, Amanda, Clarissa, Hannah, Sam, Steffan, and Tanya, thank you for chasing the gloom away. Thank you, Ben, for filling my life with the perfect balance of pancakes and laughter, and seeing my dreams as facts and not wishes, even when I'm swamped by the deepest of doubts.

Thank you to my entire Velez Zavala family, but especially Victoria and Marita. You are the best sisters in the world, sorry to everyone else's families. Thank you to my parents, who raised their daughters to believe no dream was impossible and then led by example. Thank you for ending every phone call with, "So where's my book?" Here it is, finally written, with paciencia y buen humor, just as you taught me.